THE
HOUSE
SITTER

BOOKS BY ELLERY KANE

ROCKWELL AND DECKER SERIES

Watch Her Vanish

Her Perfect Bones

One Child Alive

THE
HOUSE
SITTER

ELLERY KANE

bookouture

Published by Bookouture in 2022

An imprint of Storyfire Ltd.
Carmelite House
50 Victoria Embankment
London EC4Y 0DZ

www.bookouture.com

ISBN: 978-1-80314-207-4
eBook ISBN: 978-1-80314-206-7

For Gar
My partner in crime

The arc of the moral universe is long but it bends toward justice.

—Dr. Martin Luther King Jr.

PROLOGUE

The dispatcher heard the breathing first. The frantic gulps of panic. Then, a woman's voice.

"Help me." Two small words, made even smaller by her hoarse whisper.

"What is your emergency?" the dispatcher asked again, when the woman said nothing more. The silence stretched, taut as a bowstring, with only the woman's breathing to mark the seconds ticking by. "Ma'am, are you still there?"

The dispatcher waited, attentive to the quiet maelstrom of the woman's terror.

"Someone's in the house. I have to keep quiet."

With a wary glance at the clock, the dispatcher began a mental countdown at eight minutes, the target response time for Priority A emergency calls in San Francisco. A lot could go wrong in eight minutes. "Help is on the way, ma'am."

"Please hurry. *Please.*"

"Are you somewhere safe?" True safety didn't exist, of course. Not even in posh Pacific Heights, where the call had originated. A place like that lured its natives into a naïve slumber only to shake them awake at 2:57 a.m. with a knife blade to the throat of their own mortality.

"I'm in my bedroom," the woman answered, finally. An *old* woman, the dispatcher decided. Her voice, wavery. Her vocal cords, weakened and stringy with age. "But it's not safe. I'm not safe anywhere. I tried to go out the window, but it's too high."

"Find a place to hide," the dispatcher urged, realizing a frail woman would be helpless against an intruder. "Quick."

Moments later, a door groaned open.

The dispatcher listened to the whining tremors from the woman's throat. Powerless to stop the inevitable, the dispatcher could only follow protocol.

Then, the woman's breathing stopped altogether. In its absence, an unfathomable stillness.

Without warning came a gasp and a scream—long, shrill, and terrible—followed by the sharp and unmistakable pop of a gunshot.

"Ma'am? Are you still with me?"

Another wail, more primitive than the last, coursed down the wire, raising the fine hairs on the dispatcher's neck. It went on too long to bear. The woman kept screaming, even as the gun blasted again and the line went dead.

PART I

ONE

BEFORE

Iris caught a glimpse of herself in the café window. The sun-spotted face of an old woman frowned back. Funny how the soul stayed young, while the rest of her careened like a runaway train toward birthday number seventy next month. The white cast on her arm served as another dim reminder of her fragility. Of the sudden, final stop at the end of the track. Her lonely visit to Piedmont Cemetery that morning hadn't helped.

"After you." A fit young man in cycle shorts and a bright yellow jersey held the door for her with one hand, keeping his bike upright with the other. Effortlessly, he lugged the thing inside, leaving it propped by the door. Necessary here in down-town Oakland, where an expensive toy like that would surely disappear.

"Do you take that thing everywhere?" she teased, appreciating the way his biceps flexed, enjoying the sheen of sweat on his strong calves. He reminded her a little of her Dean. God rest his soul.

"No, ma'am." He practically shouted it at her, enunciating each word. "It's not in your way, is it? Do you need any help?"

With an exasperated shake of her head, Iris waved him off

and headed straight for the counter, taking the center stool with the best view of the open kitchen. Better than sitting alone at a table with that Lance Armstrong wannabe pitying her.

She plonked her Mulberry bag—an early birthday present to herself—onto the adjacent stool and waited for the server to notice her. The girl moved like a fawn, skittish and clumsy, as she balanced a tray of drinks on her arm.

As the girl neared the oversized corner booth, Iris sensed the inevitable. Her blundering foot set on a collision course with bicycle boy's helmet. Before Iris could think what to do, foot met chinstrap, and the tray went airborne, sending four glasses flying. The girl managed to save the fifth. It sat on the tray like a lone soldier on a bloodied battlefield. The last man standing.

"Lydia!" The cook's voice bellowed from the kitchen. His red face got redder. "Not again!"

"Sorry, Burt. I'll fix it." Lydia scurried to clean up her mess. Though Iris couldn't see her face, the slump of the girl's shoulders hinted at an impending meltdown. Iris shimmied off the stool, frowning at bicycle boy as she passed, his helmet now safely tucked beneath his chair. Just like Dean indeed. Handsome but oblivious to those around him.

With the ease of an unoiled tinman, Iris lowered herself to a crouch to retrieve one of the glasses that had tumbled nearby. She placed it on Lydia's tray. "Rough day?"

The girl looked up at her, defeated. She wiped a rogue tear from her cheek. "Rough life, if I'm being honest."

Lydia laughed but it didn't cover the bitter sting of truth. Iris understood that better than anyone. She picked up another errant glass and followed the girl back toward the counter. When she returned to her stool, Iris felt accomplished. Even with a distal fracture of her radius, she could get things done. Slowly, painstakingly. But done, nonetheless.

"Thanks for your help." Lydia set the tray on the counter, sniffling, and passed Iris a menu.

Iris flipped through its laminated pages, her sapphire cocktail ring glinting beneath the pendant lights. A forty-fifth wedding anniversary gift from Dean, she rarely wore it. It felt too much like showing off, which was exactly what Dean had intended. "So, what's good here?"

"Obviously not me. I'm not cut out for this job. Seth told me I need to be more like a diamond. Good under pressure."

"At least you didn't fall off a ladder trying to clean the gutters." Iris tapped her fingers against her cast. "And wind up lugging around this monstrosity. Since my Dean died, I can't seem to do anything right. Widowhood bites."

Lydia gave a forlorn smile, but curiosity sparked behind her watery eyes. "How did you fall?"

"It's almost too embarrassing to admit."

"Well, now you have to tell me."

Iris leaned in, lowered her voice. "I was attacked by a seagull. That damn bird flew right at me. A premeditated onslaught."

Lydia guffawed, drawing Burt's attention. He glared at her from behind the grill. "Sorry to interrupt your social hour, but those drinks aren't gonna remake themselves."

Iris peeked over the top of the menu and flashed a wry smile at Lydia. "Duty calls, my dear."

"Try the pancake combo." Lydia glanced back over her shoulder, nearly running into the kitchen door. She shook her head at herself, and Iris chuckled. "Seth says it's even better than IHOP."

Iris gaped at the feast Lydia laid before her. A short stack of blueberry pancakes drowned in syrup and two eggs scrambled. Her doctor would most definitely not approve. But to hell with him. Isn't that what those damn medications were for? Besides, Dean's strict diet and exercise routine had earned him nothing but a massive heart attack.

"Excellent recommendation," Iris pronounced, after the first bite had gone down the hatch, spiking her blood with sugar and dopamine. "*See?* You're not so bad at this waitress gig."

"Tell that to Burt. He said, 'One more mistake and you're toast. No pun intended.'"

"I've known some Burts in my day, and I guarantee you he's bluffing. He needs you more than you need him. Good help is hard to find." Iris took another luxurious bite.

"Sadly, I do need him. Between you and me, we've already drained the last drop of our savings. My emergency coffee can is nearly empty, and a few weeks ago, we had to move into the Blue Bird Motel. If I lose this job, Seth will never forgive me."

"Seth. Is he your husband?" Iris didn't wait for an answer. She hoped she didn't appear nosy. "You look too young to be married. But then, when you get to be my age, anybody under thirty looks like they should still be in high school."

Lydia raised her hand sheepishly. "Twenty-four-year-old junior college dropout here. Jeez, you must think I'm pathetic, telling you my sob story. I should probably get back to work before Burt gives me the heave-ho."

Iris couldn't let her get away. It felt nice to talk to someone other than herself. "Sixty-nine-year-old retired librarian with one broken wing. All alone in a big, fancy house I can't take care of anymore. We never could have kids of our own. So, it's just me and a bunch of stuff. How's that for a sob story?"

Sharing a smile with her new friend, Iris finished the last of her pancakes. No better way to bond than over mutual misery.

"That's a beautiful pin." Lydia pointed to Iris's lapel. Her treasured butterfly. Its wings, mother-of-pearl. Its body, white diamonds. She never went a day without wearing it. It meant too much to her to ever leave behind.

"We called it a brooch back in my day."

"Well, it's lovely. The way it shimmers in the light. Did your husband—"

"Lydia," Burt hissed. "Shut your trap and move your ass. Table two has been ready to order for the last five minutes."

"Okay, okay. I'm on it."

Iris scowled at Burt. What a tyrant. She plucked a crisp one-hundred-dollar bill from her wallet and tucked it beneath her plate. Took a moment to pen a note on the back of her receipt, her phone number scrawled at the bottom.

If you get fed up with General Burt, call me. I may have the antidote to both our sorrows.

Iris collapsed onto the sofa in the sitting room, exhausted. The BART ride to Oakland and back. The trip to the cemetery to lay her hand on the cold, gray stone at the top of the hill. Her pancake-induced high that had ended with the inevitable crash, leaving her brain dim and sluggish. At least Bill Dorsey had given her a ride to and from the BART station. But even that had been a trial to endure.

The house could use a new coat of paint, Iris.

The yard looks a little untamed, Iris.

Your fuchsia needs watering, Iris.

The HOA is concerned, Iris.

She'd never hated the sound of her own name more than when it came from Daft Dorsey's mouth. He could make her feel as small and useless as a pencil nub without even trying. Though a million years had passed since girlhood, that man's voice brought her right back to the Lost Pines Girls' Home in Mendocino. To Sister Frances. To the naughty corner. And to all that she'd gained and lost since then.

Desperate to escape the memories, Iris forced herself up the winding staircase toward the third-floor guest bedroom she'd made her own. The master suite had sat empty for years now, Dean's Ferragamo loafers collecting dust in the closet. It had unnerved her, sleeping in that big room by herself, with the shadows shapeshifting, clinging to the dark corners and keeping her awake.

Iris undressed in the lamplight, wriggling out of her button-down blouse and into her flannel nightgown like a contortionist. She shuffled to the dresser, to her pillbox, where she popped a handful of different-colored tablets into her mouth, washing them down with a swig of Dean's whiskey straight from the bottle, then toddled to the bed, her worn copy of *Rebecca* waiting for her on the pillow. She could always count on the wonderfully wicked Mrs. Danvers to keep her company.

Iris read until her eyes grew heavy, the same way she had as a child. Just before sleep carried her out to sea, she thought of Lydia and a smile stretched across her face. The day hadn't been all bad.

TWO

From her perch in the attic, Iris aimed her binoculars at the street below. Her breath trembled as the pair approached in a beat-up rust bucket Dean would've called a jalopy. When they summitted the hill, the engine straining, Iris could see them clearly. Lydia rode in the passenger seat, her face as pale as the moon. Iris waved, but the girl didn't notice her there, keeping her eyes in her lap. Some people go their whole lives without looking up. It's a real shame.

Iris watched while they parked. Then, she returned her binoculars to the windowsill and prepared herself. She smoothed the silk blouse she'd chosen that morning, hoping it didn't smell musty from its years of confinement in the master closet. Its emerald color, a perfect complement to her butterfly brooch, though the fiberglass cast on her left arm took away some of its luster.

She reminded herself to move slowly, to grip the railing of the windy staircase. A woman in her condition shouldn't hurry. But she hadn't felt this giddy in fifty years, since the day she put Lost Pines in her permanent rearview. Nothing could compare to that kind of freedom. To the possibilities that branched endlessly like the limbs of the redwoods in the nearby Presidio.

Before she arrived at the front door, Iris tried on her smile in the compact mirror she stowed in her pocket. Alone for so long now, she felt out of practice. She hoped they liked her. She needed them to like her. Which also took her back to Lost Pines, the place where everything ended and began again. That scared little girl still lived inside her, even after all this time, yearning and acquiescent.

Though Iris expected it, the ding-dong of the bell started her heart racing. She waited for a while, impossible as it felt, so she didn't seem too eager.

"Good morning." She spit out the words before the door had fully opened. "It's so lovely to see you again, Lydia. And this must be—"

"Seth." He had the solid sort of handshake that would've impressed Dean, and the kind of face that would've set a younger woman aflutter. Even now, Iris could appreciate his strong jaw, the slight bump in his nose that lent a hint of rugged toughness. Seth looked like a man who got things done. "A pleasure to meet you, ma'am. Lydia can't stop talking about her new friend, Iris."

Relieved, she invited them inside. "Well, I hope you're ready to work. I have to confess I've let things go since my husband died."

"Good thing 'hard work' is my middle name." Iris laughed along at Seth's joke, and then again, when Lydia rolled her eyes, giving him a playful punch to the shoulder.

"In all seriousness, we appreciate you offering us an opportunity like this." Seth patted her good arm, the strength of him sending little quakes through her frame. "Whatever you need, Mrs. Duncan, you just say the word."

"Chocolate cake," Iris teased, pleased with herself when

they both guffawed. "And don't make me feel older than I already do. Call me Iris."

With the care of a museum docent, Iris guided them through the home that still felt too big to call her own. Attuned to their faces, she tried not to overshare, telling them only the stories that cast her in the best light. She would be an easy boss, a fun boss.

To Lydia, she pointed out the kitchen—"Dean and I ate a home-cooked meal together every night"—and the laundry room—"Our cat, Ginger, gave birth to eight kittens in that corner." She apologized profusely for the mess, confessing that the house had come to resemble her own mind, sad and scattered. Especially the guest bedroom, where she'd been sleeping since the morning Dean didn't wake up. His heart, stopped like a clock someone forgot to wind.

"I'll show you my room next time. I need to tidy it up first. I can't have you thinking I'm a total slob."

"It's no trouble," Lydia assured her. "That's what we're here for. We'll get it sorted out."

To Seth, she showed the garage, where she kept her husband's treasures, an Indian motorcycle and a 1967 Ford Mustang Convertible—"I never learned to drive. Maybe you can teach me."

"In this beauty?" Seth grinned, running his hand along the glassy-smooth red fender. "It would be an honor."

Finally, she led them to the back door that opened to the fenced yard and to the Presidio beyond it. Iris hesitated there. "The yard is the worst of it. Dean and I ventured out here every weekend, planting and pruning and getting too much sun. I haven't had the heart to do much by myself. Honestly, it's become a bit of a jungle."

Lydia offered her a reassuring nod. "That sounds familiar. It can't be any worse than our last job. Right, Seth?"

Seth only grunted, squinting to see through the small window that had grown cloudy with dust and rainwater.

"Now that the winter is all but over, my neighbors have started to complain." With that, Iris pushed the door open, revealing the knee-high weeds, sprinkled with dandelion and buttercup, that had sprouted after the rainy season and choked out the carpet grass. The fence itself, grown up with hollyhock, appeared in desperate need of a fresh coat of paint. And the birdhouse Iris treasured had fallen to ruin, toppling from its perch in a windstorm. "They've alerted the HOA."

"HOA?" Lydia frowned, making her way down the steps. Her flip-flopped feet disappeared in the overgrowth. Iris would have to warn her about the garter snakes. Harmless little buggers, but they could give you quite a fright.

"Home Owners Association," Iris explained.

"Otherwise known as the Lawn Nazis." Seth followed Iris and Lydia toward the shed in the corner of the yard, where Dean had stored the lawn tools. "Screw them and the horses they rode in on."

Iris clutched her chest, pretending to be taken aback, when in her own head, she'd uttered far worse. She couldn't have the couple thinking she was a heathen. But that's what happens when you grow up in a pound, a puppy that nobody wanted. You learn how to bite.

Seth shrugged, remorseless, and already she understood him. "Sorry, Mrs. Duncan—I mean, *Iris*. But anybody that makes you feel bad has to deal with me now. When I'm done with this place, the HOA won't know what hit them."

"That's very kind of you, dear. It's been too long since I had anybody in my corner."

The door to the shed required muscling, but Seth managed it easily. He inspected the squeaky hinges. "A little WD-40 will fix that right up."

After Seth cleared the massive spiderweb from the entrance

without complaint, Iris stepped inside, pointing to the rack on the back wall. Most of the tools were covered in a thick layer of dust. "Consider these on loan to you. Anything you need, just take it. You don't have to ask."

"I probably will ask you though. I wouldn't want you to think we were taking advantage."

"It'll be *me* taking advantage." Iris chuckled. "I can see what a help you'll be around here. Both of you. Just you wait, I'll have you so busy you'll be begging me for a day off."

"Would you mind if I stored a few things in here?" Seth asked. "Just some odds and ends we don't have space for."

"I wouldn't mind at all."

As they waded back through the thick grass, Iris plucked a dandelion, admiring its bright petals, the color of a perfect egg yolk. She tossed her head back in the breeze, gazed up at the cloudless sky, and pronounced it a superb morning.

With Seth and Lydia waiting in front of the fireplace in the sitting room, Iris arranged her cinnamon walnut coffee cake on a foil-lined baking sheet for reheating. It took some maneuvering to do on her own, but she got through it. She wanted to surprise them. After depositing the cake in the oven, she poured three cups of black coffee and set them on a sterling silver serving tray, careful not to spill a drop.

"Lydia, dear, would you help me with the coffee?"

Moments later, Iris shuffled to her armchair, with Lydia following. "I have to confess carrying a tray brings back bad memories."

"Oh, goodness. Of General Burt, I presume. I can't believe that buffoon fired you. That he had the nerve to suggest you'd steal from the register. It's his loss."

"That's what I told her." Seth roamed the shelves at the

perimeter, studying the collection of rare books Dean had gifted her over the years.

"Well, the customer is always right," Lydia replied, with a sad shrug. When she lowered herself onto the adjacent sofa, Iris patted her hand.

"Baloney. But I'll admit I'm glad you got fired. That place was sucking the life from you. And I'll bet Burt didn't give you a fair wage."

"Ain't that the truth," Seth said, taking his place next to Lydia. Iris winked at him, proud that he had called her offer of seventy-five dollars per hour overly generous.

"So, how long have you two lovebirds been together?"

Lydia sipped her coffee, her eyes deferring to Seth over the lip of her cup.

"It seems like forever. Right, Liddy?" Then, to Iris, he added, "We grew up together."

"How lovely. You must know each other very well then. The key to a successful marriage is a strong friendship. I reckon Dean knew almost everything about me. Losing that kind of closeness leaves a real void." Chiding herself for being a Debbie Downer, Iris quickly changed course. "Lydia mentioned you're staying at the Blue Bird Motel temporarily."

"Until we save up enough for a place of our own."

"But is it safe there? I swear I heard about a shooting at the Blue Bird a while back. It has something of a reputation, I believe."

"Safety is relative. Lydia and me, we can hold our own."

Iris noticed Lydia's silence. The girl had begun biting her nails. Poor thing.

"But you shouldn't have to. Nice young people like you should have a hospitable place to lay your heads. Especially if you decide to start a family." Iris smiled sweetly. She hoped not to sound too forward. "You do intend to have children, I hope. Dean and I always talked about adopting, but I suppose it was never the right time. Timing is everything. That's what Dean—"

Iris froze, mid-sentence. Her coffee cup dropped from her hand, crashing to the hardwood. The delicate china shattered. "Did you hear that?"

Lydia shook her head, already in motion, stooping to clean up the mess. But Iris stopped her, pointing a trembling finger. Her breath, shallow in her ears. "There's someone at the door."

"Sounds like a delivery to me." Unbothered by the whole dramatic scene, Seth sauntered toward the stained-glass windows. The sudden thud from the porch didn't deter him or slow him down.

"Be careful," Iris whispered. She'd gone rigid as a plank.

He pulled the door open to reveal the small brown package that had been left on the stoop. Already nearing the street, the mailman turned and waved.

Seth retrieved the box and placed it on the coffee table. "The label says it's from Easy Ship Pharmacy. Does that ring a bell?"

Iris groaned and hung her head in shame, covering her face with her good hand. "How ironic. It must be the memory supplement my doctor prescribed for me."

She lifted her eyes to find Seth staring at her. His eyebrows raised, his expression straddling the line between confusion and amusement. "Is it possible to die of embarrassment?" she asked.

"If it was, I'd be long gone." Lydia stood at the hall closet, already securing the broom and dustpan Iris had pointed out on the tour. With a few deft strokes, the broken china vanished. A puddle of coffee remained the only tangible proof of Iris's clumsiness.

"I should've mentioned the burglar," Iris said. "But I didn't want to alarm you."

"Burglar?"

"A few days ago, I found the back door open. I must've

forgotten to lock it. There goes my memory again." Iris thunked her finger against her head. "Some items turned up missing. Little things. A few forks. My first edition copy of *Great Expectations*. The television remote control." The book's disappearance, especially, worried her.

Puzzling, Lydia asked, "What kind of burglar steals the remote?"

"A burglar or a ghost. I'd prefer the former, I suppose."

From the corner of the room, Seth sniffed the air, wrinkled his nose. Concern clouded his face. "I smell smoke. Is something—"

"My coffee cake!" Iris sprang to her feet too quickly, the blood rush leaving her dizzy. She stumbled a little before Lydia came to her aid, holding her steady. Together, they trailed Seth to the kitchen. "It was supposed to be a surprise," Iris confessed.

The oven door already open, Seth waved a dish towel to clear the haze of smoke. On the counter, Iris's precious cake sat, still steaming and blackened to a crisp.

Her eyes blurred. "You two must think I'm a complete disaster. A real train wreck. I wouldn't blame you if you never came back. I should be put out to pasture."

"Don't say that." Lydia wrapped an arm around her and squeezed. Above the smoke that already clung to her pale blonde hair, Iris detected the distinct odor of Cheetos. "We'll get you back on track."

"That's exactly what we're here for," Seth added, swooping in around her other side, until she was pressed between them like a rose petal in a book. Iris had to admit, it wasn't entirely unpleasant, all this attention. "To help you. And we'll be here tomorrow morning at ten o'clock to start."

"Still think your last job as caretaker was worse?" Iris asked, eyeing the cake's charred remains.

Lydia answered first, with an emphatic head nod. "Absolutely. She was an artist. Have you ever tried to clean oil paint from beneath your fingernails? I swear my hands always smelled like solvent."

"An artist? Anyone I would've heard of?"

Seth's cough, sudden and violent, interrupted, and Lydia shrank back like he'd slapped her, leaving Iris's question unanswered.

"I don't know about you, Iris, but I need some fresh air." Seth unlatched the kitchen window and flung it open, letting the heady smells of early spring chase away the smoke.

Iris breathed in a refreshing dose, but her relief didn't last long. Lydia gaped outside at the sill, her face contorted in horror. "It's a dead bird."

Sure enough, a chickadee lay feet up in the corner just outside the window. Iris considered herself lucky to live so close to the Presidio, her own enchanted forest in the middle of the city, with its circling hawks and howling coyotes. Dean had always handled the messy bits. Like the night their cat, Ginger, had slipped through Iris's legs and disappeared into the dark spaces between the trees. If she looked hard enough, Iris could still find the stone Dean had set at the base of a redwood to mark Ginger's final resting place.

Iris sighed. "Well, what else can go wrong?"

As if on cue, the smoke detector began its incessant beeping.

Iris stood at the back door, shivering in the dark. Her flannel nightgown proved no match for the draft that streamed in through the broken window, through the hole in the glass the size of her fist. Beyond it, a patchy layer of fog had settled across the yard, obscuring the shed from her view.

Stretching the telephone cord from the kitchen as far as it would reach, Iris raised the receiver to her ear, studying the scene in front of her.

"I need the police," she told the dispatcher. "Someone tried to break in again. The glass is shattered, but the door is still locked. I must've scared them away."

She looked down near her slippered feet to the largest of the glass shards, kicking it out of her path. Outside, the breeze shifted, giving the fog a life of its own. Ghost-gray, it crawled through the grass, swallowing everything it touched.

"Help is on the way, ma'am. Is anyone in the house with you?"

"No. I'm completely alone."

Later, after the police had come and gone, Iris lay in bed, trying to fall asleep. *A ruffled mind makes a restless pillow*, Charlotte Brontë once wrote. And wasn't that the truth? Sometimes, Iris still missed the snuffles and rumbles of Dean's snoring. The casual way he flung his arm across her midsection. The scratch of his calloused heels against her legs. At night, her loneliness expanded like the ocean, fathoms deep.

Iris thought of Seth and Lydia. Tomorrow, she would insist they move in. It would be better for everyone.

THREE

AFTER

Monday, early morning

Officer Maureen Shaw drummed her slim fingers on her thighs, imagining the old Model L Steinway piano that sat neglected in the garage, covered in a thick layer of dust. She'd stopped performing three years ago, but she couldn't silence the music in her own head, much to her dismay. And right now, the music sounded a lot like the *Jaws* theme song. Two notes—E and F— three octaves below middle C. Simple and foreboding, a melody befitting her hard-nosed partner, Walter Greer.

Her playing picked up speed as Walt exited the 7-Eleven, two coffee cups in hand, and approached the driver's side of their cruiser, unsmiling. *Dun dun dun dun dun dun dun dun.* Her fingers not nearly as nimble as they'd once been, when she'd practiced four hours a day until the sides of her thumbs callused, all in the service of delivering a perfect performance at San Francisco Symphony Hall in front of thousands.

Balancing one Styrofoam cup on top of the other, Walt

cracked the door and nudged it the rest of the way with his foot. "A little help here, Boot."

Maureen grimaced at the nickname, not because it branded her a first-year cop—which she was—but because it made her seem like all the other rookies. Which she most certainly was not. Still, she ceased her impromptu concert, securing her cup of the strongest coffee in Upper Pacific Heights, a staple for the midnight shift and a necessity on a chilly spring morning like this one.

"Attention all units. Four fifty-nine in progress at 889 Archer Avenue. Shots fired. One female occupant located in upstairs bedroom."

The cup plummeted from Maureen's hand, narrowly missing her lap, and landed lid down on the floorboard, leaving a small black puddle beneath it. Already, Walt had launched himself into the driver's seat and reached for the radio.

"Three-E-Eleven, show us responding." He jerked the Crown Vic into gear and squealed out of the parking lot, bottoming out as he swerved onto Washington Street.

Maureen collected her cup—and her jaw—from the floor. In her nine months on the force, she'd never seen Walt move so fast. Apparently, even with one foot out the door to his retirement, the old guy could still haul ass if the situation called for it.

Lights flashing, they whizzed past the towering redwoods of Lafayette Park, the lush green lawn empty now in the dead of morning. Maureen felt slightly seasick as the car effortfully summited another hill and descended again, the homes growing larger and more opulent with every block. The car strained up the final rise and zipped down the long straightaway, coming to a stop at the corner of Archer and Broadway, adjacent to the heavily forested Presidio Park.

After Walt radioed their location back to dispatch, he drew his gun.

"Follow my lead," he told her, pointing to the massive Victorian that loomed like a giant among giants with its peaked roof, its elegant arches, and its gingerbread trim. In the glow of the porch light, the front door stood slightly ajar, one of its stained-glass windows smashed. "Keep your eyes up and your trigger finger ready. We've got an active crime scene here."

Maureen's blood zipped with urgency. *Finally.*

She drew her gun for the first time in her short career and trailed Walt down the sloping sidewalk. His lanky frame cut a sharp silhouette on the manicured patch of grass, on the perfectly groomed fuchsia cascading from the box planters.

Making quick work of the concrete steps, Walt pressed a hand to the iron railing. "Damn it," he muttered. His left palm came back stained with black paint.

Maureen pointed to the gallon of Flat Black Rust-Oleum set near the doorway, a brush resting atop it. The other side of the railing had been sanded and primed but remained dry to the touch, the project unfinished. Glaring at the enemy paint can, Walt wiped his hand on his pant leg, and Maureen bit back a nervous laugh. Nine months fielding mostly fluff calls—auto burglaries, drunk and disorderlies, the occasional assault—and now she teetered on the verge of the very thing she'd been waiting for. She could hardly manage the anticipation.

Behind them, the street extended like a long dark ribbon toward Fisherman's Wharf and the bay beyond. In a city of nearly nine hundred thousand, the quiet of this neighborhood had always unnerved her. The impeccable façades, like blank faces, hid all their secrets within.

"San Francisco PD! Show yourself!" Walt's bark cut her off at the knees. A holdover from his military days, no doubt.

When no one responded, Walt radioed for backup. Maureen didn't blame him for being cautious, but she charged ahead anyway, giving the door a little push. It yawned open, letting a sliver of light into the foyer.

She scanned the ground, sucking in a tight breath at the

sight of the broken glass that littered the polished hardwood. The crunch of the splintered pieces beneath her boots, the menacing glint of the shards. Out of nowhere, the memories rushed in, threatening to pull her under, and she braced herself for the wave of panic, the gut punch of grief that always followed.

"Flashlight," Walt whispered at her shoulder, bringing her back. Dropping her breathless on the shore of the here and now and her chance at redemption. Her chance to catch the bad guy. Even if he wouldn't, couldn't ever be *the* bad guy. "And remember, *I* take point."

Stepping to one side, Maureen withdrew the Maglite from her duty belt, allowing Walt to go ahead of her. With her gun raised, she scanned the front rooms, sweeping the beam across the home's sprawling innards. The vaulted ceiling. The grand fireplace in the sitting room. The spiral staircase that wound up four stories to the attic.

Her eyes landed on the first few steps, on the one-hundred-dollar bills that lay scattered like breadcrumbs. She followed the cash trail with her Mag up to the second floor, where an empty hat box rested on the landing. Beyond it, only inky shadows her light couldn't reach.

A sudden sound started Maureen's heart pounding. Somewhere between a flutter and a scrabble, it came from the darkness above them.

"Watch my six," Walt instructed, as he began the twisty climb. With each footfall, he redirected his flashlight upward with one hand, pointing his Glock with the other, while Maureen positioned her body at an angle to allow her a clear view behind them.

As they moved in tandem, she winced at the creaking of the old staircase. It whined beneath their weight, telegraphing their approach, reminding her they didn't belong there. Slow and steady they went, following the dropped money to the third floor, the sound growing more frantic, more desperate, the closer they came.

At the first door, Walt stopped her with a raise of his hand. Maureen peered past him into the dim cave of the bedroom, trying to make sense of the chaos. The lamp on the nightstand emitted a soft glow that illuminated the scene.

Blood stained the rumpled bedding. The air smelled of violence, metallic and cloying.

Drawers were flung open. Clothing strewn about. A jewelry box sat upended on the floor. Among its contents, a broken string of pearls, the ivory beads dotting the dark wood. Next to one of them lay a single shell casing. A second casing had fallen nearby.

From its plug near the wrought iron headboard, the phone cord had been stretched to the side of the bed. The receiver, discarded and lifeless. The line, severed.

Stoic, Walt moved ahead, methodically clearing the small space until he reached the bay windows and the source of the panicked noises.

A small blackbird beat its wings futilely against the glass, unable to see that freedom lay just a few feet to the right. One of the windows had been left half-open. Holstering his gun, Walt tried to shoo it but the bird only grew wilder, blinded by its fear. Maureen could relate. There had been days, right after, that she'd barely been able to find the surface. To poke her head from beneath the dark hole she'd crawled into.

"Let it be," she said. "It'll find its way."

Walt grunted his reluctant agreement. Turning to face the disheveled scene, he shook his head.

"What do you think?" Maureen asked him. But he'd already unclipped his radio, calling in the update. Behind him, the tired little bird fluttered down to the windowsill. It rested for a beat before hopping toward the cool, fresh air and taking flight into the still-sleeping city.

As the sirens wailed outside, Maureen stood at the foot-board, aiming the beam of her flashlight onto a picture that had fallen to the floor, the glass cracked right down the middle. In the photograph, a regal gray-haired woman sat on the steps of the Victorian, bookended by two smiling faces. A man and woman young enough to be her grandchildren.

"Two nine-millimeter casings in a ransacked bedroom. Looks like a burglary gone wrong." Walt stalked from one end of the room to the other. Finally, he tossed his hands in the air, exasperated. "But where's the goddamned body?"

FOUR

Maureen spotted the purse beneath the bed. Donning a set of latex gloves, she dropped to her knees before Walt could reappear in the doorway like a fin in open water. While the rest of the responding officers cleared the remainder of the house, he'd disappeared minutes ago to brief the robbery-homicide detectives prior to their walkthrough. She could already hear his lecture. He'd tell her to let someone else handle it. Someone older. Someone with more experience. Someone with a Y chromosome. But what did Walt know? Not all experience came in the field. Maureen had earned hers the hard way, trekking to the brink and back.

She snagged the purse's handle and tugged it toward her, leaving a skid mark on the dusty hardwood. A black leather Mulberry with gold hardware, she reckoned that handbag cost nearly one week's worth of her rookie cop's salary. Her pulse throbbing in her fingers, she worked the clasp open and removed the matching wallet.

According to the California driver's license tucked inside, Iris Duncan had celebrated her seventieth birthday in March and resided here at 889 Archer Avenue. Maureen studied the small DMV photograph in the lamplight. A short, silvery bob framed the woman's strong features. Time had wrinkled and mottled her skin, but her pale blue eyes had withstood the test. Light sparked from within them, glinting like sunrays off the bay. Already, she felt responsible for this woman. She felt accountable. The very thing the pre-employment psychologist had warned her about.

Maureen rifled through the rest of the wallet anyway, finding no cash, credit card, or cellphone. Only an appointment reminder from Golden Gate Neurology. Tomorrow afternoon, Iris was expected at a 2 p.m. intake with Dr. Stefano DeBorg. A well-worn set of keys lay at the bottom of the bag, each one labelled—house, bedroom, car—with a brightly colored band.

Dropping the purse on the plush blue ottoman in the corner, Maureen turned her attention to the bedroom. Now that her nerves had settled, she found a pattern in the chaos. She heard the soundtrack of Iris's life. A sprightly melody with a dark and lonely undercurrent. Mozart's Symphony in G minor.

On the dresser, between two towering stacks of paperbacks, the first mournful note: an oversized medication container. The Monday-morning slot remained unopened, of course, with nine tiny pills inside. Stuck to the wall above it, a Post-it read: TAKE MEDICATION DAILY. ASK LYDIA OR SETH FOR REFILLS. Maureen scanned the room, searching for more of the pale yellow reminders.

By the door: DON'T FORGET PURSE AND KEYS.

By the lamp: CHECK CALENDAR.

By the vintage clock: SET ALARM.

"You didn't touch anything, did you?" Walt materialized in the doorway, his eyes laser-focused on her gloved hands. Behind him, Maureen recognized the hulking frame of Detective Mark Casey.

"Her name is Iris." Maureen pointed to the Mulberry. "Her driver's license is inside."

"For God's sake, Shaw. I gave you one job." To the detective, he added, "They don't make these rookies like they used to."

"I think she might have memory problems. And she takes medication every day." Maureen hoped she didn't sound naïve, talking about Iris in the present tense, when blood had already soaked through the side of her white comforter. Too much blood. "She has a doctor's appointment tomorrow. A neurologist."

His mouth half-open, Walt shook his head at her. "I'm sorry, man. I assumed she understood basic crime scene procedure. It won't happen again."

Detective Casey gave away nothing until he winked at her. "Don't get your panties in a wad, Greer. She's got gloves on. And she saved us some time, ID'ing our possible vic."

His cheeks reddening, Walt spun around so quickly, he nearly took out two crime scene techs. Maureen forced her mouth into a straight line and hurried after him, knowing there'd be hell to pay. In his long career as a beat cop, Walt had apparently been passed over for detective a few times, leaving a sizeable chip on his shoulder. Rumor had it, he lacked people skills.

"Hey, rookie," the detective called out. "Next time, wait for CSI."

"Are you out of your mind?" Walt saved that little gem, waiting for the moment they ventured beyond Detective Casey's earshot. Maureen made a face, while she trailed him down the staircase and back to the foyer, where the techs had already started their work, collecting fingerprints.

"You're barely a cop and certainly not a detective," he said. "Your job is to preserve evidence, not destroy it."

"I didn't destroy anything." Ignoring Walt's dismissive grunt, Maureen added, "And the detective didn't seem to mind," as she sidestepped a fallen Post-it on the floor near the entryway. LOCK DOOR! Penned in black marker and under-lined twice, the note struck her as the most urgent and ominous of them all.

The cool air invited Maureen toward the open front door but she didn't walk through it. Instead, she turned back to the sitting room, drawn to the painting hung above the fireplace.

"Is that a Dolores?" she asked no one in particular, certainly not Walt, whose idea of culture was ordering 'chicken par-mig-iana' for lunch at the little Italian place on Fillmore.

"A who?"

"Dolores Peck. She's an artist. *Was* an artist. She died of an overdose about a year ago. Don't you remember? It was in the news." Maureen moved closer to the canvas, resisting the urge to touch it. The Golden Gate Bridge rose up from the colorful, textured sea of oil paint.

"Never heard of her."

"She was known for her abstract depictions of urban landscapes."

Maureen glanced over her shoulder, expecting to catch Walt mid-eye roll. But he surprised her, joining her in front of the fireplace. "My eyes aren't what they used to be," he confessed, as he leaned in, squinting. "I don't see a signature."

"Strange." Maureen studied the bottom left corner of the canvas. Instead of the artist's calling card, she found deep scratches in the chartreuse paint. "It's been removed. Inten-tionally."

"An art heist, huh, Boot? Well, we've got bigger fish to fry at the moment."

Maureen nodded but as soon as Walt left her alone, she

snapped a photo of the painting with her cell, planning to search for it later online. It looked similar to the Dolores in her bedroom, a gift from the late artist herself. The elderly woman had been a regular at the symphony.

Maureen stowed her phone and followed Walt outside. Beyond the doorway, patrol cars had taken over the quiet street, bathing the front of the Victorian in eerie swaths of red and blue light. A middle-aged man waved at Walt from across the way, calling him over. Backdropped by his urban castle, the man seemed small and scruffy in his sweatshirt and pajama pants. His salt-and-pepper hair stuck out to one side, holding the shape of a rogue wave.

"What's going on, Officer? It's not even four in the morning. And I have to be up in an hour for a global shareholders meeting." He extended his hand with expectation. "Bill Dorsey."

The man seemed not to notice Maureen, directing his inquiry and his firm handshake solely to Walt. Typical. With her occipital lobe already conjuring Bill Dorsey's music—Wagner's 'Ride of the Valkyries'—Maureen whipped out her notepad and jotted his name down.

"That's what we're trying to figure out, Mr. Dorsey." Walt gestured back toward the house. "Do you know the lady who lives there?"

"Iris Duncan? I certainly do. As the head of the Pacific Heights Home Owners Association, I'm well acquainted with most of our residents. Her husband, Dean, and I even played golf together a few times down at Pebble Beach. But that was a while ago now. He passed away a few years back. Of course, Iris had retired by then. She worked at the public library on Larkin for thirty-some years. Always with her nose in a book. Lord knows they didn't need the money. After she broke her arm a few months ago, I'd give her a ride to the BART station now and then."

"And Dean? What did he do?"

"Managing Director for Apex Investment Bank. In other words, a professional big shot." Maureen took Mr. Dorsey's dismissive tone as pure jealousy. The Duncan house was twice as big as his own castle.

"Did you hear anything suspicious early this morning?" Walt asked.

"Like gunshots?" Maureen chimed in, finally getting Mr. Dorsey's attention. Walt's, too. Both men frowned at her.

"Gunshots. *God, no.* Not in this neighborhood. I haven't heard a peep since last night, when Iris gave that fellow a piece of her mind. She hasn't been herself lately."

"What do you mean, not herself?" Maureen's small voice was lost beneath Walt's baritone asking, "What fellow?" Beneath her ribs, Maureen felt another pang of worry for Iris.

"Iris hired caretakers for the house a couple of months back, right after she hurt her arm. A big house like that, it's a lot to manage, and much to the dismay of the HOA, she let it get away from her. They seemed like a nice couple. Last night, she started yelling at the guy. Something about paint. I guess she'd told him to use the brown stain on the railing, not the black. She pitched a real hissy fit about it and demanded his keys back. She told him to get the hell off her property."

"And then what happened?"

"Well, nothing much. He left, and Iris huffed around outside awhile. I asked if she was okay. If she wanted me to help bring the paint inside. She told me not to bother. That Seth would do it in the morning. So, I guess she wasn't that mad at him."

"Does Seth have a last name?" Maureen asked, flipping to a fresh page in her notes.

"I'm sure he does, ma'am." Still smirking, he turned to Walt. "But I never caught it."

Walt gave a solemn nod, ignoring Mr. Dorsey's sarcasm, and repeated Maureen's question, passing it off as his own.

"What did you mean when you said Iris had been acting strangely?"

"Old age, I suppose. It catches up with all of us. Her house got broken into a while back. She thought the burglar might return. I saw her up in the attic with a pair of binoculars plenty of times, scoping out the neighbors."

Maureen's eyes drifted upward to the room beneath the roof. Windows on all sides, the views of the bay would've been spectacular.

"So, she was..." Walt returned Mr. Dorsey's smartass grin, winding his index finger round and round near his ear.

"Yep. Crazy as a damn loon."

By 8:30 a.m., Maureen lay sleepless in her bed, in her childhood home in San Bruno, staring at the Dolores on the wall above the dresser. Hers depicted the striking interior of the symphony hall, with its impeccable acoustics and unencumbered sight-lines. The paint seemed to thrum on the canvas, as vibrant as the music itself.

Dolores had given her the painting two weeks after the mass shooting that had claimed Maureen's parents' lives and nearly her own. When Maureen had decided to move back into their house, it was the only part of her old life she brought with her. *Music heals, dear*, Dolores had told her. *Music is in your soul. It'll get you through.*

Maureen's search for the Dolores that hung over Iris's fireplace had turned up nothing. She'd painted the Golden Gate before but never quite like that, with a palette of colors so bright and bold that it required effort to look away.

Maureen gave up tossing and turning and reached for the sheaf of papers on the nightstand. The transcript of the early-morning 911 call, with those two fateful gunshots captured neatly between two brackets. And the police report she'd printed from the attempted burglary at Iris's home in March. The window of the back door had been shattered, but the suspect never gained entry.

> *Complainant states she keeps cash and valuables in her bedroom. Complainant is fearful suspect will return.*

Maureen read the report again and again until her eyes blurred with the weight of the day. Until she heard the steady beat of her own music like a bass drum in her ears. Never beautiful, not anymore. But desperate. Raw. Unyielding.

Find Iris.

Find Iris.

Find Iris.

In the utter silence of that empty house, she had no choice but to listen.

FIVE

Lydia woke up alone in the Blue Bird Motel. A stupid name if she'd ever heard one, since the place had been repainted a sickly shade of mustard yellow years ago. She stretched her long legs across the expanse of the double bed, ignoring the scratchy sheets, the strange stain on the ceiling. The sound of a television blaring through the flimsy walls. For one luxurious moment, freedom swelled in her chest—delicious and terrifying—like a balloon waiting to burst.

"Open up, Lydia." Seth pounded on the door, rattling the room as hard and sudden as an earthquake, and took a pin to her short-lived freedom. A part of her felt relieved. Another part, defeated. "We need to talk."

Lydia sat up too fast. How long had she been sleeping? A quick check of the clock on the nightstand worried her. Only 8:30 a.m. Seth rarely got up before nine, not even to impress Iris. But after what happened last night, Lydia figured he had some major ass-kissing planned for this morning. Seth always knew how to smooth things over.

She steadied herself against the dresser and leaned in to the mirror, wiping the smudges of black eyeliner from her face with the edge of her T-shirt. Her pale blonde hair looked stringy and matted. Her face, puffy from last night's tears. No good ever came from crying. Seth had been right about that.

"Liddy! *Now!*"

Lydia hated when Seth called her that. It made her feel like a kid. Not a twenty-four-year-old woman with half an associate's degree. Even worse, she hated when he yelled. It reminded her of her father, and she had to fight the urge to cower in the motel closet the way she'd done back then, when she was still small enough to fit all the way inside it.

"What the hell is wrong with you?" she asked, flinging the door open. "You're making a scene."

"Really?" With dark circles beneath his eyes and anger pinching his mouth, Seth scared her a little. He gave her a withering look. "What's wrong with *me*? Get your goddamned phone."

Glancing at her cell on the nightstand, Lydia whimpered at the glacial cracks in its surface. "You broke it. Remember?"

"Yeah. After you got me all riled up. What did you think would happen?" When she didn't answer, he retrieved his own phone from the back pocket of his jeans and tapped his finger on the screen a few times, before holding it out to her like a rigged explosive. "We're in trouble."

Lydia gaped at the article, waiting for her brain to catch up to the rest of her. Half-asleep, her thoughts plodded aimlessly as zombies. "What is this?"

BREAKING NEWS
PACIFIC HEIGHTS WOMAN MISSING AFTER HOME INVASION

"Jesus, Lydia. Read it. Not *what* but *who*."

It struck her then—the obvious. The house in the grainy online news photo belonged to Iris. Her knees giving way beneath her, Lydia backpedaled toward the bed and felt the old mattress sink beneath her weight.

"Where were you last night?" she heard herself ask, already wanting a take-back.

"None of your damn business." Seth paced from one end of the dingy brown carpet to the other. The color of despair and cockroach shells, she couldn't believe she'd ever walked on it barefoot as a girl. "You're the one who threw a tantrum and tossed me out."

"I thought you'd come back. You always do. I tried to call you from the room, but—"

"My cell died. And you were acting like a bitch. You can't blame me for staying gone."

"I only said we have to be careful. And now look what's happened. What are we going to do?"

Seth stopped in front of the small closet, rubbing his stubbled chin in the cheap full-length mirror-door. Then, he slid it open, hard, retrieving her duffel and tossing it onto the bed closest to him. "I'll tell you exactly what we're gonna do. We're gonna shave off these whiskers, pack our shit, and go back to the house."

"Are you..." *Crazy*. That's what she wanted to say. "Are you sure?"

"Only a guilty man runs, Liddy." One of Seth's favorite refrains. And he knew plenty about guilt. "We didn't do anything wrong."

Lydia lowered her eyes and grabbed the duffel, busying herself in the search for a clean white T-shirt. At least she'd look innocent.

Satisfied with her silence, Seth stalked to the bathroom and shut the door behind him. In his absence, Lydia reached for his phone, reading the article once more.

An elderly woman is missing after a home invasion robbery early Monday morning. The robbery occurred around 3 a.m. at a residence in the Pacific Heights neighborhood of San Francisco. Authorities suspect at least two gunshots were fired during the robbery and believe the missing woman was seriously—possibly fatally—injured in the attack. Evidence found on the scene suggested the apparent victim may have physical and mental health problems. Her name has not yet been released.

The sudden vibration of the cell startled her, and the name on the screen—Vinnie—did nothing to calm her nerves. Neither did the text message.

I'm losing my patience.

When Seth whipped the door open, she dropped the phone into her lap.

"This is your fault, you know." His face covered in white foam, he looked ridiculous. But Lydia knew better than to laugh. "You got us into this mess. I told you it wasn't smart."

She didn't argue. He was right to blame her.

Seth turned back to the mirror, running the blade down his cheek until his skin appeared, smooth and pinked from the hot water. "You don't seriously think I had something to do with it?"

Lydia took a small breath and arranged her mouth into a solemn line.

"Do you really think I'm capable of that?"

"Of course not."

Seth's pick-up growled as he revved the engine, sending them barreling up the steep hill toward Iris's Victorian mansion. Every rumble of the truck jostled Lydia's weak stomach. She wished she hadn't eaten at all, but Seth had insisted, taking them through the Mickey D's drive-through before they'd hit the freeway to cross the Bay Bridge that linked Oakland to San Francisco. Now the sausage McMuffin sat like a lump of coal in her belly.

"Stop it, Liddy." Seth reached for her hand, pulling it away from her mouth. Her thumbnail had started to bleed. "You'll bite them down to the quick again."

She nodded, shoving her fingers beneath her thighs so she wouldn't be tempted, and tried to focus on the spectacular scenery out the passenger window. Usually, the view up here—the sailboats floating on the sparkling bay like tiny swans—made Lydia giddy. Today, it felt mocking. The promise of something she would never have. But when she turned away, she only felt worse.

Crime scene tape was draped across Iris's front door and uniformed officers dotted the lawn, the porch, the street. "They're everywhere," she muttered.

"Of course they are." Seth parked the truck at the curb a block away and checked himself in the rearview, smoothing his sandy brown locks. "C'mon."

Lydia watched him, jealous of the way he moved. Confident, effortless. Unburdened. Meanwhile, her legs had turned to lead. It took all her effort to crack the truck's door. To make her way over to the sidewalk, where he stood, waiting.

He grabbed her hand and tugged her along toward the house. It seemed bigger, taller than she remembered, as if it had grown overnight. The attic loomed above them in the cloudless sky; the empty windows felt like eyes on her back. Time seemed to slow as the man approached them from across the street. A mountain of a man with a badge on his belt. And a shiny bald head that reflected the sun.

"Should we tell them that—?"

"Hell, no. We stick to the story, no matter what."

Her breath trembled.

"Pull it together," Seth seethed through his teeth, already set in an aw-shucks grin. He extended his hand to the man. "Seth McKay. This is Lydia. We came as soon as we heard."

"Detective Casey. San Francisco PD."

After Lydia said nothing, did nothing, Seth nudged her forward, and she stuck out her hand, feeling like a scolded child. She made a face when she noticed the dried blood on the knuckle of her thumb, her nubbed nails disappearing in the man's palm.

"You'll have to forgive her, Detective." Seth wrapped an arm around her shoulders and gave her a tight squeeze. "She's a little out of sorts this morning. Morning sickness. It's common in the first trimester."

Lydia felt relieved when Seth stopped talking.

The detective matched her grimace with a polite smile. "I see. And what is your relationship to the homeowner?"

"To Iris?" Seth asked. "We live here. With her."

The detective cocked his head like an old dog, studying Seth with a mixture of apprehension and curiosity. Though Seth seemed calm as ever, Lydia worried the cop would see right through, all the way down to the rotten core.

"Iris hired us in late February," she blurted, drawing the detective's all-knowing eye. "We're the caretakers."

SIX

Lydia shivered in the stark interrogation room, cursing herself for her bad choices, starting long before the day she'd met Iris, and ending here, with the thin white T-shirt and cut-off jean shorts she'd chosen from her duffel. As she rubbed her arms for warmth, she looked down at her stomach, her breakfast still sloshing around, roiling and pitching in the angry sea inside of her.

An hour ago, Seth had driven them here to the Northern Precinct at Detective Casey's request. Lydia had spent the fifteen-minute ride practicing her breathing, trying to keep the wolf of her anxiety at bay. In his attempts to make it better, Seth had only made it worse. He'd told her not to worry. That it would all be over soon. That they had nothing to hide.

Now, Seth sat in the room adjacent to this one, reciting the story. Their story. The one they'd agreed to stick with, come hell or high water. She laid her head against the wall, pretending she could hear him. His voice, warm and rich as honey. Seth had the kind of voice that made just about anything sound like the truth.

When Detective Casey appeared in the doorway, folder in

hand, Lydia offered him a weak, "Hi." Already, her voice branded her an amateur.

"You feeling better? Can I get you anything?"

Lydia shook her head, trying to look strong. "I'll be okay."

"Morning sickness can be a real drag. When my ex-wife was pregnant with our oldest, she puked up her guts like clockwork for the first six weeks." Detective Casey made a face, then laughed at himself. Lydia wished he wouldn't be so nice. "Of course, that was a long time ago. That same little girl who gave her mama hell started high school this fall."

Lydia tried to laugh, but it came out wrong. All dead-sounding. "Just worried about Iris, is all."

"Of course, you must be very worried. You all got to know each other quite well, I imagine, living in the same house."

"A little bit. She's a real nice lady." Lydia shrugged, praying he wouldn't press her for more.

"We're hoping you and Seth can shed some light on what's happened here. The shooting this morning. Iris's whereabouts. We've got quite a mystery on our hands."

"I—*we* don't know anything about that. But we'll help in any way we can, of course."

Detective Casey scribbled a few lines in his notebook. Lydia wondered what he'd written about her. Not two minutes in, and she'd probably blown it. Seth would be pissed.

"Tell me about yesterday." He set his pen down and sat back in his chair to listen.

"It was a pretty normal day, I guess. I made Iris breakfast in the morning, helped her with her medication and her physical therapy exercises. She broke her arm in February. That's why she needed a caretaker in the first place. Seth cut the grass and started painting the stair railing, just the way Iris had asked him to. She could be forgetful sometimes. Confused, you know? She had me schedule an appointment with a neurologist to see if there was something wrong with her."

The detective nodded at Lydia, easing her. Maybe she could do this after all.

"Anyway, Seth finished the first half of the painting around eight or so, and Iris came out to look at it. She got really angry. I'd never seen her quite like that before. She said he'd done it wrong. That he hadn't used the proper color. When Seth suggested that she'd probably just forgotten what color she'd picked, that really set her off. She told Seth she wasn't crazy and her memory was just fine and then she kicked us out. She even made Seth give his key back."

"Sounds like quite an episode. I can certainly understand why you're concerned."

The tight coils in her shoulders loosened; the churning in her stomach slowed. She felt proud of herself.

"So, where did you two spend the night?" he asked.

"The Blue Bird Motel in Oakland."

Lydia could tell by Detective Casey's frown that he knew it well. Most cops did. "Quite a step down from a mansion in Pacific Heights."

"You're right about that. I used to call it a roach motel. But Seth says even roaches have standards." She laughed again, a real one this time. "We've lived there before when we were down on our luck. It just seemed like the easiest place to go."

"And you both stayed there? All night?"

The lie worked its way up her throat and sat on her tongue. Sour and hot, it demanded release. "As far as I know. And I'm a light sleeper."

If Detective Casey didn't buy it, he gave no sign. He made a few more notes, before he glanced at the observation window, then reached for the folder on his lap. From it, he removed a single sheet of paper. "Take a look at this for me, will ya."

Lydia knew no good would come from looking, so she wrung her hands together, keeping them in her lap. The voice in her head sounded like her father. His words cut like lashes, the way they always had. *Stupid girl. It's a set-up. Seth would've seen this coming a mile away.*

Detective Casey placed the document on the table in front of her, where she had no choice but to lay her eyes on it. She recognized Iris's signature at the bottom. The tall loops of the I and the D. A notary stamp, next to the date—three weeks prior.

As Lydia stared at the page, the room closed in around her. Four white walls and that creepy mirrored window. Seth had warned her they would be watching her. Detective Casey, at the center of it all, looming large and sucking up all the oxygen. His massive hands, like lions' paws, resting on the table.

"Do you know what that is?" he asked.

"Last Will and Testament of Iris Duncan," she read aloud, barely recognizing the sound of herself. "I didn't know Iris had a will."

The detective gestured back to the paper, leaving her no choice.

"I, Iris Duncan, being of sound mind..." She skipped ahead, scanning the type, squeezing her eyes shut when the letters blurred together.

"Keep reading," he prompted.

"...leave all of my interest in any property whether real or personal, including but not limited to my home on Archer Avenue, all of my cash and investments, and all the rest of my property wherever located, in equal shares, to Seth and Lydia McKay."

Lydia expelled a shaky breath and prayed she would disappear. Sadly, she remained seated in that cold, metal chair with Detective Casey waiting for her to compose herself.

"Take your time," he told her. "I'm sure it's a lot to digest."

"I had no idea about this. I mean, she talked about taking care of us. She didn't have kids of her own. But she never mentioned..."

The detective's head bobbed up and down, reassuring her,

and it hit her like a Mack truck how badly she wanted out of that room. She gazed longingly at the door.

"Tell me, Ms. McKay, how did you meet Iris Duncan?"

Lydia flashed back to the Sunrise Café, her own personal hell on earth. Come to think of it, that job had been Seth's idea. To improve her people skills. What a crock. When you got right down to it, the whole thing had been *his* fault. Just like the last time. *The last time.*

Her mouth went dry.

"Could I get some water?"

After Lydia stuttered through her story, Detective Casey offered nothing but a noncommittal, "Hmm."

Lydia tucked her lower lip between her teeth to keep from saying more. Best not to ramble like she usually did.

"So, Iris offered you a job. Out of the blue. Never met her before."

"That's right. We hit it off."

"And you quit the café?"

"That very same day. The job seemed too good to pass up. Honestly, I told my boss to shove it." Lydia tried not to smile— she didn't want to oversell it—but she couldn't help herself.

"Same story Seth told us." The detective's mouth twisted like a worm, quirking to one side then the other. "But there's one little problem. Your boss, Burt Marino, swears he fired you. That a customer called that day and told him you'd been spotted taking money from the till."

A hard swallow couldn't rid Lydia of the lump in her throat. But Seth had warned her. *Don't pull the chute unless the plane is crashing.* Surely, he would consider this a crash.

Lydia mustered her bravest face and jerked the rip cord. "Tell me, Detective, am I free to go?"

SEVEN

BEFORE

Iris lay in bed, listening to the glorious din outside her door. Pots clanged against each other, doing battle in the sink, while Lydia tidied up the kitchen and prepared breakfast for the three of them. Already, the smell of bacon wafted up the stairs. Outside, the low growl of the mower threatened to lull Iris back to sleep, as Seth steered it across the backyard wilderness. She imagined him there, her fearless weed-fighter, wiping his brow. The cuffs of his jeans darkened with grass stains that Lydia would scrub out later.

Iris threw off the covers, eager to start the day. In the three weeks since the attempted burglary, the McKays had moved their meager belongings into the master suite, and she had never been more pleased. Life had purpose again. *She* had purpose.

After putting on her slippers, Iris shuffled to the dresser and opened the Sunday a.m. slot of her oversized pillbox. She swallowed the handful of tablets without looking twice and made her way downstairs, humming her favorite tune, Louis Armstrong's 'What A Wonderful World'.

The first time she fell in love that song had been playing. And she'd danced and danced, as giddy as a clam at high water.

If she closed her eyes and let her mind go, she could picture herself there, twirling at sweet sixteen. Which wasn't so sweet at all. Not at Lost Pines. Girls could be so cruel. And orphan girls were the cruelest.

"Iris, watch out!" Lydia caught her by the arm before she missed the bottom step and wound up with another broken limb.

"Goodness. Silly me, I was a million miles away."

"Daydreaming?"

Iris gave a wistful smile as Lydia led her into the kitchen. "More like reminiscing, I suppose. That's what happens when you get to be a lonely old biddy like me. Your best years are behind you. And your birthdays are more countdown than celebration."

"Well, we won't let you get away with that kind of thinking. Besides, they say seventy is the new forty. A celebration is definitely in order. This Saturday, right?"

A grin crept across Iris's face when she realized she wasn't dreading the day as much as usual.

"So, I tried a new recipe today." Lydia presented her morning's work: a steaming pot of coffee and a breakfast fit for a queen. "I give you blueberry lemon ricotta pancakes. The low-fat version, of course. Since we're keeping an eye on your cholesterol."

"It looks delicious." Iris didn't bother to carry her plate to the formal dining room. She preferred to eat at the island where she could enjoy the vase of fresh flowers and the view from the window. "And to hell with my cholesterol. I have to die of something."

"Speaking of which, did you remember your pills this morning?"

Iris stuffed a forkful in her mouth, puzzling while she chewed. Not nearly as delectable as that tyrant Burt's. Barely edible, in fact. But she kept her criticism to herself. Best not to hurt the girl's feelings. At Lost Pines, girls like Lydia were a dime a dozen. Heck, she'd been one herself at first. Girls like that broke easy. With a mere flick of Sister Frances's wicked tongue.

"I think so. But... oh, darn it. I can't be certain."

Lydia patted her shoulder. "You eat up. I'll double-check your pillbox for you."

After Lydia vanished up the stairs, Iris turned her attention back to the window just in time to watch Daft Dorsey emerge in his silk robe to retrieve the newspaper. She stuck out her tongue at him, knowing he couldn't see her. Childish, yes. But it felt damn good. Especially after the snide little darts he'd shot at her yesterday. *I see you cleaned up those leaves just in time for spring. The HOA will be pleased to see you finally got some help around the place.*

"Good morning, Iris." Iris heard Seth before she saw him, clomping in from the back in his work boots, leaving a trail of grass and dirt behind him. He glanced at her half-eaten breakfast and raised his eyebrows. "What'd ya think of the low-fat pancakes?"

"An honest effort, I'd say."

"Tastes like sandpaper if you ask me." Seth pulled a face. "I won't tell if you lose them down the disposal. Liddy can't cook for shit."

"Keep that to yourself, dear. Unless you want to sleep on the sofa tonight."

Seth busied himself at the sink, washing the grime from his hands and face. "I have a little surprise for you," he said. "I finished the garden. Rebuilt the frame, pulled out the weeds, and put down some fresh soil. I even managed to save a few of the tomato plants. And I fixed the birdhouse. Would you like to have a look?"

"The garden!" Iris chastised herself for squealing like a

schoolgirl. "Have you ever had a fresh tomato straight off the vine? There's nothing like it."

With Seth beckoning, she sprang to her feet. Suddenly, she felt wobbly. Like one of those inflatable tube men. Still, she trekked on, intent on following Seth's blurry figure toward the back door. When he opened it, Iris gripped onto the frame, trying to regain her balance. He seemed too preoccupied with the yard to notice her struggle.

"There's still quite a bit of work to be done. Nothing I can't handle. But I'll need some cash to buy a few more things at the hardware store."

"How much?" Like a boat on a stormy sea, she leaned against the door frame to anchor herself, but the world kept pitching and thrashing around her.

"A grand should do it."

Iris realized that nodding only made her dizzier. "Whatever you need," she said, keeping her head still.

"Are you okay?" Lydia appeared at her side with a frown that came in and out of focus. "You seem a little shaky."

"She's fine." Seth too seemed faraway now. Just a black speck floating in and out of her vision.

"I'm splendid." Iris managed the few steps down toward her beloved garden before she dropped into the grass like a sack of potatoes.

The promise of air and sunlight drew seven-year-old Iris to the surface. But she stayed hidden beneath the deck, treading the icy water in the lake behind Lost Pines. She wanted to hear the voices. Two of them—no, three.

So, what do you think of the new girl? I heard her mama dropped her off at the gate. Made her walk the rest of the way on her own and didn't even wave goodbye.

Damn. That's cold.

I ain't surprised her mama don't want her. She's a real dweeb.

Whoever said words can't hurt you didn't understand the sucker punch, the wind-gone-straight-out-of-you feeling. The way a single word could devastate your foundation, rock your core as soundly as an earthquake. In the aftermath, Iris gulped in a mouth of lake water that went straight down the wrong pipe and left her hacking and flailing her arms with all her might.

When she surfaced, two pairs of blue eyes awaited her. A welcome sight, since she'd been expecting those horrid little wenches: Mathilda, June, and Alma.

"Iris?" A familiar voice called to her.

Iris tried to raise her head but it weighed a thousand pounds. A gentle hand gripped hers. She turned toward it, relieved to see them. "Lydia, Seth. Where am I?"

"It's okay. You're in the emergency room at San Francisco General. We brought you here after you fainted in the yard. Do you remember?"

"It's all a bit cloudy."

"I'll bet it is. You took quite a fall, and the doctor said your blood pressure was dangerously low. That you probably double-dosed yourself."

"Double-dosed?"

"Took too many blood pressure pills."

"But, I'm always careful. I count them out myself every Monday morning. I—" Her voice trembled.

"Tell her what you found, Liddy."

"Not now, Seth. Let's give her some space. She's probably—"

Iris finally managed to sit upright, relieved to find all her limbs intact. Only the one cast in sight. With her good hand, she pointed to herself. "*She's* right here. And *she* can hear you, so out with it."

"Well, it turns out you did remember to take this morning's medication, which is a good thing, I suppose. But when I checked a few of the other slots, the meds seemed off. A few of them had three of the white blood pressure pills instead of two, and some didn't have any."

"Oh, dear. You didn't tell the doctor, did you? He'll try to put me away in some old folks' home. A place like that, I might as well be in prison. Or taken out behind the barn and shot. One bullet right between the eyes."

"Iris, no! Don't say things like that." Watching Lydia's eyes well, Iris regretted being so harsh. That girl wasn't made for a world as cruel as this one.

"I didn't mean to upset you. I was just being dramatic." Iris sighed. "But this old noggin of mine doesn't work like it used to. If you two hadn't been there..."

Seth took a step toward the bed, moving Lydia out of the way. "I've got an idea. Since we're living in the house now, what if Lydia and I help you out with your meds? Lydia's done it before, with the last lady we worked for. And she's real good with details. She'll keep you on track. We both will. Right, Liddy?"

As Seth issued his proposal, Lydia squirmed next to him, all the color draining from her face. She reminded Iris of Ginger, the way the cat would dart under the bed at the slightest sound at the door.

"That's really unnecessary," Lydia said. "I'm sure Iris can do it. She wants to be independent."

"Actually, that's a wonderful idea. One less burden to trouble my mind."

Iris settled back against the brick that passed for a pillow and tried to clear away the cobwebs from the awful dream she'd had. Which wasn't a dream at all, but a memory. She played the rest of the scene out to its bittersweet end. The way she'd surfaced too fast, gasping like a hooked fish. The way the others had cackled when they spotted her, giggling while they gathered up her clothes and tossed them onto a low-hanging branch. The way she'd shivered in the lonely lake, as the sun dipped below the horizon, until a voice had warmed her. *You look like you could use a friend.*

As Iris drifted to sleep, she heard Seth's insistent voice. "She needs us," he said.

Truer words had never been spoken.

EIGHT

AFTER

Monday, late morning

Lack of sleep made Maureen bold. Bold enough to venture back into the city, braving the tail end of rush hour traffic on the 101. Bold enough to evade the media vultures that circled the periphery. To park her Volvo by the curb, flash her badge to Morales—the officer on duty—and skirt the crime scene tape, waltzing right back into Iris's Victorian like she belonged there among the rich hardwood floors, the ornate scrollwork that adorned the ceilings. The leather-bound books and Persian rugs.

Maureen didn't waste time in the third-floor bedroom, certain it had already been searched within an inch of its life. All the evidence, gathered and catalogued, and the blood-soaked bedding collected for DNA analysis. Instead, she wandered around downstairs, guided only by her instincts and that vicious drumbeat in her head. *Find Iris!*

First stop, the kitchen, with its swivel counter stools on

either side of a massive center island and a rolling ladder placed beneath the highest shelves. The wilted flowers on the countertop filled the room with an earthy sweetness. Maureen stood in awe for a moment, letting the sun warm her through the window. She closed her eyes, imagining Iris puttering in the kitchen yesterday evening, never dreaming what awaited her come morning.

Tacked to the refrigerator, Maureen spotted another of Iris's reminders—TURN OFF STOVE AND OVEN—and several homemade cards. Construction paper embellished with glitter and markers. One read: *Thank You, Iris!* Another: *You are a blessing!* Every card bore the same signature beneath a misshapen heart: *Lydia and Seth.*

Maureen donned the latex gloves she carried in her back pocket, opening the kitchen drawers one by one. With each tug on the decorative drawer handles, her stomach bottomed out, as if she might yet find Iris hiding inside. In the fourth drawer, she hit paydirt in the form of a stack of loose photos. Though she intended to sort through them all, she couldn't tear her gaze from the first. In it, Iris waved sheepishly from the edge of the bed with her good arm, where she sat atop the familiar white comforter. She wore a cheap birthday crown, a gold number 70 positioned at the center like a gaudy jewel.

Maureen studied the photo in the sunlight, suspicion nagging at her gut like an itch she couldn't scratch. Finally, she released a frustrated groan and surrendered to her intuition, hustling back up the stairs and into the third-floor bedroom.

Breathless, she stood in the doorway and held up the photograph, the anomaly smacking her upside the head, blatant as a brick to the face. Maureen ran her finger along the left edge of the picture, where she could just make out a vibrant blue rug. A perfect match for the ottoman in the corner.

But here—she peered above the photo and into the room beyond—the floor was bare. The condition of the wood, pristine.

Running her fingers along the smooth planks, an uneasy feeling took hold. As far as Maureen could tell, the rug had vanished along with Iris.

Raised voices from downstairs pricked Maureen's ears. She cringed at the cacophony, as discordant as a cracked cymbal.

"We live here too. We have a right to go inside."

"Not unless the detective gives me the okay, sir. You're welcome to call him yourself if you'd like."

Maureen snapped a quick photo of the room with her cell-phone, then crept downstairs toward the racket.

"Don't need to, Officer. We just spoke with him, gave our statements. The old lady that lived here, she left the house to us. To me and Lydia. So—"

"*Lived?*" Maureen pushed through the front door and onto the porch, where she found the officer toe to toe with the male half of a couple. The woman waited a few steps behind him, rocking from one foot to the other and nibbling at her thumbnail. "As far as I'm aware, Iris Duncan still *lives* here. We haven't found a body. Unless you know something we don't."

Bolstered by her not-so-subtle allegation, Officer Morales took a step forward, leaving the man no choice but to retreat onto the staircase, one step, two steps, below them. Lean and lanky, he could still look Maureen in the eyes. His were impossibly blue and twinkling like the sun off the ocean. His face, vaguely familiar.

"What's your name?" she asked him.

"Seth McKay. I *live* here." The guy sure couldn't take a hint. But at least she'd placed him as the man in the framed photo she'd found yesterday.

"Well, Seth McKay, you shouldn't be here right now. The detective will let you know when it's permissible to return."

"And who are you? You're not even in uniform."

Maureen took him down a peg with a show of her badge. It

still felt good to wield it like a talisman that could stop bad guys in their tracks.

"I'm sorry, Officer. Lydia just needs to grab a few things she left behind. We were in a bit of a hurry last night, and, well..." He dropped his voice to a conspiratorial whisper. "She's got a bad case of pregnancy brain. Can't you just cut us some slack?"

Maureen brushed past Seth to face a doe-eyed Lydia. The woman covered her stomach with her hands, wringing them nervously. "I'm only nine weeks along."

"Which room were you two staying in?"

As Lydia glanced up at Seth, Maureen positioned herself between them. But Seth barely noticed. He'd already turned back to plead his case to Morales, not recognizing a losing proposition.

"Third-floor bedroom. The master suite," Lydia blurted. Up close, Maureen could see the streaks of mascara she'd wiped from her cheeks. "It used to be her and her husband's room, but she wanted us—"

Seth cleared his throat, silencing her. Behind him, the officer spoke into his radio.

"And what exactly did you leave behind?" Maureen asked.

"Um, some clothes and stuff. It's kind of hard to explain. It'd probably be easier if I went in to look for it."

"No can do." Morales joined them on the sidewalk, ushering Seth along with him. "Now, do you two have somewhere else you can stay for the night?"

"Back to the Blue Bird," Seth muttered.

"Then, I suggest you go there."

Seth nodded his agreement. Still, Maureen caught the indignation in the flex of his jaw. As she watched him move, she heard the rapid fire of the violins, the grave and dizzying melody that left her head spinning. Rimsky-Korsakov's "Flight of the Bumblebee." "But we'll be back tomorrow. You can make book on that."

"I've already radioed Detective Casey, and he's on his way here. I'm sure he'd be happy to discuss your situation."

Grabbing Lydia by the arm, Seth tugged her toward the street, pasting a thin smile on his face. "That won't be necessary."

"Figured," Morales muttered, giving Maureen a wry smile. But she didn't stop to return the gesture. No time for high fives, since the detective would be here soon. Though he hadn't been too hard on her that morning, she didn't want to push her luck. She rushed back inside, taking the stairs two at a time.

Maureen stood in the center of the master suite, finding a small clearing in the middle of the chaos, like the eye of a hurricane. Seth and Lydia had staked their claim to the place, piling their clothing and food wrappers on every free surface, but traces of the old life remained. Wingtip shoes dulled by dust. Silk ties on a rack, the material dotted by mold spots. On the nightstand, a framed black and white wedding photograph that belonged to another era, another Iris. Latched to the arm of a strapping young man, she beamed at the camera, all light and lace.

Maureen did a slow turn, taking it all in, her eyes landing on the mahogany dresser, where Iris's pill bottles stood side by side. Maureen scanned the labels, snapped a photo. A few of them she recognized from her parents' medicine cabinet. Another bottle read: *Hydrocodone, take as needed*. Likely for the pain from her broken arm.

As Maureen hurried toward the closet, her foot slipped from beneath her, sending her skidding on the hardwood. Cursing, she reached down to retrieve the culprit that had nearly put her on her ass. A Golden Gate Fields daily horse racing form. When she raised her eyes, she spotted another and another and another, the papers scattered across the floor like dead leaves in the fall. She followed the trail to the closet door and opened it.

Unlike the rest of the bedroom, which smelled of Cheetos and hairspray, the closet reeked of the past. Bone-cold air spilled from inside it. The light didn't work. When she pulled the string at the center, it stayed black as a tomb. Maureen shivered as she crossed the threshold, goosebumps raising on her arms when her shoulder brushed against Iris's fur coat. She wondered how long it had been like this, years of memories stowed in darkness.

"Officer Shaw? Are you up there?"

Damn it. Detective Casey had arrived. There was no mistaking that bellow or the thud of his approaching boots.

Maureen backed out of the closet quickly. Like something might follow her home. On her last step, she pulled up short. Tried it again, tapping at the board with the toe of her sneaker. The plank beneath it wobbled slightly when she put her weight on it. She dropped to her knees, attempting to wedge her gloved fingers beneath the board.

"What the devil are you doing back at my crime scene, rookie?"

No need to look up. The detective's scuffed boots and long shadow signaled his arrival.

"There's something beneath the floorboard," she said, hoping like hell she was right.

Maureen kept her mouth shut, while Detective Casey worked, donning his own set of latex gloves and slipping the blade-end of the pocket knife he pulled from his khakis into the tight groove between the cherrywood planks.

"Well, I'll be damned."

Her lips still zipped, Maureen's eyes widened as she peered down into the rectangular hole. A gun lay in the shallow grave.

The detective snapped several photographs before removing the weapon. He ejected the clip from the chamber, cleared the gun, and removed the bullets, counting them out loud.

"It's a nine-millimeter ghost—no serial number—with two fired and one in the chamber. Looks like a perfect fit for that gun case our boys found in the closet."

Still, Maureen didn't speak, watching as he deposited the gun into a plastic evidence bag. He held it in his hand with reverence.

"Don't let me catch you snooping around this house again or I'll have to inform the lieutenant. You've got to earn your stripes. And keep this little discovery between us. The media's already gotten wind of the shooting. Elderly female victim, Pacific Heights. Enough blood loss to indicate a fatal injury, according to CSI. It's bound to be a circus."

Though she'd fully expected a dress-down, Maureen's heart sank anyway. "Yes, sir. I'm sorry, sir."

"Off the record, well done." His voice softened, lifting her spirits. "I think you just found our murder weapon."

NINE

Maureen rode her high back to the station, singing along with the radio. It had been a long time since she'd felt like this. As if she had a purpose, a direction. As if she could make a difference. Even when she drove past San Francisco Symphony Hall, she didn't tense up, didn't clench the wheel, didn't avert her eyes like usual. Instead, she let herself look. She let herself remember.

The glorious hall adorned for Christmas with twinkling lights and pine sprigs and red velvet bows. Her parents beaming at her from the second row. Pre-show jitters had given way to the flow, the rapturous state where the music absorbed her completely. Halfway through her third solo concert, in the middle of "Silent Night," she'd seen him enter from the side door, a shadow man dressed in black. *Is that a gun?* She'd pushed the thought away, dismissed it as a trick of the light. Admonishing herself for losing focus, her fingers kept playing and playing and playing. Until.

Maureen made the left turn off Fillmore into the Northern Precinct parking lot, without knowing for certain how she'd arrived there. Her heart snare-drummed in her chest, echoing the rat-tat-tat of gunshots. The kind that come from a long gun with a shit ton of bullets. A quick glance in the rearview mirror at her dazed green eyes confirmed what she already knew. Another flashback. It had been at least a year since her last, but the pre-employment shrink had warned her about that too. *You can't white-knuckle it forever*, she'd said.

"Watch me," Maureen muttered to herself, shaking off her hundred-yard stare, and headed into the station bullpen to find a computer.

Securing a spot in the corner, Maureen typed *Seth McKay* into the police database. She tapped her foot against the gray epoxy and waited while the screen populated its results. Three prior arrests in the last five years, forgery and false impersonation, but no convictions. A slippery fellow then. No surprise there. Lydia, on the other hand, came out clean as a whistle.

Maureen printed the details of Seth's arrest record and returned to the main screen, surveying the row of his mug shots and enlarging them one by one. At age twenty, Seth's dark hair kissed his shoulders, matching his thick scruff of beard. By age twenty-one, he'd chopped off those chestnut locks, shaved them down to a buzz. Only the beard and those blue eyes remained, glinting back at her with mischief.

Maureen clicked on the third photo to find still another version of Seth, nothing like the clean-cut choirboy who'd tried to bully his way past Morales that morning. A stark contrast to his tan skin, the spikes of his bleached hair stood at attention. A blond soul patch sprouted on his chin. He had the look of a man who spent his days on a surfboard at Ocean Beach and his nights singing in a washed-up boy band.

Barely breathing, Maureen gaped at the screen, leaned in closer, until she could count every freckle. She couldn't pull herself away. Not now. Because she knew this man, this chameleon. If only she could remember where she'd seen him before.

. . .

Maureen tried to focus on the road, but the mug shot on the passenger seat wouldn't let her rest. Seth's eyes seemed to follow her, taunt her. Still, she couldn't say why he looked so familiar. Only that she knew him. *That* she'd stake her life on.

After circling the block for fifteen minutes, Maureen got lucky. She zipped into the newly vacant parking spot across from Civic Center Plaza and jogged across the street to the San Francisco Public Library. Behind its majestic granite façade lay the portal to another world, an escape from the bustle of downtown.

Maureen stepped into the lobby, gazing upward at the skylight five stories above her and the grand staircase that swirled to the top floor. When she displayed her badge to the weary librarian behind the counter, he didn't blink. Librarians weren't so different from cops. They didn't shock easy. They saw all kinds.

"Is there someone I could speak to about a former employee? A manager, perhaps."

"Darcy's on her lunch break." He didn't miss a beat, peeling a wad of gum from the cover of a returned paperback, while he gestured over his shoulder to the closed office door behind him. "She doesn't like to be disturbed."

"I wouldn't ask if it wasn't important."

"It always is, Officer. It always is." With that, he dialed Darcy's extension, summoning her to the front, and shoved a hardback copy of *Ulysses* into Maureen's hands.

"Armor." With a wry smile, he added, "You'll need it."

When the door flung open, Maureen found herself clutching the book to her chest. No matter Darcy's diminutive size or her frumpy bowl haircut, she had the scrappy scowl of an old alley cat.

"I'm sorry to bother you," Maureen said.

"Can we skip the pleasantries and get to the point? My lunch break is only thirty minutes." She frowned at her watch. "Down to twenty-two now. And you don't look nearly as tasty as my bagel sandwich. No offense."

Maureen extended her hand, then quickly thought better of it. No pleasantries. "I'm investigating a shooting. A homicide." She hoped Detective Casey wouldn't mind her taking liberties. Desperate times and all.

"And how's that my problem again?"

Sheesh. Maureen needed a bigger book. "The victim is missing. She worked here for a long time, and I'm hoping to learn more about her. Know the victim, know the killer. That sort of thing."

"What's the name?"

"Iris Duncan." Maureen displayed the photocopy of Iris's driver's license she'd printed from the database.

"Not one of ours. I've never heard of her." Her verdict pronounced, Darcy retreated toward her lair.

"Well, according to her neighbor, Bill, she worked here for thirty years. And she's got stacks of books in her bedroom." Clinging to the hardcover, Maureen tempted fate. "Is it possible you might be mistaken?"

Wide-eyed, the librarian grimaced. *Big mistake*, he mouthed.

Darcy stopped short of her open door. Her half-eaten bagel sandwich rested on a greasy square of wax paper behind her, awaiting her return. "Excuse me. Did you say *'mistaken'*? I've worked at the main branch for thirty-five years. Twenty as manager. I've had a hand in hiring every bibliothecary who's had the good fortune of standing behind this counter. I don't forget a face or a name. I am most certainly not mistaken."

Maureen lowered her armor. "Are you a Yanni fan?" She pointed to the poster of the famous long-haired musician hanging above Darcy's desk.

When Darcy's beady eyes lit up behind her glasses, Maureen pressed on, cautiously nudging the photo of Iris across the counter. "Before I joined the police force, I used to play piano at Symphony Hall. I *know* Yanni. In fact, we performed together once. I'm sure he'd be honored to meet a patron of the arts like yourself."

Darcy snatched the printout and scurried off with it.

"She owns every album," the librarian whispered. "And a tote bag."

Before Maureen could get through the second page of *Ulysses*, Darcy returned, looking sheepish. In her hand, she held a printout of her own. Staff records from 1985, along with a volunteer badge photograph.

"Iris Duncan," Darcy said. "I thought she looked familiar."

"This can't be right." Maureen stared at a young Iris, trying to reconcile the rest of what she saw in front of her. "According to your records, Iris was a *volunteer*, not an employee. And only for one year."

"Maybe that nosy neighbor didn't know her as well as he thought."

Still speechless, Maureen could only shrug.

"Now, I've got fifteen minutes left on my lunch break. Tell me more about Yanni."

TEN

Lydia sighed at the blinking red VACANCY sign. It meant more than the prospect of another dismal night at the Blue Bird. It meant her plan had turned into a big, fat failure. Worse, even, her plan had ended them up in the police station, where Detective Casey had caught her red-handed in the middle of a lie. Her father would've wriggled out of it, talked in circles until the detective believed him or just got plumb tired.

Seth returned to the truck with a room key card and an unreadable poker face. When he pointed to the corner suite, Lydia had no choice but to crack the passenger door and accept her fate. Since they'd been turned away from Iris's house, he'd said nothing and shushed her every time she tried to talk. But she'd known Seth long enough to read all his tells. The clench of his jaw. The twitch of his hands on the wheel. The feverish rage that wafted from his pores and stained the pits of his T-shirt.

When the door closed behind them, Seth marched straight to the lamp on the nightstand and ripped the cord from the wall. He held it above his head like a trophy and unleashed a string of expletives in one long breath. Then, he hurled it at the floor, releasing a triumphant grunt when the ceramic cracked.

Lydia hung back and tried to quiet her own trembling heart until Seth stalked away looking for another victim. After he'd flung the desk chair a few times, he collapsed into it, breathless, and Lydia started cleaning. Piece by broken piece, she collected what remained of the lamp base and deposited it in the small bathroom trash can. Luckily, things like this happened all the time at the Blue Bird. In fact, a lamp or two smashed in anger was the very least of what happened here.

"I can't believe those cops." Seth sounded like a man who'd gone nine rounds in the ring. Lydia half expected his eyes to be blackened, his lip swollen and bloodied. Lucky for him furniture didn't hit back. "I don't trust them. Not one bit. You watch, they're gonna try to pin this on us."

Lydia nodded. Best to agree when he got like this.

"Well, I did exactly what we talked about." Managing to keep her voice steady, she looked away so Seth wouldn't see the lie on her face. She couldn't admit she'd let him down. That she'd let the detective get the best of her. Sure, she'd lied about getting canned from Sunrise, but it didn't make her a killer. "It wasn't as hard as I thought it would be."

"Good girl. So, what did he ask you?"

"Just the basics. What we did last night. Where we stayed. How we met Iris."

"Alright, same here." Seth's breathing quieted, but the red flush in his cheeks remained. Like a pot set to simmer. "Just remember, every word out of your mouth is ammunition. The less you give them, the less they have to use against you."

Lydia sat lightly on the precipice of the double bed. She chose her words just as carefully, hoping not to trigger him. "Do you think they found it?"

"How the fuck would I know, Liddy?" Seth burst up out of the chair, pacing like a tiger in a cage. She'd never seen him quite this unhinged and it made her wonder. Wonder and worry. "You're the one who wanted to hide it in the first place."

"Because I didn't want Iris to hurt herself by accident. You know how confused she gets."

"Yeah, well, you better pray they don't find it. That cop is sniffing our trail like a bloodhound in heat, and we already look guilty."

"Guilty of what, exactly?" Lydia knew what. But she didn't want to think it. Not about sweet Iris, her only real friend. Some friend she'd been in return.

Seth cocked his head at her. "Don't tell me you're *that* stupid."

"You think she's..." Already, she felt the tears coming. A hot ball formed in her throat.

"Dead? It sure as hell seems like it." He shook his head, disbelieving, a slimy grin wiped across his face. "Can you believe she named us in her will?"

Lydia winced. "So, you didn't know?"

"Of course I didn't. If she had spilled her guts to anybody, it would've been you. Once you told her about the baby, you had her eating out of your hand."

"Really?" She hated the way it came out. As if he'd pinned a blue ribbon on her shirt. It had been the same with her father, always praising her for the wrong things. Like convincing the tourists at Fisherman's Wharf to give her money for the dying sister who didn't exist.

"Goddamn right."

"And what about the painting?"

"What about it? Cops don't know jack shit about art. That detective couldn't pick out a Dolores if he fell over one. Trust me. That painting is the least of our worries."

The way he said it, Lydia almost believed him. Groaning, she laid back and buried her head in the pancaked pillow, the scratchy comforter that smelled faintly of cigarette smoke. "I feel so bad though."

"Listen, Liddy, I'm sorry I freaked out. You know how I get. But, I'm not sorry for breaking that piece-of-shit lamp. I did that thing a favor when I put it out of its misery." Seth bounced down next to her and tugged on her arm until she relented and glanced up into his still-smiling face, into the bright blue sunbursts of his eyes that made it impossible to keep herself from smiling back.

"So, how much do you think she's worth?" Seth asked. "A couple mil?"

Lydia had seen the bank and brokerage account statements Iris left lying around her room. Chiding her for being so careless, Lydia had always folded them carefully and tucked them back into their smooth white envelopes, stacking them inside the dresser drawer. "More. A lot more."

At that, Seth jumped up from the bed, wide-eyed, and grabbed the keys, calling to her over his shoulder. "Put some ice in the bucket. We need to celebrate."

Lydia left the room open, with the security latch wedged between the door and frame, her flip-flops smacking the warm sidewalk on the way to the ice machine around the corner. As she filled the plastic bucket, she scanned the parking lot for any sign of Seth's shiny new truck that stood out like a sore thumb in the beater-filled Blue Bird lot. Seth should've been back by now, and she worried his quick trip to the minimart across the freeway for cheap champagne had turned into an afternoon at the races.

She stood in front of the vending machine, the ice glistening like glass at her feet, and surveyed the picked-over remains, uncertain what to choose. Stale corn chips. A lone Snickers bar. Or the sad little packs of dried fruit nobody wanted. Still sober as a judge, her head felt foggy, tired. Her thoughts swam lazily in the mire of the day until they sank down to the cold, murky bottom. It always happened this way. After the adrenaline surge of panic wore off, she crashed hard.

Scrounging in her jean shorts, Lydia dug up the one dollar and twenty-five cents she needed to liberate that Snickers. When it plunked into the drawer below, already she felt better. Chocolate could fix anything. Iris had said that sometimes, on days when her memories slipped through the cracks, unreachable.

Still no sign of Seth, she carted her loot back to the room, pushing the door open with the ball of her foot.

She smelled Vinnie—the stench of cigars and cheap cologne —before his hand clamped down over her mouth and he pulled her up against the protrusion of his pot belly. Her body woke up too fast, leaving her dizzy, and she dropped the bucket right there on the carpet, sending a few ice chips over the side.

"Where is he?"

Lydia kicked her legs until he set her free and tossed her onto the bed like a rag doll. "Who?"

"Don't play with me, Lydia. You know *who*." Vinnie stalked toward her, his corn-kernel teeth bared beneath a wiry mustache. "And you know why. He owes me. And I don't care if he is family. I gotta eat too, ya know."

"Well, I can't help you. He went out a while ago. I'm not sure when he'll be back." Lydia pushed herself back against the headboard, as far out of Vinnie's reach as she could manage. The sight of his nubby fingers creeping toward her legs made her skin crawl.

"Call him."

"My phone's broken."

"Sure it is." Vinnie's belabored sigh turned into a smoker's cough, his plump face reddening as he hacked. Finally, he stood up and spit a wad of phlegm into the trash can.

Lydia pretended his showing up here didn't knock the wind from her. "He's got your money. He's good for it, I mean. We need a few weeks though. That's all."

"A few weeks." A laugh clunked from Vinnie's throat. It sounded as dead and slimy as the glob he'd hocked up. "Look at you, covering for him. Your old man would roll in his grave if he knew what you turned into. He had high hopes for you."

Lydia had been eleven years old and panhandling at Lake Merritt when her father handed her a square of cardboard and a stinky black marker and told her to write something that would make the rich folks fork over their filthy money. *Who's cuter—me or my brother? Vote with your quarters.* They'd taken in over one hundred dollars that day, and Lydia earned herself an ice cream sundae at Fenton's. So what if her side of the shoebox had far less money? Her dad had doled out something better, rarer. Those exact words: *I've got high hopes for you, Liddy.*

"I'm not covering for him. It's the truth. But you've got to be patient. Right now, we're dead broke." She said a silent prayer of thanks that she'd left her coffee can bank in her bag. Vinnie would've taken what little they had. Even as a girl, she remembered him—*Uncle Vinnie*—circling like a shark.

He moved back toward the bed, resting his hand on her bare thigh, his pupils big and black as raisins. He dug his too-long fingernails into her flesh. "Don't bullshit me. He's been gallivanting around Oakland in a sixty-thousand-dollar truck. You expect me to believe he needs a few weeks?"

Though her leg burned, Lydia didn't move, didn't wince. It wasn't only fear that fixed her there, a deer in the headlights. Stubbornness ran thick in her blood, and she'd be damned if she gave him the satisfaction. "Believe what you want, that truck was a gift. We don't have your money."

Vinnie dug in deeper, his lips curling like a worm. "And do you really think he'd tell you if he had the cash? Hell, no. It'd already be used up, chasing the next winner. Hoping to finally be in the money. It'll always be a couple more weeks with him. A couple more weeks with nothing to show for it. I can't believe you're stupid enough to think any different. You really do take after your mama."

"I'm not stupid. You're the one who loaned him the money. How *stupid* is that?" Lydia had had about enough. Through gritted teeth, she added, "And don't talk about my mom, asshole."

Before Vinnie could make his next move, Seth burst through the door, fisting two brown paper bags. The gold wrapper of André Brut visible between his fingers. "Vinnie? What the hell are you doing here?"

Vinnie retracted his claws, and Lydia sucked in a tight breath, rubbing the red half-moons he'd left on her skin.

"I'm here on business. You know that."

Seth frowned at the marks on her leg. At the ice bucket still plopped on the floor, the carpet wet around it. "That don't look like business. That looks personal. Real personal."

"When you put it like that, a man's money is about as personal as it gets, I'd say. And you're twenty thousand short. Now, if you want *her* to work off your debt, I'm sure we can come to an arrangement."

The fire crept up Seth's neck and into his face. His grip tightened around the bottlenecks. "You pervert."

"So, *now* you've got a problem with it?" Vinnie guffawed. "You're just jealous that she likes me better. A lot better."

Usually, Lydia would try to douse Seth's flame. She'd gotten good at putting out his fire. But not this time. Instead, she directed his wrath at Vinnie. "He already copped a feel," she told him.

Like an angry bull, Seth's nostrils expanded with each breath.

"Easy. Easy now." Vinnie backpedaled toward the door, his

hands raised in surrender. "It ain't like I haven't already sampled the merchandise."

Lydia's smirk flattened, shame curdling her stomach. She wished the floor would open up beneath her and swallow her whole.

Seth reared back and took a vicious slice with one of the bottles, missing Vinnie by a hair's breadth. While Vinnie fumbled with the door handle, Seth lined up strike two. The blow glanced off his shoulder, leaving the bottle still intact.

Finally, Vinnie pulled the door open. But in his rush, he stumbled on a ripple in the carpet. A meatball right down the middle, Seth took aim and swung for the fences. The bottle shattered against Vinnie's bald head, and he fell to his knees on the sidewalk just outside the room. Blood dripped from beneath a gash above his ear.

"Get out of here. Now." Seth stood over him and wielded the broken bottle top.

Leaving the safety of the bed, Lydia retrieved the ice bucket and joined him there. "And don't come back," she added, upending the bucket.

Vinnie scrambled to his feet, slipping on the ice, and wobbled through the parking lot to his gold-trimmed Chrysler. By the time Lydia shut the door, Seth had retrieved the two plastic cups from the bathroom, freeing them from their sanitary wrappings and filling them to the brim with cheap bubbles.

He raised his cup, tinking it against Lydia's. "To Vinnie."

Already, Lydia regretted drinking too much champagne. She lay on one of the double beds with a raging headache, while Seth sprawled on the other, snoring like a freight train. When she tossed another pillow in his direction, he groaned and shifted. Then, he picked up right where he'd left off with his nasal droning.

More brutal than the throbbing behind her eyeballs, Lydia's conscience had begun its incessant nagging. Vinnie hadn't been wrong about Seth—he'd already burned through the haul from their last con—or her, for that matter. Though Lydia preferred to think of herself as loyal, not stupid. A razor-thin line she'd been skirting for as long as she could remember. First, with her dad. Now, Seth.

Annoyed with herself, Lydia rolled onto her side and forced her body upright. Seth didn't stir, not even when she prodded him in the ribs with her knuckle. A lightweight herself, he'd finished off most of the bottle, along with the remnants of the flask of vodka he kept stashed in the truck's glove box.

Lydia crept toward the small closet, where they'd deposited their bags. Seth's black backpack sat in the corner, the top half unzipped in invitation.

Vinnie's question played on repeat in her head—*Do you really think he'd tell you if he had the cash?*—until she had no choice but to satisfy her doubt. With the care of a cat burglar, Lydia tugged the zipper the rest of the way and pulled back the top flap. She rifled through the loose racing forms, the extra T-shirts and boxers, to the bottom.

Her hand froze on a fat white envelope with Iris's handwriting. She drew it to the surface, to study it beneath the flickering closet light. It read: *For when the baby comes.* The withdrawal slip tucked inside showed the date.

The walls of the motel room closed around her, trapping her in that ratty closet where a dead cockroach lay belly up in the corner. Her mouth went dry as talc. Couldn't feel her fingers, as she opened it. It took her nearly two minutes to count the hundred-dollar crisp bills, another two to recount them, convinced she'd been wrong the first time.

One day before she disappeared, Iris had given Seth twenty thousand dollars in cash, the exact sum he owed Vinnie Frank.

ELEVEN
BEFORE

Chuckling under her breath, Iris steered her binoculars away from Daft Dorsey's picture window, where she'd just born witness to his abject humiliation. Mrs. Dorsey suffered no fools. And she'd sent her husband away from their shouting match with his tail between his legs. Iris couldn't remember ever having a cross word with Dean, much less yelling at him. But the past always sparkled, coated in its sheen of unreality.

Iris rested her good arm for a bit, massaging her shoulder. It was a bother, holding the binoculars in one hand. But she had to face the music. The cast wasn't coming off for another six weeks. At least her medication mix-up and subsequent zonk-out hadn't caused any further damage. While Seth and Lydia stood by her bedside, the ER doc had delivered the news, droning on about how lucky she'd been. *At your age, Mrs. Duncan, hip fractures are quite common. You need to be more careful.*

Raising the binoculars once more, Iris aimed them at the horizon. Past the dome of the Palace of Fine Arts to the shimmering blue waters of the Bay and beyond to the Marin headlands. She never tired of that view. Few paintings could do it justice.

When she heard a soft whimper from below, she froze, her heart skipping like a stone. Seth had left hours ago for the hardware store on Fillmore, armed with a thick wad of her cash, and she'd left Lydia dusting in the library. But she couldn't deny her ears. Someone was crying.

Iris left the binoculars on the ledge and followed the sound to the master bedroom. Through the crack in the door, she spotted Lydia curled like a snail atop the covers, her shoulders gently shaking. Iris knocked but she couldn't wait. Couldn't just leave her alone to suffer. Her time at Lost Pines had taught her well. Trouble shared was trouble halved.

"What's the matter?"

"Nothing." Lydia sat bolt upright, wiping beneath her eyes with a dust rag. Her cleaning supplies sat in a plastic bin on the dresser.

"It doesn't look like nothing. I heard you from the attic." Iris nudged the door open and entered the room. She'd thought it would be harder to see it this way, with the belongings of strangers strewn across the oak hardwood that Dean had restored.

"I'm sorry I disturbed you. I thought I shut the door. I'll get back to work." Lydia made a move to get up, but Iris stopped her.

"No, no. It's no bother. Take a break. Besides, I've got two good ears and nothing but time to listen." She joined Lydia on the bed, propping herself up with a pillow.

"I suppose it would be nice to talk to someone. It's been me and Seth on our own for so long, I hardly have any friends. To be honest, I'm not sure I've ever had one. The girls in high school all made fun of me. And at community college, everybody seemed so busy with their own lives."

Iris nodded and clasped Lydia's hand. "It was the same for me, dear. But all you need is one true friend. So, tell me, what has Seth done to get you so upset?"

"How did you know?"

"I know trouble when I see it. And that boy has trouble written all over him. Handsome, to be sure, and charming. The worst combination."

"Don't forget self-centered," Lydia added. "And he never keeps his promises. Never thinks of anybody but himself."

"Was he always like that? He mentioned that you two grew up together. I'll bet you know him inside out."

Freeing her hand from Iris's, Lydia busied her fingers, twisting the dust rag that was now darkened by her mascara. She wore too much makeup anyway, if you asked Iris. Smeared that stuff on her eyes like warpaint.

"I really shouldn't be telling you all this. Seth would lose his mind if he knew. He likes to make a good impression."

"It's not my place to get involved, but..." Iris chose her words carefully, knowing how skittish Lydia could be. "Well, it's just that for two young people in love, you sure don't act like it. When I was your age, Dean couldn't keep his hands off me. But I haven't heard a peep from this bedroom. You won't make any babies that way."

A rash flamed across Lydia's cheeks. "Um, I..."

Iris smacked her own hand, wincing as a jolt of pain travelled up her fractured radius. "Jiminy Cricket, Iris. What's wrong with you?" Then, to Lydia, "Don't pay any mind to this old fuddy-duddy."

"You're not a fuddy-duddy." Lydia turned to face her in earnest. "You're the coolest lady I know. And you've been so kind to us, taking us in like this. We couldn't have dreamed of staying in a house this fancy. Not in a million years."

"I just want to see you happy. Especially since you've both been so helpful, agreeing to take on extra work." Iris gestured to the array of pill bottles on the dresser. That morning, Lydia had finally agreed to Seth's suggestion that they arrange them in

Iris's medication box each week. "Maybe a little bundle of joy would be just what the doctor ordered. It would certainly take my mind off the break-in. And think of all the fun we could have fixing up a nursery in one of the guestrooms. Of course, you both would need a raise so you can start saving for a college fund."

"You'd do that? For us?"

Iris smiled. "As long as I get godmother status."

They sat for a moment, both quiet with their thoughts, until Lydia squeezed Iris in a side hug, careful not to jostle her arm. As she held her there, captive, she whispered, "I didn't want to tell anyone yet, but I'm pregnant."

While Lydia slaved away—cleaning the oven, reorganizing the refrigerator, folding the laundry—Iris kept her entertained, regaling her with stories about Dean and the library and their life in San Francisco. Eventually, Iris settled at the island counter in the kitchen, pleased with herself for lifting Lydia's mood. Even the TURN OFF STOVE AND OVEN Post-it note Lydia had insisted on didn't irk her like it usually did. But as the hours dragged on with no sign of Seth, Lydia closed up like a clam, her eyes cutting to the window as she chopped vegetables to add to the beef stew, and Iris sat alone with her thoughts.

Just as the pot had reached a simmer, Seth appeared at the door, dropping two bags from the hardware store on the stoop before entering the house.

"Sorry I'm late." With a rueful grin, he deposited a handful of coins into Iris's hand. "Here's your change. Supplies these days cost a fortune."

Lydia kept stirring the stew without looking up. "What took you so long?"

"Damn engine's acting up again. The thing overheated in the parking lot. I swear, some days I'd like to watch that hunk of junk burn." Seth retrieved a spoon from the drawer and sidled up next to Lydia, sneaking a taste of the steaming brown mixture even as she swatted his hand away. "I'm starving."

"Car trouble? Oh dear. You should've called. I would've sent a taxi and had it towed to the shop. Or Lydia could've driven us over in the Mustang." Iris chuckled. "Now that would've been a sight."

"Trust me, you don't want to get Liddy behind the wheel. She's an anxious driver. A real menace to the road." Seth pulled a face as he joined Iris at the counter. But Iris kept her eyes on Lydia. Hunched over the stove, she still hadn't stopped stirring.

"It was no biggie," Seth continued. "I walked over to the gas station and got some coolant. Fixed 'er right up."

"Well, you two need a reliable vehicle. Especially now."

"Why's that?"

Iris winked at him, the news brimming over in her smile. "Lydia told me your little secret."

"She *what*?"

The stirring spoon fell from Lydia's hand and clattered onto the stove. "Iris—"

"Your bun in the oven. Your pea in the pod. Your bundle of—"

"Iris, no!" Lydia spun around, pale-faced and stammering. "I... I didn't tell him yet."

"Bun in the oven?" Seth sprang to his feet, grabbing the girl by the arms. He didn't shake her, but her whole body trembled anyway. "What the hell is she talking about, Lydia?"

"I was going to tell you." It slipped from her mouth like smoke, barely a whisper.

Iris grimaced at them both. At the unspoken words that passed between their eyes. "My goodness. I seem to have opened my big mouth and stuck my foot right in it."

Seth released his grip. Still, they stood there, limbs taut as rope, facing one another in silence. Iris could see what needed to be done. "I'll leave you two to talk this out in private."

TWELVE
AFTER

Tuesday, early morning

Maureen couldn't focus. And a slow crime night in the Northern Precinct didn't help. Two DUIs, a domestic disturbance, and a public urination call couldn't cut through the noise in her brain. Not even close. Nor could Walt's endless droning about the Warriors come-from-behind victory.

"...And then, Curry shakes off VanVleet and drives to the bucket. Kicks it out to Thompson. *Splash*. Three points, and we win by one." Walt pumped his fist in the air with such exuberance Maureen feared he'd thrown out his shoulder. "What a game. Reminds me of my playing days at Lowell High. District champs three years running."

She waited for the dust to settle on Walt's championship trophy, then came right out with it, unable to contain herself a moment longer. "Have you heard anything more about Iris Duncan?"

"Iris *who*?" Walt piloted the cruiser toward the station with twenty minutes left on their shift. Desperate for any distraction, Maureen didn't even mind the arrest paperwork that awaited them.

"The elderly woman shot inside that Victorian in Pacific Heights early yesterday morning. They still haven't found the body. And she didn't work at the library like the neighbor said."

"Aw, jeez, Shaw. Give it a rest."

"I will," Maureen began. "Eventually. I care what happens to these people, Walt."

He shook his head like a disappointed father. "Well, that's your first mistake. You gotta shut that shit down. If you want to last at this job—and I think you do—then you have to treat it as just that. *A job.* No different than an auto mechanic or a ticket taker. First rule of policing, you don't get attached."

"And second?" Maureen asked.

"Huh?"

"What's the second rule of policing?"

Walt sneered. "Never agree to take on a smartass boot as your partner, that's what."

*Smart*ass. Not a total insult then. "Do you think we could roll by the Duncan house tomorrow? Canvass the area. See what we see."

He replied with a heavy sigh.

"C'mon, Walt. You're set to retire in a few months. Let's shake things up a little. What do you have to lose?"

"My pension, for starters." Maureen kept her puppy-dog eyes trained on him. "If I agree, do you promise to shut up about it?"

She ran two fingers across her lips, zipping them closed.

"Fine. A quick drive-by." As he piloted the cruiser into the lot, Walt gave her a stern look. "Until then, let it go."

. . .

Letting go didn't come easy to Maureen. Which was how she'd learned to play Ligeti's "The Devil's Staircase" by the time she'd turned eleven. And why she'd sat through every excruciating day of the murder trial of Adam Waddell, the seventeen-year-old kid who'd mowed down her parents and ten other concertgoers with an AR-15 at Symphony Hall. Maureen had the tenacious spirit of a bulldog with a bone. A bulldog who found herself in plainclothes outside the Blue Bird Motel at 9 a.m., waiting for Seth and Lydia McKay to show their faces.

Maureen knew the Blue Bird. What cop didn't? Though she'd never patrolled the streets of Oakland, legends of the no-tell motel had whispered their way across the Bay Bridge. Murders, prostitution, drug deals gone bad. The kind of place "you can never leave" that the Eagles sang about. When Seth told Officer Morales where they'd be staying the night, Maureen could've guessed she'd end up here eventually. *Bulldog, meet bone.*

As she counted the minutes, humming "Hotel California" and watching the dreary rooms for signs of life, the sun disappeared behind a wall of clouds. The sky turned slate gray and started spitting rain. Just enough to muck up her windshield, but at least the squeak of the wipers kept her alert. She hadn't had a proper rest in over twenty-four hours. And a bowl of Fruit Loops and half a doughnut barely counted as a meal.

When Seth emerged from the corner suite, Maureen hunkered down in the Volvo. Steadying her hand against the wheel, she snapped a few pictures on her cell as he walked to his truck, the black GMC that towered like a giant in the parking lot, where most of the cars looked one joyride away from the scrapyard. Later, she'd enlarge the photos on her computer. Maybe it would jog her memory.

Seth tossed his backpack onto the passenger seat and climbed inside the cab. He started up the truck and eased it out of the lot, heading toward the freeway. Maureen followed, of course. The unexpected May drizzle slowed traffic to a crawl, and the truck's size allowed her to keep a safe distance, easily tracking it down I-580 to the Gilman Street exit.

Maureen had Seth's destination figured. Golden Gate Fields rose up on the side of the highway, adjacent to the bay. She trailed the truck into the parking lot, ducked into a spot several rows away, and tugged on the ratty Giants baseball hat that once belonged to her father. As the bugle made its regal pronouncement—ten minutes to race time—Seth hurried inside the venue with Maureen behind him.

While Seth jogged toward the counter, he rummaged through his backpack, leaving a trail of daily horse racing forms behind him. Finally, he produced a thick white envelope. Maureen posted up nearby, her ears pricked.

"Put it all on Skydancer to win the first race." Breathless, Seth shoved the envelope through the slot.

The female teller counted the large stack of bills, unfazed, and issued his ticket. "Good luck."

Ticket in hand, Seth beelined it for the stadium and disappeared into the stands. Maureen approached the counter.

"That gentleman that just left, what was the amount of his bet?" Maureen flashed her badge as she spoke. The teller regarded it no different than she had Seth's greenbacks. Unimpressed, her mouth remained a flat line drawn in red lipstick.

"He placed twenty thousand on Skydancer. At sixteen to one, she's a long shot. But that's the way he likes it."

"So, you've seen him before?"

"Seth?" She lifted one corner of her lip, attempting a smile. But it came nowhere near the rest of her face. "Does a horse have four legs? He's here damn near every day, just like his daddy before him."

"Is it typical for him to bet that kind of money?"

"Not especially. Then again, have you seen Skydancer?"

Maureen shook her head.

"He's a gray thoroughbred." At Maureen's perplexed silence, the teller widened her heavily lined eyes, repeating herself like a kindergarten teacher. "*Gray*."

"I'm sorry. I don't really follow horse racing."

"There's this old superstition. 'When the track is wet, gray's your bet.' Gray horses are mudders. That means they like getting their hooves dirty."

"So, Seth bet twenty thousand dollars on Skydancer because of a racing folk tale?"

Maureen caught a whiff of cigarette smoke in the teller's staccato laughter. "You're not much of a gambler, are you, hon?"

She thought of all the risks she'd taken in her twenty-five years. Youngest student accepted into the Conservatory of Music. First solo performance at Symphony Hall at age fifteen. Concert pianist turned mass shooter survivor turned rookie cop. "Not that kind."

"Is Seth in some kind of trouble?"

The starting bell sounded and the gates sprang open, rescuing Maureen just in time. "I better get out there."

"Word of advice. Steer clear if he loses." The teller lowered her voice so that Maureen had to strain to hear her over the din of the small crowd. "And even if he doesn't."

Maureen rushed outside, scanning the mostly empty bleachers until she spotted Seth standing at the railing. Eyes transfixed on the muddy track, he seemed not to notice the misty rain that slicked his hair and darkened his T-shirt.

"Past the half mile pole, it's Lady Macbeth by a length and a half, and Brown Sugar in second…"

Maureen spotted Skydancer near the back of the pack. Kicking up a dirt storm behind her, the gray horse made her move.

"On the far outside, Skydancer is moving up. Lady Macbeth still out front, with Brown Sugar close behind."

Seth unleashed a sudden yowl that rose up above the sparse group of onlookers. "Go! Go, goddammit!"

"At the far turn, here comes Skydancer, gaining on Lady Macbeth." The two horses raced nose to nose, driving hard toward the finish. Maureen didn't breathe, didn't move. As they rounded the final turn, their hooves pounding the dirt, she half expected the bleachers to tremble beneath her. Travelling the length of the stands, Seth waved his hands in the air, willing Skydancer forward.

"And down the stretch they come. It's Skydancer by a nose, with Lady Macbeth trailing. Now, Lady Macbeth pulls ahead. It's Lady Macbeth gaining steam in the final furlong. But here comes Skydancer. It's Lady Macbeth and Skydancer down to the wire. And it's... it's too close to call, ladies and gentlemen."

Seth paced at the railing, looking as keyed up as if he'd run the race himself. When his eyes cut to the leaderboard, Maureen stifled a gasp.

"And Lady Macbeth wins in a photo finish!"

Slinging his backpack over his shoulder, Seth stomped up the bleachers toward her, radiating heat. It was too late to turn tail, so Maureen pulled her cap down low and hoped like hell he wouldn't recognize her.

No need to worry, she realized, when Seth ripped the door open with a growl. He moved like a missile intent on destruction, launching himself through a group of spectators with such force that he nearly knocked an old man to the ground. The man steadied himself with his cane, as Seth scowled at him.

"Get out of my way, clown."

Maureen lagged behind Seth's trail of fire as he blazed back to the parking lot, oblivious. When he reached his truck, she ducked down behind an SUV in the adjacent row and waited, peering around the side to witness the show.

Seth dropped his backpack on the wet concrete and stalked toward the car next to him. He glowered at the little Kia, like it had just insulted his mother. Taking a quick glance around him, Seth reared back and nailed the side mirror with his heel.

"It's all..." He punctuated it with another foot strike.

"Your..." And another. Finally, taking his fist to it a few times.

"Fault..." Dangling by a wire, the mirror hung loose, waiting for Seth's paws to rip it free. He held it above his head and smashed it to the concrete, yelling, "Iris!"

His chest heaving, Seth grabbed his bag and climbed into the cab of his pick-up. Maureen watched him go, too stunned to follow.

As she examined the damage to the hapless Kia and its amputated digit, her mind went right back to Symphony Hall. To the last time she witnessed that kind of rage. And to the courtroom, where she'd waited patiently, willing Adam Waddell to turn from the defendant's table and look at her. She knew a killer when she saw one.

THIRTEEN

Maureen loitered outside the entrance to the Robbery-Homicide Division, second-guessing herself. She had to admit she'd crossed a line following Seth to the track, flashing her badge to get intel on her prime suspect. Even so, Detective Casey needed to know about the tirade she'd witnessed. And the big money Seth had dropped on Skydancer. Maureen shuffled from one foot to the other, trying to decide. Go in or go home.

She reached for the door handle. Just then, it opened, forcing her to yield her section of the polished tile floor to a pair of black boots and broad shoulders. To look into the familiar, unsmiling face of Detective Peter Diedrich. The same face that had once been her port in a storm, now churned her stomach like a maelstrom and made her wish she'd gone home instead.

When Diedrich looked at her, his frown deepened. She might as well have stomped on his toe. Before she could flee—which she fully intended to do—Detective Casey appeared in the doorway.

"Well, if it isn't the rookie gumshoe." At least Casey looked amused. But then again, that irked her too. No one took her seriously. "What are you doing skulking out here in street clothes?"

"I wanted to talk to you, sir." She purposely avoided Diedrich's eyes. She knew what he thought of her. *Mentally unfit for duty.* He'd had no qualms about sharing his opinion with her field training officer and the lieutenant. The worst part was that she couldn't blame him. "In private, if you have a moment."

"We were just on our way out." The detective glanced down at his watch, while Maureen questioned her life choices. *We.* So, they were partners. Which meant that the odds of her impressing Casey had taken a sudden turn for the worse. She'd become the cop equivalent of the long shot, Skydancer.

"I promise I'll be brief. It's about the Duncan case."

"Of course it is," Diedrich muttered. Mercifully, Detective Casey ignored him and pointed up ahead.

"Walk and talk."

Maureen launched right in, staying glued to his shoulder as she gave him the full debrief about Seth's meltdown at the track. She even threw in her observation about the missing rug for good measure. Behind them, Diedrich lingered within earshot. Once, she swore she heard him scoff, but when she spun around, he showed her the same blank face. By the time she finished her story, they'd reached the Crown Vic in the parking lot.

"I know I violated procedure."

"That's putting it mildly." Diedrich shrugged off her glare.

"But it seemed important. I couldn't keep it to myself. Not with the stakes so high."

Detective Casey nodded, buoying her hopes. He understood her need to catch a killer. How it consumed her, drove her. Defined her. "I told you to stand down, Shaw. And what did you do?"

She gritted her teeth. Her hopes sank back to the murky bottom. "The complete opposite."

"Exactly."

"And it's not the first time," Diedrich added. "She's got a history of—"

Maureen couldn't let him say it. Couldn't let him do it. He would unearth her ugliest skeleton and make it dance. "Can you at least tell me if you got any prints from the gun? Was CSI able to match the weapon to the casings we found at the scene?"

"Yes and yes."

Detective Casey opened the driver's side door and lowered his long legs into the seat. Diedrich stood across the car from her, casually watching her implode. He'd borne witness to her desperation before, and now he'd never let her forget it.

Maureen leaned down, peering into the cab of the vehicle, both to avoid Diedrich's judgment and to plead her case. "C'mon, sir. Don't leave me hanging. After all, I did find the gun, didn't I?"

"Officer Shaw, we have a job to do. And so do you. Now, questionable methods aside, I appreciate the information. But we follow the rule of the law here. We have to. Anything less, and we jeopardize our investigation." Detective Casey reminded her of her father—firm but kind—and that same ache in her ribs returned with a vengeance. Thinking of her parents still felt like pressing a bruise.

"Surely you, of all people, can understand that." Diedrich drew Maureen's eyes upward to meet his own. She saw herself reflected there. The girl she'd been, barely twenty-two when her life blew up. He held her gaze for one devastating moment before he climbed into the car alongside his partner, satisfied she understood too well.

"I know I overstepped. I just got carried away with finding out what happened to Iris. You can't fault me for that. What kind of cop am I if I don't do whatever it takes to catch the bad guy?"

With a sigh, Detective Casey shut the door in her face and fired up the engine. Maureen kicked at a pebble, hoping to disappear, but the *shush* of the window brought her back from the brink.

"Ballistics confirmed that the two shell casings we collected from the bedroom came from a nine-millimeter handgun, which is consistent with the weapon you found beneath the floorboard."

"And the prints?" Maureen heard the excitement in her voice. "They're Seth's, aren't they? Have you requested his cell-phone records? I bet you'll get a hit on the tower near the Presidio at the time of the murder."

"His cell was apparently out of juice for most of the night. And forensics detected only one set of fingerprints on the grip of the gun. We found a match in IAFIS. Live Scan data from a job application at a daycare facility a few years back."

"Daycare?" Now, she just felt stupid.

But Detective Casey regarded her as something worse. Someone to be pitied. "If you want to be a detective someday, you have to learn to check your assumptions at the door. You follow the evidence. You go where it leads you. Not the other way around."

He fired up the engine and pulled away, leaving her standing there, speechless. As the car made the turn out of the station, Diedrich rolled down his window and shouted to her.

"Go home, Maureen."

Maureen jerked in and out of a fitful sleep. When she flopped to her right, she met with the brutality of the nightstand. The framed photo of her parents on their twenty-fifth anniversary, with her positioned between them, her face a peculiar amalgam.

Mother's eyes. Father's nose. And a foolish smile all her own, a smile that tempted fate. When she spun to her left, the bright light of the computer awaited her, where she'd resized Seth's old mug shot until it filled the entire screen. Still, he eluded her. Flat on her back proved no better. The Dolores hung there, above the dresser, reminding her of her old friend and of all she'd lost.

Maureen tugged a pillow over her head. But the memory still found her. It knew all her hiding places because it lived inside her, an uninvited guest. The crack of gunfire, confusing at first. The wave of terror that knocked her down to her knees beneath the piano. The dark figure, moving with purpose. Row by row, spraying his bullets, until he reached the front of the auditorium. Her mother and father huddled together under the seat, her mother's wide eyes trained on her. A finger mashed to her lips.

Bolting upright, Maureen chucked the pillow onto the ground. In her chest, her heart trembled like a small, frightened creature. She'd said *nothing*. She'd done *nothing*. Not when it mattered most. So, Diedrich could shove it. Whatever she'd done after—no matter how bold, no matter how stupid—had been too little, too late.

It hit her then, knocked the wind from her. In the space blown clean by the bluster of her panic, she saw the moment clear as a photograph. The blond soul patch, the tousled hair to match. Blue eyes like the hot center of a flame.

Maureen fell back onto the bed, gathering herself, before she cast off the sheets and sprang to her feet, certain that she knew exactly where she'd seen Seth before.

FOURTEEN

Lydia understood when to bite her tongue. Some lessons you learn the hard way. Like the time she'd slipped her dad a Gamblers Anonymous brochure and wound up with a split in her lip that bled for three hours straight. Those kinds of lessons you don't forget. No matter how much you wish you could.

When Seth left that morning, Lydia didn't ask his destination. She saw that frenzied determination in his eyes, no different than a strung-out junkie. And when he showed up two hours later, his knuckles swollen, she didn't ask what went wrong. Instead, she slogged to the ice machine and back with a hand towel to render first aid to the bonehead, knowing they were twenty thousand dollars poorer.

"How much do we have left?" Seth pointed at the coffee can on the table, then rested the ice pack on his bruised hand.

"Ninety-eight bucks last time I counted. Enough for another night or two at this dump."

"Shit." He hung his head. "I'm sorry, Liddy. But I'm sure the cops will let us back in there tonight. Hell, they better. Or I'm gonna find us a damn good lawyer."

With what money? Lydia wondered. But she popped a

piece of ice in her mouth, crunching it to smithereens to keep it preoccupied.

"So, can I get a twenty-spot?" he asked. "I gotta clear my head."

Lydia felt nauseous, but she simply nodded, her head bobbing numbly like one of those silly toys.

"You're an angel. I'm good for it. I promise." Seth tossed the towel in the sink, leaving the ice to melt and popped the lid off the can, withdrawing a twenty-dollar bill from the money Lydia had saved. He slipped it in his pocket and ran a comb through his hair. Squirted his tongue with Minty Breeze breath spray like it mattered.

Like a dutiful dog, Lydia followed him to the door but she couldn't look at him.

"Don't be mad. You know how I am." He pecked her on the cheek and headed down the sidewalk to the infamous Room 37. Before he arrived, she turned away, unable to stomach it. Her hard-earned twenty about to be wasted on a hooker.

Lydia figured she had thirty minutes, tops. Twenty bucks wouldn't buy Seth much more than that, even at the low-rent Blue Bird. Securing the keys to his truck, she hurried out into the parking lot, approaching the GMC like a crime scene. No matter what load of bull he'd fed Iris back then, Lydia suspected Seth had handed over their old beater of a car to Vinnie as collateral.

Lydia's search began in the luxurious cab that still smelled brand new. She rifled beneath the leather bucket seats, sweeping aside a handful of racing forms, and peering into the dark underbelly. She didn't know what she might find, only that Seth had a knack for keeping secrets. And the secrets he kept could destroy them both. She slipped her arm into the crevice between the seat and the console, retrieving a lone Cheeto, and cast it onto the pavement. Nothing to see here.

The backseat felt smooth as butter beneath her hand. On the floorboard, Seth had stored a few garden tools—hedge clippers, trowel, work gloves—in a plastic bin for easy access. Iris had him working in the backyard every day, restoring it to its prior glory.

Lydia's eyes darted to Room 37. The door remained shut, God-knows-what going on behind it. Another man loitered outside, looking as nervous as her. Probably a first-timer.

After hoisting herself over the tailgate, Lydia crouched in front of the aluminum toolbox. She inserted the small key into the lock and opened the top of the box, examining the interior. Seth had the toolbox of another man. A different man. A man with a calendar and a 401K and a credit score above six hundred. Lydia pawed through the top layer, setting the items aside, careful not to scratch the paint. A set of jumper cables, a flashlight, and a couple of emergency flares led to the tools below, most of which belonged to Iris and the others who'd come before her.

The black plastic served as camouflage, so she didn't spot the bag until she reached the bottom. Weighted by a claw hammer from Iris's shed, it lay crumpled in the corner.

Lydia made a quick check of the door to 37—still closed— before she fished the bag out and stuck her hand inside the cavernous opening. Her fingers touched something strange, something repulsive. Instinct told her to pull back, to leave it alone, but she drew it to the surface instead.

She stared down at the dish towel, wanting to drop it. To hurl it. To get it as far away from her as she could manage. But her fingers felt numb. Like they'd frozen to ice around it. Like it would take one of Seth's tools to pry them off.

The towel had hung in Iris's kitchen. *Don't go baking my heart*, it read. Lydia had helped her pick it out from a little gift shop on Sacramento Street. But now, that cute white kitchen towel looked like a prop in a horror film, stiff as a bone and stained bright red. Blood red. Smelled like it, too.

When Lydia raised it to her nose, she gagged. And, finally, the acrid scent of metal startled her into action. She dropped the towel from her hand. Shoved it back into the plastic bag and balled it up tight. Rushed to arrange the tools inside the box, exactly as they'd been before. Then, she scooped up the bag and raced back to the corner suite, shutting herself in.

The thwack of the slamming door echoed the sound of her heartbeat. She stood there, braced against it, until the whoosh of blood in her ears quieted to dull roar. Until she could almost think straight.

Just then, a fist pounded behind her. "San Francisco Police. Anybody home?"

As Lydia peered out the peephole, the feather-light bag weighted her to the spot. Detective Casey looked back at her, his image warped by the magnifying glass, so that it seemed his stubbled chin, his discerning eyes consumed the entire world outside that door.

"Hellooo? We saw the truck in the lot. We know you're in there."

"Just a second." Through sheer force of will, she managed to get the words out. Strained and breathy and shaky as a tightrope but good enough to hold him off.

Lydia darted to the empty dresser, shoved the bag inside. *No, dumbass. That's the first place he'd look.* Same for the spot beneath the mattress. It was Seth she heard now, scolding her in her head. But somehow, he sounded no different than her father.

"You hiding a body?" If he only knew.

When she peeked out a second time, another man with a badge had materialized beside him. Two cops. Two sets of questions she couldn't answer. Two pairs of cuffs to hook her up after they caught her in a lie. After they caught her holding a bloody dish towel that belonged to a missing woman.

"Open the door, Lydia."

With no more time to second-guess herself, Lydia shoved the bag into the ice bucket on the table and placed the lid on top. She smoothed her hair in the mirror, dismayed to find her face as blanched and sweaty as a cooked goose.

"Seth's not here." Leaving the dead bolt firmly in place, she spoke into the slim opening between the door and the frame.

"Just as well. I came to see you. Is everything okay in there?" Damn him for seeming so nice. For nearly convincing her that he cared.

She pressed her lips together, sealing her secrets inside, and nodded.

"Can I come in?"

"Uh... I..."

Detective Casey gestured to the cop behind him. "My partner can wait out here. I promise it won't take long. I just have a few questions to follow up on."

Lydia understood this game, knew it was rigged against her. But she opened the door anyway. To refuse would only make her look guilty. Which she supposed she was when you got right down to it. She'd lost count long ago of all the bad things she'd done.

Detective Casey sauntered across the threshold as if his entry had never been in doubt. As if he'd known Lydia would cave like a house of cards. She retreated to the opposite side of the room, where she leaned against the wall, hoping it would keep her upright.

"Celebrating?" The detective took a seat at the table, and she followed his eyes to the overflowing trash can, to the empty bottle of André Brut.

"Oh." It took her way too long to get her head on right. "Not me. I can't drink, of course. Not with the baby coming."

"The baby. Right."

Lydia tried not to look at him. At his hands especially, poised like twin spiders, inches from the ice bucket of doom. "So, you had something you wanted to ask me?"

"Have you ever fired a gun?"

Lydia shrank back. "Of course not."

"Ever owned one?" When his index finger crawled toward the bucket, barely tapping its surface, she forced herself to breathe.

"No. Never."

"Held one? Even just for a moment." The hands rested now, one on either side, with the bucket between them. Horrified, Lydia gaped at a visible piece of the black plastic bag that hung over the side, beneath the lid, unnoticed. It seemed to mock her, to shimmer in the light that streamed through the curtains. To say, Here I am. Come set me free.

"Lydia." The way he said her name, she could tell Detective Casey pitied her. But she only wanted him to move his hands somewhere else. To pick himself up and go away. Leave her here with that God-awful towel, so she could figure out where it came from and what to do about it. "Have you ever held a gun?"

"Not that I remember." Once the lie had been unloosed, she couldn't take it back.

"*Interesting.* And what if I told you we found a gun in Iris Duncan's house? It was hidden under a floorboard in the room where you and Seth slept."

"It's not ours, if that's what you're asking. It wouldn't surprise me if she hid it there herself and forgot about it. She was always doing stuff like that."

"I suppose that might be a possibility." The detective finally stood up, leaving the ice bucket behind him. It didn't bring Lydia the relief she expected. "But that wouldn't explain the fingerprints, now would it?"

"Fingerprints?" Thank God for that wall. She needed it now that her knees had gone weak. "What fingerprints?"

"Not just any fingerprints, Lydia. *Your* fingerprints." Detective Casey kept his distance, lingering near the dresser. But what he said and how he said it—he might as well have grabbed her by the throat. "I have no choice but to ask you directly. Did you fire that gun at Iris on Monday morning? Did you have anything to do with her disappearance?"

"No. I would never hurt Iris, I swear. She's my friend. My only friend." Lydia heard how silly she sounded, how desperate. She'd never been a friend to Iris, not when it counted.

"Your *friend*. You're what, twenty-four?"

Lydia didn't bother to respond. He already knew the answer, already knew too much about her. And the things he didn't, she suspected he'd figure out soon enough.

"You don't hear about many twenty-somethings palling around with seventy-year-olds. Not much in common between them, I would reckon. Is Iris your first elderly *friend*?"

He made it sound like a dirty word, and the shame of it clouded her thoughts. Through the murk, a single image floated to the top. She couldn't look away from it. Sun-spotted hands, resting on a blanket, paint beneath the fingernails. A glass of water by the bed. The face, still and blank as a canvas. She hadn't been there, but she pictured it all the same.

Lydia let out a sob.

"And while we're at it, who managed her medication? You? *Seth*?"

"Of course not." She wiped at a tear, angry at herself for letting him get under her skin again. "Iris filled the box herself. We both reminded her to take it. Otherwise, she'd forget. But if the pills are wrong or something, it's her fault. She had all these old bottles she never threw away. Her husband's too, and—"

"I never said the pills were wrong."

It got hard to breathe. "Oh," barely squeezed out.

"I realize the situation is difficult for you. But I'm on your side here. You don't want to get yourself caught up in this. Seth has a gambling problem, am I right? Those kinds of people get desperate. They get greedy. They make bad decisions, and people get hurt. You're not like him. If you tell me what you know, I can help you. I can help you get away."

Through the sliver between the curtains, Lydia spotted Detective Casey's partner circling Seth's truck like a bloodhound.

"Is there a problem, Officer?" Seth appeared in the window, speaking so loudly she could hear him through the paper-thin walls. With his shirt untucked, his belt unbuckled at his waist, he approached his vehicle. "As I understand it, you can't go poking your nose in my property without a warrant. And if you don't mind my asking, when can we return to *our* house?"

Detective Casey cleared his throat, drawing Lydia's ear. "This is your chance, Lydia. It's a limited-time offer. And if I was you, I'd take it. I'd leave his ass and never look back. You're too good for that lowlife."

Lydia shuffled past him and opened the door, barely feeling her legs beneath her. She told him what he wanted to hear, what she needed to say to get the hell out of that room. "I'll think about it."

But as sharp as he seemed, the detective didn't have a freaking clue. She could no sooner leave Seth than she could cut off her own arm.

"What did you say to that cop?"

Seth disgusted her. With his hickey-spotted neck and his shirt reeking of cheap perfume, he still had the nerve to question her. He hoisted himself up on the dresser, smug as a despot on his throne.

"Nothing. *Why?*"

"Because he told me they were lettin' us back in the house as of this afternoon. And I don't trust him as far as I could throw him. They're up to something."

"Well, I didn't say anything. But he sure said plenty." Lydia slumped into the chair at the table, feeling strung out. Her nerves, frayed. "They found the gun, Seth. I told you they would."

He shrugged it off, but she caught the way his jaw twitched. Like someone had started retightening his screws. "Well, a gun don't mean shit. They can't prove who bought it. Hell, they can't even prove we knew it was there. For all they know, Iris put it there herself."

"That's what I told them. Too bad they already ran the prints." She stared down at her hands in her lap, remembering the weight of the weapon. The feel of it against her skin. How she'd suddenly understood its intoxicating power.

"Jeez, Liddy. I told you to wipe it down. You can't just let them railroad you. I'd like to fucking strangle that old broad."

"Don't call her that."

Another twist of the screw, and Seth scowled at her. Like she'd been the one to buy the ghost gun off Vinnie. Untraceable, it had been assembled from a DIY kit, no different than a doll-house or a model airplane. "Whose side are you on?"

"I could ask you the same." Lydia jerked the lid off the ice bucket and whipped out the plastic bag, damp now from the melting ice. She tossed it at Seth, pleased with herself when he recoiled. "Go on. Look inside."

"What is this?" He wrinkled his nose at the towel, keeping it at arm's length.

"You tell me. I found it in your toolbox. It smells like blood."

Seth descended his makeshift throne and stalked toward her, waving the thing in her face. When she held up her hands to keep him at bay, he cackled at her. "And what—you think I killed Iris? Is that about the size of it? You think I shot her and used a dish towel to wipe up the blood? C'mon, Liddy, give me a little credit. I have no clue how that thing got in there."

"I don't know what to think. This is her dish towel. I recognize it."

"Well, what the hell were you doing in my toolbox anyway?" he asked.

Lydia recognized her father's uncanny ability to deflect. To jab a finger back at her so that she would lose focus. "That's not the point, and you know it. You should be thanking me. If those detectives had a search warrant, you'd be celled up in Santa Rita by now. And if you must know, the sink sprang a leak again. I needed the pipe wrench to tighten the nuts."

Seth huffed as he slunk around the side of her, disappearing the towel inside the bag and returning it to its ice bucket grave. He paced his well-worn track to the bathroom and back. Until finally, he seemed decided. "Promise me you won't freak out."

"I promise." But already, her worried mind had taken off like a jet engine, spinning a flurry of thoughts in its wake.

"You're right. The blood on that towel belongs to Iris. And unless you want to spend the rest of your life in the big house with me, we have to get rid of it."

FIFTEEN

BEFORE

"Excuse me, sir? Will you please point me in the direction of Archer Avenue?"

Manners maketh the man. Even now, fifty years removed from Lost Pines, Sister Frances's colloquialisms stuck in Iris's head like a catchy melody. Like one of those rigged claw games, the mind had a strange way of holding onto the bad things and letting the good ones drop out of reach forever. Try as she might, she couldn't conjure her best friend's laugh.

"It's about a half mile that way." He pointed up a steep hill. Then, frowned at the cast on her wrist. At the slippers on her feet, their bottoms worn with wear. "Are you lost?"

Iris stooped to pet the gentleman's bulldog. It gave her a hand a slobbery lick. "Perhaps. I went for a walk in the park, and I... well, here I am. With you and this handsome fellow."

"And you live on Archer? *Alone?*" The man looked worried. "Is there someone I should call?"

"Um..." Iris shrugged, grimaced with embarrassment. "I'm not sure."

"Do you have a cellphone, ma'am? Maybe we can look at

your contacts." He reminded her of Dean, always trying to solve a problem. "Or your recently dialed numbers."

"Heavens, no. Once Dean purchased one of those cellular devices, it attached to his hand like a barnacle. I never could pry it off."

In spite of Iris's straight face, the man chuckled. He spun around, surveying the street, his dog watching him intently. "Her," he said, suddenly. "She looks like she knows you."

"Iris!" Breathless, Lydia came running up, with Seth lagging two steps behind her. "Where were you? We looked everywhere."

Before Iris could muster an answer, Lydia enveloped the Good Samaritan in a bear hug, trapping the poor man's arms at his waist like a straitjacket. "Thank you for finding her."

"I—I didn't really do..."

Seth arrived on scene, taking ahold of Iris's good arm like she might bolt. "Are you sure you're alright?"

The dog growled at him. A rumble that built to a sharp bark. With a sudden jerk of the leash, the man hissed, "Quiet, Wilson!"

Startled, Iris managed to find her voice again. "I'm perfectly fine, dear. I just got a tad bit turned around with all the new construction. I would've found my way eventually."

"Iris, you've been gone for four hours." Seth guided her away from the grumbling bulldog. But Wilson pulled at the lead, insistent. And Iris couldn't look away from his eyes, laser-focused on Seth's ankles. "You could've been hurt."

"Four hours?" Iris repeated, frowning at her watch. The damn thing must've stopped. "That's impossible."

"Are you okay now?" The man raised his voice over Wilson's protests. "Are you safe with these people?"

Seth rolled his eyes. "It's a good thing your fleabag didn't bite Mrs. Duncan. We would've sued you for everything you're worth."

Sister Frances would've been proud of the way the man coughed politely into his hand to cover his gasp. No good deed goes unpunished, Iris thought.

"'These people'?" Lydia scoffed. "Of course she is."

"She can answer for herself, can't she?"

With all eyes on her, Iris nodded. She wouldn't have anyone thinking poorly of her caretakers. "Seth and Lydia? I trust them with my life."

Iris rested on the sofa in the sitting room, her favorite blanket draped across her lap. Her old bones ached. And yet, she felt twelve again. Sitting in the naughty chair across from Sister Frances, awaiting her punishment.

Seth began, "Iris, you can't just wander off without telling us."

"In your pajamas," Lydia added. "And your slippers. Those shoes aren't meant for walking outside the house."

"I didn't mean to go so far or to stay gone so long. I'd never want to make you worry. But it was such a nice day that I lost track of time." Iris heard her voice crack. She worried they would get fed up and leave her. And what then? "Let me make it up to you both. Put on your fancy clothes, kiddos. I'm taking you to dinner at Gary Danko."

"Gary *who*?" Seth asked.

Lydia rolled her eyes at him. "No way. That place is too fancy. They've got an entire menu devoted to cheese. We won't fit in there at all."

"Speak for yourself." Seth laughed. "I love cheese."

"He's right. That's nonsense, dear. Everyone deserves to be spoiled. Now, Lydia, I'm sure I have a nice dress you could wear. And would you like to borrow my Hermès bag? It would look lovely on your arm."

"Really?" Lydia squealed.

Iris hoped she could find that old thing. Dean had purchased it for her a lifetime ago after his first promotion. She'd worn it once to make him happy, so it wouldn't seem a waste. But now the bag had found its purpose after all.

"I'll take that as a *yes*."

Across the table, Seth stuffed an entire dinner roll in his mouth, softly moaning while he chewed. Lydia sat paralyzed by Iris's side, surveying the forks. To reassure her, Iris patted her hand. The first time Dean brought her to a place like this, she'd resembled a fish out of water, flopping around awkwardly while everyone else seemed to know exactly what to do and when to do it. She'd eventually learned the dance, but she'd never felt entirely comfortable. As if at any moment she might be exposed for what she really was. A little orphan girl nobody wanted.

"It's the smaller one," she whispered to Lydia.

Lydia managed a smile, before taking the fork in her hand and cutting a dainty bite of lettuce. Iris watched her chew, swallow. Sip from a glass of sparkling water.

"This is too much," Lydia finally said, cutting her eyes to the five-hundred-dollar bottle of Dom Pérignon chilling in the ice bucket, then back to Seth. "Won't you let us chip in?"

"She said to order anything we wanted. Right, Iris?" Seth bit into his third roll, talking as he chomped. "Don't ruin my fun just because you can't have any."

Iris shook her head, troubled. Since she'd spilled the beans about the baby, she could feel the tension between them. They were a team. They were in this together. She wanted them to realize that. "I'm the party pooper here. This should be a romantic dinner for the two of you. You both look fantastic. You should be enjoying each other, and here I am, getting in the way. Why don't I go sit at the bar? That way you can be alone."

Lydia blinked at her in surprise, clinging to her arm like a life raft. "No way. We want you here."

"Trust me, once the baby comes you'll be wishing you spent more time together. Besides, I don't mind eating alone." Iris signaled to the server. "But first things first, get a little closer, Seth. Put your arm around her. She needs to be touched."

Lydia groaned.

"C'mon. Humor a lonely old widow."

"If you insist." Seth scooted his chair closer to Lydia, but she stuck out her hand to keep him at a distance.

"Lydia, he's trying. Don't push him away. Look at him. Look him in the eyes." Iris directed the scene to her liking. Seth and Lydia side by side, gazing at each other. His arm around her chair, grazing her back. A flickering candle at the center of it all. "Now, that's a proper young couple in love."

Iris found a seat at the bar with a view of the table. While she savored each dish from the three-course tasting menu, she couldn't stop smiling at them. Every so often, she gave Seth an encouraging nod. She never once thought of the past, of how she didn't really fit in here among the other diners with their caviar tastes. Truth be told, she couldn't remember enjoying a dinner quite so much.

SIXTEEN

AFTER

Tuesday evening

As Walt steered the Crown Vic in the direction of Iris's Victorian mansion, Maureen wriggled in her seat like a kid at Christmas.

"Settle down, Shaw, before you pull a muscle. You get to play detective for exactly thirty minutes. Not one second more." Maureen had been certain Walt would change his mind, so thirty minutes seemed generous. Like a big box with a shiny bow that rattled when you shook it. "Then, we get back to our real job. Patrolling."

Ignoring Walt—*what a killjoy!*—Maureen kept her focus on the street ahead. The attic came into view, the elegant spire towering above the other houses. "I'm telling you, he's our man. What I saw yesterday at the track. *Sheesh.* That guy is a walking time bomb."

Walt seemed as unimpressed as usual. "Didn't you say the prints on the gun belonged to someone else?"

"Her, I'm assuming. Lydia. His crime partner." Maureen couldn't prove it, of course. But, it seemed to fit. "Not to mention the fact that I know him. Well, I don't *know him*, but I've seen him before. I put in a call to Detective Casey as soon as I realized. This is not Seth McKay's first rodeo. Who knows how many bodies he's left behind him?"

"You *what*?"

"I've seen him. At Symphony Hall. Back when I used to..." Maureen searched for the right words and came up empty. She'd lost so much, left so much behind. Sometimes, she wondered if a part of her still lay beneath that piano with a bullet to her head. "He was there in the audience, cutting up and having a good ole time with the Friends of the Symphony group. The Friends of the Symphony, Greer. Average age... *old*."

Walt shook his head with the vigor of a man trying to expel a demon. "I meant, you called Detective Casey? Didn't he tell you to lay off?"

"Technically, yes. But then, he told me to follow the evidence." She shrugged, refusing to let her partner—or Detective Diedrich with his condescending scowl—bring her down. "It's a bit of a mixed message."

Walt positioned the car in the fire lane adjacent to Presidio Park. The vast expanse of wilderness took on an eerie feel at night. A solid black hole in the middle of the city, it seemed like the kind of place a person could wander into and never come out.

"So, what's your plan, Columbo?"

Maureen popped the door and exited the vehicle, turning toward the house. While she contemplated how best to admit to Walt that she had no plan, a light appeared in the attic revealing two silhouettes. Seth's truck sat in the driveway.

"Unbelievable," she muttered. "They let them back in."

Already, Maureen had started walking. Fast.

"Where the hell are you going?" With his long legs, Walt easily caught up to her, close enough to give her an earful. "Whatever you're thinking, it's not a good idea."

"I'm thinking you gave me thirty minutes. That's plenty of time to rattle some cages." And there was one cage in particular she intended on giving a Loma Prieta-sized shake.

Walt distanced himself at the railing while Maureen pounded on the front door. The broken panel of stained glass had been patched with cardboard and duct tape, giving the otherwise impeccable façade an unsightly black eye. She wondered if the McKays had bothered to straighten Iris's bedroom. If they'd returned the framed photograph of themselves to the nightstand, despite the deep fissure down its center.

Maureen had no intention of going away. She kept up her incessant rapping until the bolt unlatched and the door opened.

"What can I do for you, Officer?" The saccharine harmonies of Seth's smile didn't reach his eyes. She only found dissonance in those stormy blues. The rough kind of chord that had made her cringe when she'd played it.

"Good evening, Mr. McKay." Maureen extended her hand. "Officer Shaw. We met yesterday morning when you stopped by the house to gather your things."

Seth gave no sign of remembering her. "We weren't expecting anyone. It's past nine o'clock, and Lydia needs to get to bed. She's—"

"Pregnant. Right. I remember." Maureen matched his false simper with one of her own. "You know, I couldn't stop thinking about you. About where I've seen you before. It kept me up at night until I realized."

Now she had his attention. "Well, you don't look familiar. But then, I ain't from around here. Grew up in Oakland. I doubt we've met."

"Have you ever attended a concert at Symphony Hall in San Francisco?"

Lydia let out a sudden laugh, materializing from behind him. The whites of her eyes glowed in the dim light.

"Nah. Liddy will tell you. I ain't exactly the concert-going type. I'm more of a Lynyrd Skynyrd guy myself."

"Funny. I could've sworn I saw you there. You looked different back then. Spiky hair, a soul patch. You were sitting with the Friends of the Symphony. I rarely forget a face."

Seth shrugged, unaffected. "Wasn't me, Officer Shaw. Unless I've got a long-lost twin. If you find him, let me know. I've always wanted to meet my doubleganger."

Another awkward laugh from Lydia. "*Doppel*ganger," she corrected under her breath. "And it's bad luck if you ever see him."

"Must be my mistake then." Maureen peeked around the door and into the foyer. "Do you know where Mrs. Duncan got that painting? The one hanging over the fireplace."

Without looking, Seth replied, "No clue."

"I assume she bought it," Lydia offered. "Or maybe her husband gave it to her before he died. I think she mentioned he was into the arts. Right, Seth?"

Seth gave a noncommittal grunt and pushed the door closed slightly so that Lydia—and her mouth—all but disappeared behind it. Maureen stuck the toe of her boot against the frame to prevent him from shutting it further.

"It's just that the artist's name is scratched out. It looks like a Dolores. Ever heard of her?"

"Doesn't sound familiar. But then, the only painting I know is *Dogs Playing Poker*. Now, that's a classic." The smile reappeared, stretching his handsome face obscenely. Maureen wanted to look away. "If that's all, Officer Shaw, we'd really like to settle in and get some shut-eye."

Peering past him into the hallway and up the winding stairs that led to darkness, Maureen fought off a shiver. Only one kind of person could sleep at the scene of a murder. A guilty one.

Maureen turned to find Walt shaking his head at her. "You've got a one-track mind, Shaw. What does that damn painting have to do with anything?"

"I'm not sure yet." Maureen headed down the steps toward the sidewalk, empty in both directions as far as she could see. Pacific Heights was the kind of neighborhood with an early bedtime. Even the dogs had gone quiet. But Maureen knew that if they waited around long enough, they would hear the coyotes. That the high-pitched howls would sound a lot like screams. She and Walt had responded to plenty of false alarms near the Presidio. "It could be a clue. On the other hand..."

"A fool's errand?" Walt offered.

"You're such a pessimist, Greer."

"Ain't that the truth." He chuckled, and followed her down the sidewalk toward the gated entrance to Presidio Park. "That's what happens when you spend thirty-five years on patrol. The glass goes from half-full to half-empty to 'fill 'er up with vodka, please.'"

Maureen removed a small flashlight from her duty belt and aimed it into the murk.

"Don't tell me you're thinking about going in there. That place gives me the heebie-jeebies at night. Didn't you see the sign about the coyotes?"

"Oh, c'mon." Maureen *had* seen the sign and promptly gone right past it. "It could be a possible exit route for the perp. Or a place to stash the body."

Walt's sigh sounded more like a death rattle. "That's your theory? Seth McKay lugging Mrs. Duncan out here in an area rug. I seriously doubt it. Rumor is that none of the neighbors' cameras had a view of the road and nobody spotted him or his truck. Not to mention the cadaver dogs they brought in here yesterday apparently led them on a wild goose chase that turned up nothing."

Peering into the darkness, Walt added, "Besides, I'd rather take my chances with the bipedal wildlife. You know, the kind without claws and sharp teeth."

Maureen readied a saucy comeback—*have you seen some of the folks in the Tenderloin?*—but it went unsaid. A sound, small and insidious, beckoned her into the park.

The side gate whined in protest when she pushed it open. Her boots crunched against the underbrush, too loud for comfort. Behind her, she heard Walt's do the same. She moved to the first line of tree cover and waited, still as a sapling. When the sound came again, she readied her Glock. Though she'd only drawn it twice now, it already felt familiar to her. The weight of it in her hand, a reassurance. False though it may be.

"Psst. Over here."

Maureen spun toward the voice, aiming the gun at its source. A spindly old man with knobby limbs that resembled the trees where he hid himself. He raised his hands, dropping a crumpled flyer to the forest floor. The rest of his body wobbled to and fro like it belonged to someone else. "Don't shoot."

Lowering her weapon, Maureen took in a whiff of the cheap alcohol that emanated from the man's mouth. Beneath a nearby redwood, she spotted his tent and the empty tall cans of Pabst Blue Ribbon that dotted his makeshift front yard. A shopping cart rested in the tree cover, stuffed to the gills.

"What's your name?" Walt approached from the other side with his gun still drawn.

When the man spotted him coming, he nearly lost his balance, stumbling ahead until he anchored himself against the tree trunk. "Oughta let a fellow know you're coming. Not just sneak up on 'em."

"Your name," Walt repeated.

"Charlie Cochise, reporting for duty, sir. But around here, they call me Tallboy."

"Tallboy, huh?" Walt raised one bushy eyebrow.

"That's right." Tallboy pointed over his shoulder to the cart. "Can I sell you somethin' from my collection? I got new merchandise. A Frisbee, a rosary. And a couple pairs of sunglasses. It's amazing what people leave behind."

Walt grimaced. "Tempting, but no."

"I see. You must be lookin' for that old lady."

"What's it to you?"

Maureen wished she could tell Walt to shut his trap. At least he put his gun away. "Do you know her?"

"Nah. Fancy lady like that livin' in the Heights wouldn't give a guy like me the time of day."

"Then, why do you have this?" Walt had retrieved the flyer and held it out, revealing the unsettling headline: POLICE OFFER $10,000 REWARD FOR INFORMATION ON MISSING ELDERLY WOMAN. Beneath it, Iris's face smiled at them, completely unaware of the cruel twist of fate that awaited her in her seventieth year. Maureen recognized the photo from the nightstand. Seth and Lydia had been cropped from view.

"I thought you'd never ask. Do ya know if that detective got my tip?"

Maureen tried to tamp down her excitement but the sparks had already caught fire and started to burn. She could feel herself hot-stepping across the flames. "*Tip?* Did you call the tip line?"

"Sure did. Had to use my last two bucks to call. And ain't nobody ever followed up. Prolly didn't take me too serious." Tallboy staggered to his tent, lowering himself partway and falling the rest, like a skyscraper set for demolition. He laid back, his head resting on his pack, and let out a thunderous belch.

"I can't imagine why," Walt muttered. "How would they even know where to find you? Walk ten paces and make a left at the first big tree?"

"Well, *we* take you seriously." Maureen cut her eyes at Walt. "And we'll be certain to pass any information along. If what you have to say is useful, you might be eligible for the reward."

"Now you're talkin'. I could buy me some high-dollar wine and a couple weeks at the Ritz." He grinned, and his thick beard parted, revealing a fence of broken teeth. "It was a couple weeks back at Lafayette Park. I saw that lady. The one who got shot. She was sittin' on the bench underneath my tree. Well, it ain't mine, but it's where I usually lay my head after the free meal at the Rescue Mission. I noticed her on account of the cast. Plus, there usually ain't nobody in the park on Monday afternoon."

"What happened next?"

"She stayed there looking real, real peaceful... had a book with her..." The pace of Tallboy's voice slowed, and Maureen hoped he could stay awake long enough to reach the end of his story. "I'd had a few... by then... and I... I drifted off."

Tallboy's head lolled to one side, emitting a shallow snuffle.

"Sheesh." Walt consulted his watch. "You sure this is how you want to spend your last ten minutes? With a man named after the size of his beer cans?"

"Charlie!" Maureen nudged Tallboy's tattered sneaker with her boot, and he startled awake. "...a cheeseburger, hold the onions, and a chocolate—oh, crap. I think I was dreamin' about food again. What were we talking about?"

With a sigh, Walt waved the flyer in his face. "You said you had a tip for us. About the missing woman."

"Right, right. The old lady. There was a guy with her."

"A guy?" Walt laughed to himself, all breath and judgment. "Well, that's specific. I'll bet his name is Joe Average and he lives in the suburbs with his wife and 2.5 children."

Maureen winced at her partner's bedside manners. Luckily, his scorn seemed lost on Tallboy. "Did you get a good look at him?"

"Middle-aged white guy in sunglasses and a ball cap. Your standard mystery man. Except for the ear. Now that I remember."

"You remember his ear." Walt let out a full-on guffaw.

"Well, yeah," Tallboy answered. "'Cause he didn't have one. Just a nub. Those two folks didn't go together, if you know what I'm sayin'." He propped himself up and reached for one of the Pabst cans, jiggling it a little and taking a swig of whatever remained. "The old lady gave him an envelope, and he left. Money, I'm guessing, based on the looks of him. I had a whole story made up about it. I do that sometimes. Make up stories about folks, about their lives. I had him figured for a PI, out to dig up some dirt. Maybe find her long-lost kid or something."

"What did she do after that?" Maureen asked.

"The darnedest thing. She must've been watchin' me like I was watchin' her, cuz she marched right up to me and said, 'You should be careful sleeping out here in the park with all the thieves running around the neighborhood.' And then, she slipped me a fifty. A fifty! I ate like a king that night."

Walt tapped his watch. Jerked his head toward the car with such force that Maureen figured he'd be in need of a chiropractic adjustment. Regretfully, she gave Walt a small nod, thanking Tallboy with a hardy handshake before retreating toward the car.

As she reached the gate, he called out to her. "Hey, I'm workin' on a story about you too, ya know. You ain't like the rest of them cops. No siree. You take your job personal. Like it means something to ya. You must be trying to right a wrong, Officer Shaw."

Maureen smiled to herself. Not because she felt on the verge of a breakthrough with a case that inexplicably meant everything to her. But because tonight, Charlie "Tallboy" would eat like a king again.

"You gave that bum money, didn't you?" Walt waited until she sat captive in the passenger seat to look down his nose at her. "If you ask me, he was full of it. With brain cells so pickled I doubt he can remember what happened a few hours ago, much less a couple of weeks. I'd take his so-called tip about a one-eared man with a mighty big grain of salt."

"But you have to admit, a lot of it sounds like Iris. The reading. The mention of a burglar in the neighborhood. Her naïve generosity."

Walt shrugged, then fired up the engine, guiding the Crown Vic back down Archer Avenue. "Was old Tallboy right about you too?"

"How do you mean?" She knew exactly what he meant, and already, she felt his eyes on her like a spotlight.

"I realize you've been through some messed-up shit. That Symphony Hall shooting—I remember it like yesterday. Thank God I wasn't on patrol that night. Something like that, you never shake it."

"I know."

"*Do you?*" He slowed as they passed the Duncan residence. The windows in the attic had gone dark, along with the rest of the house. "Even if Seth McKay *is* guilty, nailing him to the wall isn't going to fix anything. It certainly won't bring you any peace."

Maureen remembered that last day in the courtroom. The sentencing of Adam Waddell. She'd never made it past the metal detectors. The security guard had alerted Detective Diedrich, who'd escorted her out of the building with a stern warning about the eleven-inch blade in her purse. The blade she'd fully intended to stick in any or all of Waddell's soft places.

"Who says it's peace I'm looking for?"

SEVENTEEN

Lydia waited in the dark, huddled on the bed, while Seth peeked through the slit in the bedroom curtains. "They're gone," he said, finally. But Lydia felt no relief. "I told you not to turn on the attic lights. Now, we've got another cop on our asses."

"It's creepy up there. It smells like her." Lydia shivered, conjuring the scent of the lilac perfume that still lingered in the house. The attic, especially. Which had been shut up like a tomb until Lydia had unlocked it an hour ago at Seth's urging. "And her binoculars were just lying on the ledge, waiting. Like she might wander in at any minute."

"So, you're worried about Iris's ghost. Is that what you're telling me?" He shook his head at her, disgusted. "You're such a child."

Lydia wanted to stop him right there, to catalogue all the ways he acted like a two-year-old. Case in point, the tin of chocolate chip cookies he'd pilfered from Iris's cabinet shortly after their arrival. But what good would it do? A leopard can't change his spots.

"I guess I'm just wondering... should we even *be* here? It feels wrong."

"Think of us as house sitters, Liddy. We're looking after the place until Iris returns. I even found my set of keys in the kitchen drawer, so we're both legit."

"*Until* she returns? Don't you mean *if*? She's not on vacation, Seth. You said yourself that she's probably..." Lydia watched as Seth sprawled on the mattress next to her, fluffing a pillow behind his head. House-sitting did sound sort of glamorous. It helped to think of it that way. To ease her mind. And Iris *would* want the house looked after.

"*Dead*? I don't get why you can't just say it."

Lydia groaned at his indifference. "Do you know that lady cop?"

When Seth stiffened, she continued her prodding. She had to get her little cuts in where she could. To prove to herself he still bled. "She said she recognized you from the symphony. What if she saw—"

"I heard what she said. And she didn't *see* anything." The way Seth's eyeballs bugged out, he didn't seem so sure.

"But she asked about the painting too. Don't you think that's strange?"

He smacked the mattress, his fist causing a small shockwave beneath her. "Goddamn it, Lydia. Lay off. I've got enough to deal with right now with that..." he lowered his voice to a whisper, cast his gaze on the drawer where he'd hidden the plastic bag with the dish towel inside it, "...*thing* you found."

"Alright, alright. I'm just worried, is all. It's been a stressful couple of days." Lydia shoved off the bed and headed for the door, eager to be free of him. Even in a house as big as Iris's, Seth took up all the air. No way would she be sleeping in the same room with him tonight. "Should I keep searching for those papers?"

"Hell, yes. Who knows what kind of treasures she left behind? Are you sure you're looking in the right place?"

Lydia nodded. It had dawned on her during the ride over, halfway across the Bay Bridge, as she'd stared out at the light on Alcatraz Island. *I hid all my important documents in the attic. Just in case that burglar comes back.* Iris had been on edge that day, more paranoid than usual.

"And use the flashlight this time. With all those windows, that place might as well be a homing beacon for cops."

Securing the flashlight Seth had retrieved from the shed, Lydia made her way toward the staircase. But first, she paused outside Iris's bedroom. She had to see it for herself. Gathering her courage, she turned the knob and thrust the door open. Though Iris had been gone for less than forty-eight hours, the room had a soulless, empty feel. Uneasy, she traced its boundaries with the light, chasing the shadows. But for every dim corner she illuminated, she cast another in darkness.

The bed drew her in like a vortex. The sheets, stripped. The mattress, bare. A hunk of it had been cut away like a cancer. Lydia could imagine the reason why but didn't want to think too long on it. It would only make her nauseous. Also missing: the pillbox and the blue rug Iris had bought at a flea market in Berkeley despite her husband's disapproval. *I called it cheerful; he called it cheap,* she'd told Lydia.

Atop the disfigured mattress, Lydia found the frame that had once held a photo of the three of them. The glass had been broken; the photograph, removed. Lydia picked it up and examined it, remembering the way Iris had set the old-fashioned camera on the tripod, hurrying to position herself between them on the steps. She'd had her cast removed that day, and she'd seemed happier than she'd been in weeks. Before the camera had flashed, Iris put an arm around her and Seth. Not to claim them as her own, not to suffocate them. But to show she cared. Lydia doubted anyone else had ever cared about her like that.

"House-sitting," Lydia whispered, realizing how stupid it sounded.

The faint smell of lilac and metal became suffocating. Lydia dropped the frame back onto the bed and hurried out of the room, anxious to shut it all away. Up the stairs she went. Though the footsteps were her own, their thudding echo still gave her goosebumps. Every creak of the house's old bones sounded like a protest. Like it didn't want them there.

Lydia wouldn't dare look behind her. Petrified, she rushed toward the attic, dimming the light beneath her T-shirt and stepping inside the room.

Though the room had been finished, it had no furnishings, only a few banquette benches with storage beneath their velvet cushions. Lydia had already searched them all and found only cobwebs and dusty paperbacks, their pages thick with age. Not the treasure Seth hoped for.

Lydia scanned the walls and walked the floor, listening for a loose plank that might disguise a hiding place. But the only sounds she heard came from the television in the third-floor bedroom. The low hum of the program, punctuated by Seth's raucous laughter. She imagined him lying there, his feet propped on a pillow, watching *South Park* as he munched on the last of Iris's cookies and swept the crumbs onto the sheets.

"Find anything yet?" he yelled up to her. She could tell he had a mouthful.

"Still looking."

Lydia lowered herself onto a bench, laid her cheek against the soft velvet, and closed her eyes. Her head felt heavy, weighed down with regret. Now that she'd told Seth about the documents, he'd never leave it alone. But they needed money and fast. And who knew how long it would take for Iris's estate to be settled? No matter what delusions Seth entertained, Lydia knew Iris would have to be declared dead before they'd see a cent. That could be weeks or months or half past never, if the cops thought they had something to do with it.

Dead. She hated that word. So short and so final. It sliced right through her, sharp as an axe blade, and left her suddenly cold. As if Iris had laid a phantom finger on her spine.

When Lydia opened her eyes, she saw it in the dim glow of the waning flashlight. It had been waiting for her all along.

She dropped to the floor and crawled toward the heating vent on the opposite wall. With shaky fingers, she loosened the screws and tugged off the cover, releasing a flurry of dust motes from the filter. After laying it aside, she shined the light into the cave beyond, where Iris had left one of Dean's Ferragamo shoeboxes. The bright red color evoked a shudder.

Lydia lay on her side and reached into the vent, dragging the box toward her. She didn't call for Seth, didn't say a word. Just swiped a hand across the top to remove the dust and tugged it open.

As she sifted through the papers Iris had left behind, her eyes welled with tears.

"Wake up, Seth." Lydia prodded his shoulder until he groaned and rolled away from her. But a hard smack with a throw pillow did the trick.

"Leave me alone." While he grabbed for the covers, ready to disappear beneath them, she dangled the box like a carrot, giving it a little shake. "What the— *Shit.* You found it."

Already, Seth stuck out his hand. Then, he reached for it, swiping the air as Lydia pulled it out of his grasp.

"We have to think about what to do," she said. "We have to be careful about this."

His curiosity piqued, Seth sat upright, scattering the crumbs from his T-shirt. "Well, what the hell have you got in there? A damn severed head?"

"Worse." Lydia sat on the corner of the bed and prepared herself with a deep breath. She chose her words with care, doling them out in small bites so Seth wouldn't get ahead of himself. "Iris had a life insurance policy."

"And?"

"And, what do you *think*? We're the beneficiaries, Seth." Lydia opened the shoebox and removed the thick envelope that had arrived at 889 Archer Avenue just one month earlier, according to the postmark. She laid it on her lap.

"How much?" Seth asked.

"Is that really all you care about?" As if she didn't already know the answer. Seth had a one-track mind.

"How much, Liddy?"

The answer waited on her tongue, a bitter pill, until he grabbed her arms and gave her a shake.

"Two million."

"Two freakin' million dollars?" Seth jumped up and stood on the bed, giddy as he bounced. "Plus the house and her estate. We're gonna be filthy rich. We'll never have to spend another night at the Blue Bird. Hell, we can buy that shithole. Tear it down and build us a mansion with one of them in-the-ground swimming pools."

Lydia wrung her hands together, too tired and anxious to play along, even when he tried to pull her up to join him. "Maybe."

"Maybe? C'mon, where's that McKay spirit?"

She directed the corner of her mouth upward, attempting a smile.

"Is this about that detective? Because he can't prove a goddamn thing. Cops ain't as smart as people think, you know. They just get lucky. I'm telling you, we're through the worst of it. Now, we just get rid of the *thing*, and we bide our time."

"There was a lot more stuff in the box." She passed a gleeful Seth the remaining documents. He rifled through them, tossing most of Iris's precious papers aside. "The title to the Mustang. And a bunch of savings bonds for the baby. *See.*"

On the front of an envelope, Iris had written: *For Baby McKay. From Your Future Godmother.* Seth counted out ten thousand dollars in bonds. "That lady was a fucking nut. But God bless her."

"*Was.*" Lydia repeated it under her breath, cradling her knotted stomach. For a horrifying instant, relief washed over her. She would never have to look Iris in the eyes again. She would never have to tell her the truth.

EIGHTEEN

Wednesday

When Lydia opened her eyes, she cried out in alarm. Seth stood over her. Backlit by the morning sun streaming in through the front window, he looked like a shadow man. A monster. And worse, the scowl on his face told her something had him riled.

Lydia sat upright and groaned, realizing her neck ached from the stiff arm of the sofa. After tossing and turning for hours, listening to every little sound, she must've finally fallen asleep. The clock on the mantel read 9:05 a.m. "How long have you been standing there?"

"Long enough." Seth had that look. The one that warned her any furnishings within a six-foot radius might be in jeopardy. "We've gotta do it today. *Now*."

"Do what?"

He grabbed the plastic bag from beside him, securing it in a stranglehold, and shook it in her face. She heard a strange rattling sound from inside that confused her. "You let somethin' slip to that detective, didn't you? You told him somethin'. You must've. That's why you were freakin' out last night."

Lydia felt outmatched. Barely awake, she struggled to catch up to him. To remember all the things she'd withheld before they tumbled out into the open. "What are you talking about? I told you, I didn't say anything."

"Then, explain this." Seething, Seth reached for another prop in his maniacal show. The *San Francisco Chronicle* had been delivered to Iris's door that morning and every morning before it. He tossed it at her, curling his lip in disgust.

As Lydia read the headline, numbness spread upward from the tips of her toes until she felt as dead as a slab of meat. "Persons of interest?"

Her eyes scanned the rest of the article, but her brain got stuck, spinning its wheels on the first two sentences.

The San Francisco Police Department has identified Seth and Lydia McKay as persons of interest in the suspected homicide of Pacific Heights resident, Iris Duncan. Duncan, an elderly widow, has not been seen since early Monday morning, when authorities believe she was shot while contacting 911 to report a possible burglary in progress.

"Yeah. Persons of interest," Seth scoffed, snatching the paper from her hands. "That's what it says, alright. But you know what that really means. They've already decided we're guilty of something, and they won't stop until they prove it."

"We *are* guilty of something." Lydia didn't know why she said it. It just slipped out. She hurried to cover up her big mouth. To sweep all the muck they didn't speak of back under the rug where Seth preferred it. "We lied to Iris."

"Hell, that ain't a crime. So, we fudged the truth a little. Who doesn't?" The newspaper drew his gaze like a magnet. "This is something altogether different. This is murder, Liddy."

"I thought you weren't worried about it."

"I'm not. I mean, I won't be. As soon as we get rid of that damn bag." Seth paced to the window, pulled the curtains shut. "The cops could be here any minute. They're gonna want to talk to us again. And if they find that thing, we're toast."

"Okay, we'll go." Lydia tossed off the throw blanket she'd retrieved from the hall closet last night. The one Iris always laid across her lap while she read. "Are you going to tell me how her blood got all over it in the first place?"

"It was an accident, okay. And before you go gettin' any ideas, I have no clue how it ended up in the truck." With a huff, Seth turned on his heel and headed into the kitchen. Which Lydia understood as clearly as if he'd spoken the words out loud. *Drop it.*

She followed him anyway, pressing her luck. "What do you propose we do with it? Bury it? Burn it? Toss it in the trash?"

"No on all counts. Jeez, Liddy. Haven't you ever watched *Forensic Files?* We bury it, they dig it up. We burn it, they spot the smoke. We throw it in the trash, it's fair game, ripe for the picking. I want that thing as far away as possible."

"The cops could be watching for the truck. They're probably just waiting for us to do something..." The word stupid came to mind. "*Foolish.* Who says we need to get rid of it anyway? You said yourself it was an accident."

"Do you actually think the cops are gonna buy that? Once they figure out it's her blood on the towel, they won't hear anything else we have to say. We're doing this for you, you know. Your fingerprints are on the gun."

"Yeah, well. The detective made it pretty clear he thinks we're in this together. I just hope you know what you're doing."

Seth grumbled as he poured two cups of coffee. Lydia hoped he wouldn't have one of his fits and break Iris's china. Already, she could hear the violent crack of it meeting its end against the hardwood. But his hand remained surprisingly steady when he passed her the cup. She wanted to ask him what else he'd put in the bag, but she knew better than to court disaster.

"Don't I always have a plan?" Reaching into his pocket, he dangled the keys to Iris's Mustang and pointed toward the garage.

Heavy as a lead ball, dread nearly dropped Lydia to her knees. The last time Seth had a plan, someone ended up dead.

Lydia watched Seth buckle his seatbelt. She knew he wouldn't take any chances getting pulled over for a minor infraction like that. With a press of a button, the garage door opened, but he didn't pull forward. Not yet. Instead, he rolled down the window and casually leaned out, appearing more like James Dean than a criminal with a blood-soaked dish towel in the trunk. He winked at her, before he donned an Oakland A's ball cap, identical to the one he'd given her.

"You ready?"

Ready to vomit. To go hide in a corner. But she nodded, holding tight to the keys to Seth's truck. "I guess."

"You're either ready or you're not, Liddy." He ignored her tired sigh, oblivious to her silent breakdown. "Put the cap on. If the cops follow you, all the better. Just take 'em for a drive. I'll see you in a bit."

Lydia tucked her hair inside the hat and pulled the brim down low to disguise her face. "Promise you'll come straight back. No detours."

And by detours, she meant one. The racetrack. She kicked herself for showing Seth the savings bonds, certain they'd disappeared while she slept. When would she ever learn?

"No detours. Cross my heart."

Her legs dragging beneath her, Lydia exited the garage and walked toward the sleeping beast parked in the driveway.

Gingerly, she pressed the key fob, startling at the sound, even though she'd expected it. She opened the driver's door and boosted herself up on the running board to climb inside.

Lydia sucked in a breath and started the engine, while she tried to remember all the rules Seth had taught her years ago. Rules he never followed himself. Hands at ten and two. Eyes on the road. Check your blind spot. She knew all the basics. But every time she got behind the wheel, the past came flooding back in a single indelible image—her father's lifeless face—and she couldn't focus. White-knuckling it through three failed driving tests had certainly proved that.

"We can do this." She gave the console an encouraging pat, imagining the truck purring beneath her. "Work with me, please."

Lydia inched out onto the quiet street. She covered the brake as the truck crept down the hill, and kept her gaze straight ahead. When she reached the bottom, she finally allowed herself a backward glance but found only asphalt in the rearview.

Her reassurance didn't last long. Several blocks down, just past the house with the fancy Greek columns, a nondescript gray sedan turned out behind her and followed at a respectable distance. When she made a right turn onto Washington, the car did the same.

Lydia sped up, hoping to lose them. She made another turn and another. But the car stuck close. Too close.

Her grip tightened on the wheel. She felt fifteen again, her thin frame swallowed up by the bucket seat in her father's decrepit van. His lucky rabbit's foot swaying from its hook on the rearview mirror. The cut above her eye, where he'd back-handed her, had wept blood down her cheek.

Her breath came in shallow gasps. She'd only wanted to get away. Then and now.

Her field of vision narrowed, and the houses on either side

of her disappeared, until she saw only blacktop. She knew it wasn't real—it couldn't be—but in the center of the road stood her father. His arms waved wildly; rage colored him red. She heard Seth's voice implore her from the passenger seat. *Drive! Drive!*

The thump beneath the truck's massive tires sounded sickeningly familiar, even after nine years. Like the soundtrack to a nightmare, you hear it once, and you never forget it.

Lydia yelped and slammed on the brakes, jolting her body forward and straining her seatbelt. She sat there, shaking, stuck halfway between then and now, until the vehicle eased past her. Not the gray sedan, after all, but a white Jeep, which made her more confused than ever.

A teenaged boy leaned out of the passenger window. Another stared at her from behind the wheel.

"Are you nuts? Learn how to drive!"

She felt too stricken to speak. Once they'd sped on, she steeled herself for the worst. She knew too well what awaited her: the pool of blood; the limbs, limp and disfigured. The only difference, she didn't have Seth here to help her clean it up. To lay on the guilt trip. To make her feel like an ogre.

Jesus, Liddy. Look at what you did. I never said to hit him.

Whimpering, Lydia stepped out onto the street and forced herself to peer beneath the truck. Her tears turned to laughter, her laughter to tears again. Wedged under the front tire, the body of her victim. The dented lid of a garbage can.

Hands still shaking, Lydia restarted the truck. She wished she had a working cellphone to call Seth. But she had him to blame for that as well. She wanted to scream at him until his ears bled. Until he begged for mercy.

When she glanced up into the rearview mirror to wipe the mascara streaks from beneath her eyes, she spotted the flashing lights. The unmarked gray sedan pulled up behind her. Moments later, another followed, a familiar face at the helm.

With his long strides, Detective Casey floated toward her effortlessly. While she struggled to regain control over her breath, he tapped on the window.

"Uh. Hi." A pathetic attempt to sound normal, even for her. She looked straight ahead, uncertain where to put her eyes.

"You okay?" He didn't wait for her answer. "We got a report that you were driving pretty erratically. Where were you headed in such a hurry?"

"A report? That's impossible. I hardly passed any other cars."

"Are you calling Detective Casey a liar, Ms. McKay?" Lydia recognized his smartass partner from the Blue Bird.

"No, I just—well—"

"Were you planning to leave the scene of an accident?"

Lydia searched out Detective Casey's eyes, hoping at least he would have mercy on her. "I didn't hit anyone. Just an old plastic lid."

"It's okay, Diedrich. I've got this." But Lydia's relief didn't last long. "That plastic lid belongs to the City of San Francisco, which means you've damaged city property. I'm afraid I'm going to have to ask you to step out of the vehicle." Detective Casey took a step back, waiting for her to comply. "You have your driver's license with you, I assume."

Lydia struggled to swallow a beach ball-sized lump. "I don't have a license. I never have."

Detective Casey nodded, which only made it worse. "I'm well aware of that. Because we know a lot about you... you and Seth. We're not as dumb as we look."

"Speak for yourself, man." The other detective chuckled. As if they were a comedy duo.

Seeing no other choice, Lydia popped the door of the truck and reluctantly surrendered to her fate. As the detectives walked her back to their vehicle, one on each side of her like she might bolt, she couldn't help but think of Iris. And the others before her. That *one*, especially. She wondered exactly what the cops knew. They hadn't cuffed her, hadn't placed her under arrest, which meant they couldn't know everything. Certainly not *that*.

Detective Casey cleared his throat. When he spoke, she remembered what Iris had said once. An old saying about a goose walking on her grave. A chill passed through Lydia, because the detective all but read her mind.

"We know you've been lying to us. It's about time you told us who you really are."

NINETEEN

Maureen downed the dregs of her third cup of coffee and kept her sandpaper eyes laser-focused on Iris's Victorian. The copy of the *Chronicle* she'd swiped from the breakroom kept her company on the passenger seat. Its damning headline—TWO PERSONS OF INTEREST IDENTIFIED IN SUSPECTED MURDER IN PACIFIC HEIGHTS—had proved to be the only rallying cry she needed. After riling Seth and meeting Tallboy in the Presidio, she felt closer than ever to a breakthrough. So, after shift change, she'd half-assed her paperwork and raced here straightaway, positioning the Volvo on the hill near the park, which afforded her a clear view of the house and the garage.

Minutes ago, Lydia had left in Seth's truck alone, riding the brake and tootling along like a grandma. Predictably, after the truck had advanced a few blocks, the unmarked police tail had pulled out after her. Sheer incompetence, Maureen thought. From their ill-chosen vantage point in the valley, the cops had been unable to make out Lydia's disguise.

With the house dark and no sign of her prime suspect, the whole scene raised Maureen's antennae. She leaned forward, watchful. Her nerves teetered on a razor's edge, her body exhausted, impatient, and keyed up all at once. But when a vintage cherry-red Mustang exited the garage with Seth at the helm, she pumped her fist in the air. *Take your peace and shove it, Walt.*

Maureen eased the car down the street, keeping the Mustang in her line of sight. As she followed Seth out of the city, she replayed the article's finer points.

Lead Detective Mark Casey identified the two persons of interest in a briefing to the media late Tuesday evening, indicating that Mrs. Duncan, who had no close friends or next of kin, had hired the McKays as caretakers approximately two and a half months prior to her disappearance. Detective Casey was reluctant to cite specific evidence of their involvement, but he noted that the circumstantial case against the McKays is mounting. "One key piece of evidence is all we need. That's why we're offering the reward and urging the public to come forward."

Short but pointed, Maureen reckoned Detective Casey had chosen his words with great care, intending to smoke the rat from his hole. And right now, said rat sped toward the Bay Bridge in the direction of Oakland, oblivious to the Volvo on his tail.

With Golden Gate Fields in sight, Seth took the Fourth Street exit and parked in front of Bay Area Bank and Trust. Maureen ducked down as she drove past and settled into a spot on the street to wait for him. A grin plastered on his face, Seth removed his wallet from the pocket of his jeans and bumped the car door closed with his hip. He had the look of a Broadway star on the verge of bursting into song. That kind of exuberance could only mean one thing. In the last twenty-four hours, the rat had found himself a hefty hunk of cheddar.

When Seth left the bank ten minutes later, Maureen had no doubt about his next stop. The first horse race didn't start for another hour, but the gates opened at ten. She trailed him to the mostly empty parking lot, where he zipped into a spot near the outer boundary. Just beyond it, the rocky shoreline of the Berkeley Marina.

While Maureen looked on from her own position at the entrance, Seth emerged from the Mustang. He pulled his cap down low and snuck a few wary glances over his shoulder before he popped the trunk and withdrew his backpack. Instead of heading inside the venue as she expected, Seth hopped the guardrail and began walking toward the Albany Bulb, a long piece of tree-covered land that extended into the bay. Once the sight of a massive homeless encampment, the Bulb had long been known for its unusual artwork made from the reclaimed refuse left behind.

"What the heck?" Maureen muttered under her breath.

Securing her duty weapon in her pocket holster, she opened the door and followed. Before she reached the perimeter, another man caught her eye. Well, not so much the man, but the gold-trimmed Chrysler he surfaced from. He moved faster than she anticipated, tracking Seth's footsteps in an ill-fitting jogging suit that seemed stretched to its limits. With every stride, his jowls flopped like a hound dog's. And as he pumped his stumpy arms, his jacket lifted, revealing a tactical baton nestled alongside his portly belly.

Maureen ignored the zing of fear that zipped up her spine and pressed on, careful to stay out of sight. Once Seth reached the jetty, he slowed his pace, and she mimicked his other tail, taking cover behind the trees and advancing methodically, until she found her final vantage point behind the thick trunk of a live oak. The man with the baton lingered in back of a rockpile closer to the shoreline, his labored breaths swallowed by the wind.

Seth stumbled down a small embankment toward the beach, where two makeshift soldiers—pieced together with metal scraps and bits of cloth—guarded the spot from atop a graffitied plank, and a massive driftwood dog sat on its haunches, staring out into the sea. Just beyond, near the water, the most famous of the Bulb statues, the Beseeching Woman, reached her arms out, her intentions unclear.

Maureen pressed her back into the tree, grounding herself in the present. She couldn't afford to slip up. Not now.

Seth crouched in the tall grass near the bay, opened his backpack, and withdrew a black plastic bag. As he approached the water, he reached down to add a few hunks of broken concrete to the sack, which now hung heavy at his side.

Maureen's hand rested on her Glock, unsure what to do next. The only certainty: she would see the contents of that bag. Whatever it took.

"Well, well, well." The suited man stepped out of his hiding place and lumbered down the hill, with the sea breeze whipping what remained of his hair into a frenzy. "If it isn't San Francisco PD's 'person of interest.' I knew you couldn't stay away from the races."

Seth appeared unbothered, surreptitiously dropping the bag and taking a step away from it. As if it didn't belong to him. "You back for another ass-whipping, Vinnie?"

Vinnie's chuckle quickly turned dark. "Hand it over."

"Hand *what* over?"

"Whatever's in that plastic bag you were draggin' around. It sure must be important if you hiked all the way out here to get rid of it. I'll consider it a down payment on what you owe me."

"I don't know what you're talkin' about. What bag?" But when Vinnie moved to grab it, Seth jumped in front of him, whipping out his wallet instead. "*Here.* I have your money. Part of it, anyway. It's ten thousand dollars. And I can get you more. Soon."

As Vinnie disappeared the cash into one of his meaty paws, the other seized the baton at his waist. Seth realized too late and barely raised a hand before the length of the club descended on his left knee, dropping him to the sand. Vinnie shook his head. "You really are as stupid as your daddy."

"I'll get you the rest, man. The old lady was loaded."

"I'll bet she was." Vinnie delivered another vicious strike, this time to Seth's ribs. While Seth curled into a fetal position, he loosened the knot on the bag and peered inside, a thin smile curling his lips. "I want what you owe me plus interest. Or I'm taking all your little secrets straight to the cops."

"'My secrets'? What about yours, *Uncle Vinnie*?" Seth hauled himself up and lunged forward. "You're not so squeaky clean yourself."

Vinnie slung the bag out of his reach and whacked him on the wrist with the baton. "Finders, keepers. Now that I've got this, I own you."

Maureen had recited an oath to serve and protect. But she could appreciate Vinnie's brand of street justice. It took the form of a metal baton. A sharp blow to Seth's head. A woozy freefall with a hard and sudden stop that left Seth lying there like a lump.

Vinnie rummaged through Seth's pockets, turning them inside out. Satisfied with his haul, he wiped the sweat from his face, retrieved the plastic bag, and turned back toward the path, where Maureen hunkered down and waited for him to pass.

"SFPD." She aimed her gun at his back. "Drop the bag."

He made a slow spin toward her but didn't release his grip. In one hand, he kept a stranglehold on the bag. In the other, he wielded the baton. "*SFPD?* Did you get lost, little lady? And where's your uniform?"

"I said, *drop the bag*."

"Or what? You gonna shoot me?"

"Maybe. Maybe not. But I wouldn't want to take that bet."

Vinnie leered at her. "Well, I am a betting man."

Maureen knew bullies like Vinnie. Some, she worked with on the force. She took a step forward, then another, careful to stay out of reach of his baton. The closer she came, the better she could see the glint of fear in his beady eyes. "You either hand it over and walk, or I arrest you for the assault I just witnessed and take it anyway as evidence. You spend a night in jail, miss the races. It's your call."

The bag fell from Vinnie's hand.

"And the baton. Go on."

Cursing, he flung the weapon in her direction.

"Now, get outta here."

Vinnie started up the trail, pausing after a few steps to give her his middle finger. But when she lunged at him, he took off running like a wild hog through the brush.

Collecting the bag, Maureen hurried down the embankment toward Seth. He lay flat on his back with a nasty bump swelling on his temple. A nudge of her foot produced a barely audible groan; an unexpected pinch of pity pained her heart. Until she found a spot on the plank alongside the soldier statues, where she sat and worked the bag open. Until she discovered exactly what Seth had been trying to bury in the cold tomb of the sea.

The salty wind whipped against Maureen's face as she dialed her cellphone. Held it to her ear. Waited for the ringing to drown the perpetual drumbeat, louder now than ever. *Find Iris!*

"Albany Police Department. How may I help you?"

TWENTY

BEFORE

Iris screamed, emitting a shriek so shrill it scared her. She stood there, dumbfounded, and gaped at the dresser in her bedroom until Lydia burst through the door with Seth at her heels.

"What is it? What's wrong?" Lydia asked. The poor girl looked terrified.

"The burglar. He's been in the house again." Iris pointed, her lower lip quivering. "He's taken my pillbox. And worse, my precious butterfly brooch. He must know how much it means to me."

Seth and Lydia exchanged a worried look. They thought she'd lost her mind. Wrapping an arm around her, Lydia guided her to the ottoman, helping her to sit.

"We have your pillbox," Lydia said. "Don't you remember? We took it last night to refill it."

Iris shook her head, glumly.

"The doctor thought it would be best if somebody helped you keep track."

"I suppose he did, didn't he? And I imagine you've reminded me of that before..." A pained lilt in her voice hinted she knew the answer.

"Only a few times." Lydia patted her shoulder. "But that's what we're here for. I tell you what, I'll put a note on the box to remind you. Like the one we made for the oven, after you burned the coffee cake. And the alarm, after you overslept."

"Oh, goodness me. I am a hopeless case."

"Now, about your brooch." Waving Seth over, Lydia scanned the room. "I'm sure it's around here somewhere. You've probably just misplaced it. Seth and I will help you look."

"Are you sure the burglar didn't steal it? I can't imagine I'd lose something so valuable."

Seth poked through the jewelry box on the dresser. Opened and shut the top two drawers. Glanced in the closet. "Is there a place you might have hidden it? For safekeeping."

Iris puzzled for a bit. "Maybe in the hat box beneath the bed. I keep some of my cash there."

Lifting the bed skirt, Seth dropped to one knee and peered into the shadows. He reached until his shoulder disappeared, retrieving the dusty hat box. "In this old thing? It doesn't look like it's been touched in ages."

"Be a dear, and check it anyway." Iris clutched at her lapel. "I won't be able to rest until I've found it."

A dust cloud plumed when Seth lifted the circular lid. He coughed a few times, his eyes widening. "No brooch. But holy smokes, Iris, that's a lot of scratch."

"I suppose it would be safer in the bank. But my husband always used to say that it was good practice to keep some money on hand. In case of—"

"A quick getaway," Seth offered, with a sly grin.

"*Emergency*," Iris corrected. "But with a burglar in the neighborhood, I'm certain Dean would reconsider."

Lydia continued the search, stopping to collect a pile of mail that had toppled to the floor. She shook her head at the bank statement visible on top. "I told you to be careful with these, Iris. You don't want everybody knowing your business."

"I know, I know. But who'll see it anyway? Just the two of—"

With a gasp, Lydia crossed the room in two eager steps. She reached beneath a crumpled tissue atop the towering stack of paperbacks on the far nightstand. "Um, Iris... does this look familiar?"

"My brooch!" Iris sighed with relief, straightening her blouse to ready its usual place of honor. "How in the world did it get over there?"

Pinning it for her, Lydia shrugged. "I'm just glad we found it. I know how special it is, it being from Dean and all."

"No, no. It wasn't from Dean."

"Sorry. I just assumed. A secret admirer, then?"

Iris's chest tightened. She felt the tears coming. "A special friend."

"How mysterious," Lydia cooed. "Now, finish getting ready and come downstairs. We have a surprise for you, *birthday girl*."

"It's my birthday?" Iris scrunched her forehead in confusion, waiting until Lydia looked sufficiently stupefied to add, "Kidding. I'm only kidding, dear. I couldn't forget the big 7-0 even if I wanted to."

When Iris rounded the corner to descend the final flight of stairs, they started singing. *Happy birthday to you...* It reminded her of her last birthday, and she could hardly bear it. But she commanded herself to smile. To wear the silly paper crown Lydia had laid out on the table. It was expected of her.

"You're queen for the day, Iris." Lydia placed a handmade card next to her plate. *You are a blessing*, it read. "This is from me and Seth."

With ceremony, Seth laid a napkin on her lap. "And the pancakes are courtesy of Dottie's Café, since you know Lydia's cooking could kill a horse. Sorry, Liddy."

"Whatever you wish today is our command."

Iris's true wish couldn't be granted. No one could bring back the dead. Not even Seth with his angelic smile. So, she would have to settle. "I'd like to take a stroll in the Presidio. Or maybe over to Lafayette Park. And if it's not too much trouble, Seth, could I help you with the gardening? It's been so long since I felt the dirt between my fingers."

"I'm not sure that's a good idea. With the cast and—"

Lydia cleared her throat, gave Seth a pointed look.

"But I'm sure we can make it work."

"Is that really all you want?" Lydia asked, squeezing Iris's shoulder. "What about some more of those cute little dish towels we found on our walk yesterday? Or a girls' night out at the movies?"

Iris patted her hand. "Your company is the best gift an old woman could ask for."

"If you say so."

"I *do* say so. But I am a little chilly, dear. Would you mind getting my sweater?"

The moment Lydia's footfalls landed heavy on the stairs, Iris turned to Seth. Uncertain how he'd react, she hesitated. She didn't want to scare him. "There is one more thing. If you can keep a secret."

Seth dipped his head in a mock bow. "Name it, my lady."

Iris leaned on the hoe, resting. She felt Seth's eyes on her, just waiting for her to take a spill, and she couldn't blame him. She was seventy now, with the crown to prove it. The age when everybody gives you that look. Like you're nothing more than a lame duck. An accident waiting to happen. And with one arm already in a cast, they wouldn't be wrong.

"Make sure to give them space," she told Seth, as he dropped the cucumber seeds into the row he'd dug in the soil.

She followed behind him, tamping down the earth. Firm but not too packed. "The seeds need room to grow."

A hint of amusement played on his lips. "So, this is what you wanted to do on your birthday? Plant cucumbers?"

Iris took another break, dabbing her sweat on the back of her glove. "You know, I never celebrated a birthday until I turned eight. We were so poor that I hadn't even heard of a birthday party. And presents? Forget about it."

Seth chuckled, emptying the remainder of the seeds from the packet. He reached for the hoe but Iris waved him off. Nothing quite like hard labor on her birthday to remind her that she wasn't dead yet. "I didn't realize you grew up like that, Iris. But look at you now. Queen of Pacific Heights with a fancy house and a hat box full of dough."

"Life is funny, isn't it? Even though I didn't have two nickels to rub together back then, that first birthday celebration at the orphanage was my favorite. Well, if you could call it a celebration."

"At the orphanage?"

Iris got back to work. Because busy hands helped her to wall off the memories. Best to keep the past at a safe distance. It didn't hurt as much that way. Still, she allowed herself a small reminiscence. "I had one friend. The best friend I ever had. And on my eighth birthday, she snuck out with me and we shared a Moon Pie by the lake. She told me to make a wish, though we didn't have a cake. Or any candles. Or any friends to join in the singing. We had each other, and that was all we needed. It was the best birthday ever. Do you know that I spent every birthday with her, even if it was sometimes just a phone call?"

"So, this friend, will she be stopping by? Lydia would love to meet her. You know she'll go gaga over a sentimental story like that. Especially now that she's preggo. The hormones..." Seth made a face, while he retrieved the hose, tugging it toward the garden. "It's probably good that you made her take a nap. She's been on edge since I found out about the baby."

"Thanks to me and my big mouth. I'm glad you finally came around, in spite of me spoiling the surprise. The two of you as parents, that will be a sight to see."

"Aw, I was just worried, is all," he said, watering the first row of seedlings. "I mean, how am I gonna afford a baby? I can hardly take care of myself. And kids are expensive. I don't want to be a fuck-up like my dad. Pardon my French."

"Don't you fret about that." Reaching the last furrow, Iris packed the dirt with her blade. As she worked, she lifted her face to the blazing sun, so she could explain away the tears in her eyes. "And as for my friend, she passed away last year, a week or so after my birthday. The brooch was a gift from her, so you can see why it's irreplaceable."

A sudden, sharp pain sliced through the front of Iris's right ankle, and her knee buckled, sending her—and her birthday crown—tumbling to the ground. At least the freshly tilled soil made for a soft landing.

"Iris! You're bleeding." Dropping the hose, Seth hurried toward her. He bent down to examine the cut. The smear of red on the hoe's sharp end. The rivulets running beneath the strap of her sandal and into the ground. "I told you to wear boots."

Wincing, Iris snuck a glance at the wound. She'd never seen so much blood. "Goodness. That's what happens when you get old. Your skin turns thin as paper, and you bleed like a stuck pig."

"Do you need a doctor? Stitches? Should I call someone?"

"Heavens, no. It's not as bad as it looks." But Iris's hand was already covered—red and sticky. "Just grab a towel and help me get cleaned up. There are some bandages in the first aid kit in the kitchen. And don't tell Lydia. She'll only worry. Worry isn't good for the baby."

Seth took a deep breath and stood up, glancing over his

shoulder at the house. The windows he'd cleaned last week remained empty, the glass polished smooth as fine silk. Still, Iris hoped Lydia hadn't heard the whole scene.

Before Seth headed inside, she grabbed for his hand. She needed to get this out. To make him understand.

"You're such a lifesaver, dear. And please, don't worry about your expenses. You know Dean and I never had children of our own, and I've been itching to spoil a little one." Iris pointed to her fallen crown with a wry smile, and Seth returned it to its rightful place atop her head. "As long as I'm around, you and Lydia and the baby won't want for anything."

"But you won't be around forever. Then what?" he asked.

Lying there like a felled tree, Iris felt the truth in his words more than ever. "The closer I get to the grave, the more I realize you can't take it with you."

TWENTY-ONE

AFTER

Wednesday afternoon

"Who is Gene McKay?" Detective Casey asked Lydia. Like it was a perfectly natural place to begin. And she supposed it was, since Gene had been the beginning and end of everything for as long as she could remember. Even after he died, he lived on in her head.

"Seth's father." Lydia grimaced at her bitten-down thumbnail, sucking a smear of blood from the quick. It felt like an eternity since the detective had escorted her back to the stark interview room and told her to wait for his return. She'd sensed him there all along, behind the one-way mirror, watching her slow unraveling. By now, she'd been boiled through and through. Like a frog in a pot of hot water. The sweat pooling beneath her armpits proved it.

"*Seth's* father?"

Lydia wrapped her arms around herself. Her pale flesh, her only armor. "That's what I said."

Detective Casey looked plumb tired. "Drop the act, Lydia. I've seen the records from social services. I already know. I just want you to tell me the truth. Is that too much to ask?"

Lydia screwed her mouth up tight. The way she'd done at five years old, when Gene had accused her of stealing the last of his money. In truth, he'd been too drunk to remember gambling it away the night before.

"Fine. You don't want to say it? I'll say it. Gene McKay and his wife, Joni, had a son. Joni died giving birth to their second child—a daughter—and old Gene never did recover. Or hell, maybe he always was a sorry bastard. Those kids had to fend for themselves, depend on each other. Thick as thieves, am I right? You and Seth. Brother and sister."

Lydia didn't have the strength to deny it. Maybe if she simply nodded her head, he would go away.

"Why did you lie about it?"

She shrugged, helpless. How could she explain without looking like a monster? That she'd just followed Iris's lead that first day in the café. That it was all part of the con. And a good one. A young couple in distress tugged at the heartstrings. The purse strings, too.

"I understand family relationships can be complicated. Confusing. Embarrassing, even. I hope I'm not making you too uncomfortable."

A nervous laugh fluttered from Lydia's throat. "Too late for that."

"You said you were pregnant. Now, I have to ask. Did Seth—"

"God, no. Nothing like that." Lydia's face flushed. She hung her head. "I don't really want to talk about this anymore."

"Alright, I get it. It's a lot to process. But I want you to know, Seth has been detained. Albany police caught him down at the Bulb, right near the water. He had a bag with him. Do you know what was in it?"

Lydia shook her head so fast, she felt dizzy. She never thought Seth would go *there*, of all places. *Not a lick of good sense,* her dad would say.

"Evidence," the detective told her, enunciating every syllable.

"Evidence of what?"

"You tell me." Detective Casey retrieved his cellphone from his pocket, scrolling his finger across the screen before he held it out to her.

The black plastic bag lay splayed on a metal table. Next to it, the bloody dish towel and several large chunks of broken concrete.

Lydia enlarged the right corner of the photo, disbelieving. She tried to make sense of it, but there could be only one explanation. Seth had promised her that he wouldn't hurt Iris. That he wouldn't do what he'd done before. But she couldn't deny her own eyes.

She counted at least ten packets of the little blue pills. More than enough for an overdose. "I—I... I'm not sure what to say..."

"It's Valium."

How about we give her a little something to take the edge off? Make her more... open to suggestion. Even now, the memory of Seth's voice made her sick. That lying sack of shit. He must've snuck them in the box somehow.

"But Iris wasn't prescribed Valium." As the detective nodded, Lydia realized she'd spoken out loud.

"You're right. She wasn't." The way he said it, being right didn't seem like a good thing. "Then, you can imagine our concern when we found three Valium pills in every remaining slot of her pillbox."

While Lydia waited in the lobby of the police station, she counted all the ways she hated her big brother. All the things he'd done, the messes he'd dragged her into. At the top of that very long list: Seth reminded her of their father. Handsome, charming when he wanted to be, with a mean streak half a mile wide. A shiny red apple with a rotten core. She planned to tell him just that and more.

But when Seth approached the door, with Detective Casey and his partner stanchioned beside him, Lydia lost her resolve. No one had prepared her for the egg-shaped bruise on his forehead, the limp in his gait. Still, she glared at him, hoping he would at least feel the heat of her stare.

"You're getting off easy today, McKay." Detective Casey had dropped his nice guy act, going full bad cop on Seth. It gave her a tiny bit of satisfaction to watch him squirm. Even though she knew that whatever happened to him now, whatever humiliation he suffered, she'd be the one to pay for it later. "We could ship you back to Albany, let them book you for possession with intent to distribute."

"Not to mention evidence tampering," his partner added. "Driving a vehicle without owner consent."

"But we're not. You know why?" Detective Casey cast a pointed glance at Lydia, and she dropped her eyes to her feet. "Because there's a murder charge headed your way. I don't know when or where or how, but the other shoe is gonna drop sooner or later. And I can't wait to see the look in your eyes when I show up at Iris Duncan's house with a warrant for your arrest."

"Is that all, Detective?" Seth grimaced, holding his hand at his side, and Lydia wondered who had bested him.

Detective Casey gave a smug nod. "All for now."

"What about my backpack?"

"It's been logged into evidence."

"Then, can I at least get the keys to my truck?"

"We've obtained a search warrant on both vehicles. They've been impounded."

"The Mustang too? How are we supposed to get home?"

Turning to his partner, Detective Casey shrugged. "Good question. There's a bus stop about a mile from here."

Seth let out a huff. "Well, when can I get my truck back?"

The detectives had already walked away, their footsteps pronouncing the conversation over. But hearing Seth's question, they both stopped short at the door to Homicide. Detective Casey didn't bother to turn around.

"When we're done with it."

The number 22 bus to Bay Street smelled like sweaty socks and cigarette smoke, but at least it would get them within walking distance of Iris's house. Lydia still couldn't manage to think of it as theirs. Right now, she wished she could be rid of it. Rid of Seth, too.

As soon as they boarded, he pointed to the seats in the back row. So far, he had said exactly nothing about the plastic bag. Or the Albany Bulb. Or the injury to his face. By the time the half-empty bus lurched to a start, the silence threatened to overwhelm Lydia.

"They know," she hissed. "They know who we are. And who we aren't."

Seth stared straight ahead, but the flex in his jaw told her he'd heard her loud and clear. The bus rumbled on for a few more blocks before she poked him again.

"Detective Casey showed me what was in the bag. You've been lying to me."

"And you haven't?"

His accusation had a sting that surprised her. Like he'd been waiting for the chance to bite back. Like he might really know all that she'd been hiding. But he didn't—*he couldn't*—so she kept her mouth shut. "What are you talking about?"

"You think you're the only one the cops have been talking

to? You lied to that detective. You told him you quit your job at the Sunrise. Why would you lie about something stupid like that? It makes us look guilty, Liddy."

"Oh. *That* makes us look guilty." From a few rows in front of them, a head turned to look, but Lydia didn't care. And when Seth pressed an admonishing finger to his lips, she raised her voice an octave. "Because I thought that what made us look guilty was the bloody rag in your truck. And the Valium you never told me about. You drugged her! You promised me you wouldn't."

Seth gave her the look. The incredulous one that preceded every lie he'd ever told her. The look that made her feel crazy. "Yeah, and I *didn't*. I mean, I'll admit I thought about it, but I didn't need to this time. You know what Iris was like. She trusted us."

"And the money," she added, ignoring his lame protest. "The twenty thousand dollars you took from Iris that you neglected to mention."

"Shit. The cops know about that?"

"No. Not yet anyway. But I do." The implied threat settled uncomfortably between them like an unwanted guest. "I saw it in the envelope in your backpack on Monday morning. I'm guessing it's gone now though. Like those savings bonds. You're so selfish."

Lydia turned away, looking out the grimy window at the beautiful city. At the lavish homes of Pacific Heights, one of which belonged to her now. And yet, she had never felt like such an outsider.

Seth nudged her with his elbow, whispering, "This is what they want. Remember what Dad always told us. Stick together."

"Look how that turned out. I can't believe you'd go back to the Bulb. After what we did."

"It's by the track, okay? I thought I could park there without drawing too much attention to myself. Besides, that was nearly ten years ago. It's not like they're gonna find—"

"Alright, I got it." Lydia regretted bringing it up at all. She preferred that particular topic stay at the bottom of the bay, exactly where they'd left it. "So, what happened to your face? Clearly, something went wrong."

"Not a what, but a who. *Vinnie.*" Seth reflexively rubbed the bump on his head. "I'm gonna kill that asshole."

TWENTY-TWO

Maureen sat on a cold metal chair in the SFPD Homicide Division waiting room, feeling very much like a suspect. The lieutenant had ordered her here an hour ago. *Detectives Casey and Diedrich would like a word.* And Maureen suspected they might choose a word like insubordination. Still, she didn't regret a thing. Thanks to her, the moment Seth had awakened from his stupor on the beach, he'd been greeted by a pair of handcuffs and a free ride in an Albany PD cruiser. As the car pulled away, she'd phoned Detective Casey and left him a crowing voicemail. She knew there'd be hell to pay, but she couldn't help herself. *I caught our guy tossing evidence at the Bulb.* Emphasis on *our*.

"Maureen." Detective Diedrich stared down at her, pronouncing her name like an admonishment. He'd come alone. So, it was worse than she'd thought. "Mark asked me to speak with you."

She followed him into an office and took the chair he pointed her toward. "You know, I've been thinking about Seth McKay. He came to one of my concerts, sat with the Friends of the Symphony. Most of those folks are over age sixty. I'll bet this wasn't the first time he—"

"Enough." Diedrich silenced her, swiping the blade of his hand across his own throat. "You've done enough hypothesizing."

"It's just... that painting. The Dolores. It's been bothering me. What if Seth stole it?" Maureen didn't realize her suspicions until they dropped from her mouth. "He scratched off the name, thinking nobody would figure it out. Iris had no clue."

"No clue, huh? Reminds me of someone else I know." Diedrich shook his head and released the enormous sigh of a weary schoolteacher. "I thought you'd come in here contrite. I thought you'd apologize for walking all over our case. For undermining our authority. For doing exactly what we asked you *not* to do. Not to mention disrespecting your training officer."

"Walt?"

"Yes, Walter Greer. Thirty-five years on the force, and *this* is how you repay him. He has to put up with your nonsense. Do you really want to start off your rookie year with a misconduct complaint?"

"It's not nonsense, Pete, and you know it." Maureen drew in a breath to summon her courage. "You knew it back then, too. You were just too chicken shit to do anything."

"I was right. This is about Waddell. About the shooting, the trial. All of it."

A cymbal crashed in her head, as the old wound burst open. The scab that never healed. "And so what if it is? When your parents and ten other innocent victims get gunned down by a psychopath in front of you, and then that same psychopath manages to fool the jury into thinking he's crazy, it changes you. It changes everything."

"There are rules. You can't come into a courtroom wielding a knife. And you can't overstep your rank. The DA is going to have to explain to a jury how an off-duty cop's fingerprints wound up on that plastic bag. If the defense is worth their salt, they'll say you planted evidence. And hell, maybe you did."

Maureen's throat ached, but she wouldn't cry. She wouldn't give Diedrich the satisfaction, wouldn't crumble like she had that day outside the courtroom, blubbering as he'd led her out. "I just want some justice for Iris Duncan. And your unmarked tail car obviously wasn't going to cut it, chasing after McKay's wife in some silly disguise."

"You mean his sister?"

"Huh?"

"You heard me. You're not as smart as you think you are. This case is way above your paygrade. And if you push this too far, you'll lose the only thing you've got left."

In the barren landscape of Maureen's life, it was painfully obvious what he meant. "I won't lose my job."

"Not your job, Maureen. Your self-respect."

Maureen opened her insulated lunch box and forced herself to finish the stale leftovers of yesterday's turkey sandwich. She washed it down with a swig of warm water from a plastic bottle she found shoved beneath her seat. A fitting lunch for the day she'd had. The more she dwelled—*the McKays were brother and sister!*—the worse she felt, and the worse she felt, the stronger the drive to redeem herself. It had been the same with music. One wrong note in a performance, and she'd be up all night, practicing until her fingers cramped.

Maureen couldn't believe she hadn't spotted the resemblance between Seth and Lydia, obvious to her now, as the weary pair trudged up Archer Avenue toward the house. She dropped her head down, though she doubted they'd spot her in her Volvo, tucked in a parking spot up the street. The media vans had cleared out, no doubt heading to the site of the next tragedy with a younger, blonder, shinier victim.

"Unbelievable," she said aloud. Caught dumping a blood-soaked rag and enough Valium to kill a few horses, and the guy had still walked free. But at least Detective Casey impounded their vehicles. Watching Seth limp up the steps to the front door was a small consolation.

The knock on her window jolted Maureen upright. Wide-eyed, she stared into the frowning face of Iris's neighbor, Bill Dorsey. He wore a color-coordinated jogging suit with sneakers so white Maureen wondered if they'd come straight from the box.

"Oh, Officer... *Shaw*, was it? I mistook you for a vagrant living in your vehicle. I was about to tell you to move along."

Maureen nearly laughed. Because it felt like the truth. She desperately needed a hot shower and a meal that didn't come in a wrapper. "Off duty at the moment," she said, hoping that explained the state of her car and her face: messy.

"You're doing surveillance." He lowered his voice to a whisper. "We're not in any danger, are we?"

"Not at the moment."

Bill looked disappointed. And Maureen wondered if he'd ever lived through real danger. The kind with life-and-death stakes. Not losing ten grand in the stock market on a bad play, or scratching his five-thousand-dollar rims when he parked too close to the curb.

"I saw the news this morning. Persons of interest in Iris's death living in her house. In *my* neighborhood. It just doesn't sit right. And the HOA certainly won't be happy." Bill gazed off, looking wistfully at the house. "To think we finally got her to clean up the place. Now, this."

"You said yourself that it's a big house. A lot for one person to manage." *A grieving person*, Maureen added silently, recalling how some days it had taken the last of her energy to pick up the newspaper and retrieve the mail.

"Well, that's true. But it wasn't a problem until this year. Until she started acting kooky, talking about that burglar and perching up there in the attic like a spy. Then, the whole place went downhill. Sometimes, I think she was just trying to piss off the HOA. She even hired an attorney."

"An attorney?"

"A criminal defense attorney. Frankly, I don't understand why he took her case. He must have felt bad for her. But he could write one hell of a mean letter. He threatened to sue us for harassment and age discrimination."

As Bill spoke, Maureen's mood brightened. The gray fog of the morning lifted to reveal the dazzling sun. "You know, I'm glad I ran into you. It turns out Iris didn't retire from the public library like she told you. She hadn't worked there since 1985. And she only volunteered. Any idea why she might lie about something like that?"

Bill appeared flummoxed by the revelation. "Iris didn't tell me; her husband, Dean, did. If I recall, he wasn't too keen on her working at all. Dean had a stiff upper lip. Traditional. Conservative. You know the type."

Maureen nodded, wondering what else Iris had kept hidden from her husband and why. "And Iris? What type was she?"

"Honestly, a pain in the ass." Bill gave a sad smile. "But mostly, she stayed to herself. Especially after her husband died. She didn't have any real friends to speak of. Not that we didn't try. My wife invited her for Thanksgiving dinner the last couple of years, but she said she had plans. If you ask me, she did it on purpose, keeping people at arm's length. Dean once told me she had a rough childhood, but he didn't elaborate."

"I don't suppose you kept any of those letters from the attorney."

"Are you kidding? My wife calls me a pack rat, but the truth of the matter is that, as the chief financial officer for one of the largest software companies in the Bay Area, I understand the immense importance of record retention. I've got emails from 1998. Every report card since I matriculated at Edgewood Elementary. Receipts, newspaper articles, you name it. And I certainly saved the correspondence between Iris Duncan and the HOA. That's a no-brainer."

Ten minutes later, Maureen exited Casa de Bill with a copy of the March 30th letter from the firm of Chalmers and Pierce, the paper still warm from Bill's fancy all-in-one printer.

Maureen sat in the car, studying the communication, which had been typed on the firm's official letterhead and co-signed by Iris herself.

My client alleges discrimination and harassment by the Archer Avenue Home Owners Association, including her claim that a representative or representatives of the Association has been trespassing onto her property without her expressed permission and pilfering or moving her belongings in an attempt to frighten her.

Sure enough, the letter had ended with an old-fashioned threat.

My client has recently taken steps to remediate the Association's complaints. If the Association continues to pursue her with such aggressive tactics, we reserve all rights under the law, including but not limited to a discrimination lawsuit on the basis of age, gender, and marital status.

Maureen tossed the letter onto the seat. She glanced at the house, then at herself in the rearview mirror. At the dark circles beneath her glassy eyes. She should head home and sneak in a catnap. But she had the next two days off to sleep, and she felt a familiar tug guiding her toward downtown, to the offices of Chalmers and Pierce. Though Diedrich's voice nagged at her, she knew she couldn't stop now.

TWENTY-THREE

BEFORE

Iris gaped at the gun in Seth's hands. She had to admit, the man could make things happen. He'd answered her birthday request in only a week's time, showing up at the door to her bedroom that morning with a sleek polymer case. Finally, she felt safe in her own home again.

"How much do I owe you?" she asked, reaching for the 9-millimeter.

"Whoa." Seth snatched it back. "Easy there, Annie Oakley. Do you even know how to use it?"

"Of course I do, dear. Every Saturday at Lost Pines, the headmaster took us up to Fort Bragg for skeet shooting. Not to toot my own horn, but I won the Golden Trigger trophy five years in a row."

"Wasn't that..." Seth counted on his fingers, scrunching his face before he gave up. "A really long time ago? You wear glasses now. You've got arthritis and one arm in a cast."

"It's like riding a bicycle. The body remembers. Besides, I don't intend to fire it without good reason. But, if you really think I could use a lesson, I know a place we can go."

"It's up to you. We'd have to keep it between us, though."

Seth passed the gun to Iris. "I got you a bargain. Fifteen hundred. And that includes the case."

Iris counted out the bills from her hat box, adding an extra hundred to the pile. A small price to pay for the satisfaction it gave her. "Buy yourself something nice. Or better yet, buy Lydia something nice. That girl works harder than the devil at a sinner's convention. She needs to be spoiled every now and then."

"Yes, ma'am." He glanced over his shoulder into the empty hallway. Downstairs, the clatter of dishes gave Lydia away. "I have to warn you. Liddy doesn't like guns. You might want to keep it out of sight."

Iris returned the gun to the case and slid it beneath her pillow. "That goes without saying. Snug as a bug. I promise she won't lay eyes on it unless it's absolutely necessary."

Seth paused at the door, peeking over to her pillbox. "Did you forget to take your medication again?"

Hanging her head, Iris studied her feet. Thankfully, the cut on her ankle had healed nicely. "I'll admit it, I probably did. These days, I'd forget my head if it wasn't screwed on."

He emptied the slot into his palm and held the pills out to her. "Down the hatch," he said.

"There's something else Lydia doesn't know about." Before she downed his offering, Iris pointed to the top drawer with a mischievous grin. "A spoonful of whiskey helps the medicine go down."

Seth withdrew the bottle, and his eyes popped. "Macallan 25? Damn, Iris. You've been holding out on me."

"Go ahead, dear. You take the first swig."

"You don't have to tell me twice." He gulped down a mouthful, wiping a bit that dribbled onto his chin. "That's a helluva lot better than Jim Beam."

Iris chased her pills with a small nip. Just enough to burn

her throat. "Money can't buy everything, dear. But it can certainly buy good whiskey."

Iris hurried from her bedroom up to the attic, nearly tripping on the last step. Her heart leaped into her throat, each frantic beat issuing a warning that someday, her sense of urgency would be her downfall. With one lame arm and the other hand full, she'd narrowly avoided face-planting into the hardwood.

Positioning herself at the window, she opened the case and retrieved the gun. It felt much lighter than the Beretta shotgun she'd used as a girl, and yet, her hand shook with its weight. Down below, she caught sight of Lydia on the front steps, airing out the rugs. Shielding her face from the dust cloud, Lydia beat Iris's favorite blue throw against the bottom stair. Dean had never liked that rug, so Iris had compromised like a good wife. Kept it in the guest bedroom, where she sometimes snuck in to admire it. Not because of its beauty or expense—it was cheap and tacky—but because of what it meant to her. Dean had no idea about any of that.

Movement across the street drew Iris's eye. She pushed open the window and steadied her hand as she raised the barrel, target in sight.

Stricken with panic, the man let out a shrill yell. He waved his arms wildly, drawing Lydia's attention, and pointed up to Iris in the attic. "What the hell? She's got a gun!"

In a flash, Lydia dropped the rugs and rushed inside. Iris heard her race up the steps, listened to her ragged breathing. But she didn't lower her weapon. She couldn't. Not now. It seemed to have a mind of its own, determined and vengeful.

"Iris, what are you doing? Put the gun down."

"No, I won't." She squeezed the grip tighter. "It's *him*. It's the burglar. I saw him lurking in the backyard, and now there he is. Look for yourself."

Lydia joined her on the banquette. Placing a firm hand on the gun, she wrestled it from Iris's grasp. "That's your neighbor. Bill Dorsey. I mean, he is sort of a prick. And you don't really like him. But you can't go pointing guns at people. The poor guy just got home from work."

"I know him?"

"Of course you do. He's lived next door to you since before Dean died. He's the head of the HOA, remember?"

Iris's mouth hung open. She looked at the gun, then back to the street, where the man had disappeared inside. She raised the binoculars and found him watching from his picture window, his face stricken. "My God. You're right. It is Bill. He's going to have a field day with this one. Who knows what he'll tell those HOA heathens about me? They'll probably have me committed."

"Where did you get this thing?" Lydia placed the gun in the case and held it tight to her chest, out of Iris's reach.

"Um... the gun store?"

Lydia rolled her eyes. "I'm gonna kill Seth."

"Please don't blame him. This was all my fault." Iris smacked her forehead, hard. "My stupid, stupid fault. With everything that's happened—the attempted break-in, things turning up missing—I wanted to be able to protect myself in case the two of you weren't around. But it was stupid. *Stupid!*"

Seizing Iris's hands in her own, Lydia tried to calm her. "It's okay. Nobody got hurt. And it *was* kind of funny seeing hoity-toity Bill scream like one of those girls in a horror film, right before they get an axe between the eyes."

Unmoved, Iris didn't crack a smile. "I'm losing my mind, Lydia. This morning, I forgot my pills again, and now this. What's wrong with me?"

"There's nothing wrong with you. You're forgetful, is all. But I can call that doctor if you'd like. The neurologist the ER physician suggested. He works at Golden Gate Neurology."

Iris groaned. "What if he finds something wrong with my brain?"

"And what if he doesn't? What if he says you're perfectly normal? Wouldn't that make you feel better?"

"Oh, fine." Iris flapped her hand, as if she didn't care. "Just do it. It'll probably take forever to get in to see him anyway. By that time, you'll have shipped me off to the loony bin."

Lydia rolled her eyes. "We'll do no such thing, but..." She stood up, tucking the polymer case beneath her arm. "This is coming with me. I'll find a safe place for it."

"You think I'm imagining it, don't you? About the burglar."

After a long pause, Lydia answered. "I think you believe it, and that's all that matters."

"But what should I do if he comes back?" Iris shuddered. "*When* he comes back. The very thought of it, it's like a goose walked over my grave."

Lydia frowned for a moment, before she said, "Holler for me or Seth as loud as you can."

"And if you're not here?"

"Then, hide yourself and call the police." When Lydia squeezed Iris's shoulder, the soothing motion reminded her what it had been like to have a friend who cared. The bitter-sweet memory throbbed beneath her skin, and she could barely stand it. But she waited until Lydia had left to ask.

"What if he finds me anyway?"

TWENTY-FOUR

"I can't believe you lied to Lydia. Again." Seth wagged his finger at Iris, then he positioned one of six soda cans on a large, flat rock at the San Pablo Wildlife Refuge. "'A trip to the hardware store.' If she finds out—"

"Don't worry, dear. She suspects nothing." Iris tried to hold the gun steady with the target in her sight. "And *if* she does, I'll take the blame."

"Bend your knees a little. We don't want the kick-back to send you flying."

Iris nodded. She knew what to do. But it had been an awfully long time since she'd held a firearm. Dean would've dropped dead for a second time if he could see her now. "Here goes nothing."

Iris squeezed the trigger and stumbled back. The bullet missed the soda can target, whizzing far to the left and lodging in the nearest tree trunk instead. "Oh, dear. You're right. It isn't so easy shooting one-handed. And I forgot how powerful these things are. It's no wonder Dean never wanted one in the house."

"Told you so." Seth took the gun from her, shaking his head. "Liddy gave me an earful about what happened yesterday with the neighbor. I mean, I don't like that guy either, but that doesn't mean I want him dead."

Iris hung her head. "I had one of my spells. I didn't even recognize him. This old brain is like that car of yours. Unreliable."

"Yeah, thanks for letting me take the Mustang for a spin. I wouldn't want to break down out here in the middle of nowhere. And we'll keep the gun in our room for now. I found your hiding place, by the way. Or was it Dean's?"

Looking befuddled, Iris shrugged.

"The loose floorboard? *Genius.* Is that where you kept your diamonds?" Seth grinned, lining up the sight of the gun with the first target.

"Oh, goodness. I'd forgotten all about that. I don't suppose I ever hid anything there. Isn't that a bore?"

Seth fired, knocking the can off the boulder. It skittered back into the woods as he shot again and again, hitting every target while the spent shell cases dropped at his feet.

Iris clapped her hands, delighted. "You're quite a marksman."

"It's the only thing my dad ever taught me. Well, that and how to play the ponies."

"Ah, a betting man." Iris took a seat on a fallen tree, watching Seth line up a second set of targets. "Hopefully, he taught you the most important rule of gambling."

"What's that?" Seth asked. He loaded another clip and offered the gun to Iris.

She took a deep breath, hoisted herself up, and walked to him, firing off two more errant shots before she surrendered the weapon.

"To quit while you're ahead."

. . .

Iris clung to Seth's forearm with her good hand while he led her across the rough terrain and back to the parking lot where the Mustang waited for them. The smell of the air out here reminded her of Lost Pines with its salty breeze off the ocean.

"Feels good to escape the city, doesn't it?" she asked. "Sometimes, I wish I could live in a place like this. Quiet, serene. So pretty, it looks like a painting. *Someday.* Someday I'll dye my hair red too."

She laughed at her own silliness.

"Why don't you escape? There's nothing holding you in San Francisco." Seth laid the gun case on the hood and wiped down the barrel and the grip to a shine before he returned the 9-millimeter to its resting place. "Except me and Liddy, of course. But we could come visit you."

Iris carefully lowered herself into the passenger seat, then swung her legs around to the floorboard. The cast on her arm meant even the little things took focus, especially with a troubled mind.

"Would you, though? Come visit?" She didn't wait for an answer to add, "Did your last client move away? You don't visit her at all."

Seth positioned himself in the driver's seat. "It just didn't work out," he said, matter-of-factly. "It's not something I like to talk about."

Iris nodded. *That* she understood. "Let's put the top down, dear."

"Are you sure? I thought you said the sun might damage the leather."

She shrugged, shaking off her moroseness. "You only live once."

TWENTY-FIVE

AFTER

Wednesday, late afternoon

Seth's raised voice carried from the kitchen to the sitting room, where Lydia waited nervously on the sofa. After they'd returned from the bus stop, tired and sweaty, Seth had gone on a tear, upending the entire house, even the hallowed ground of Iris's bedroom, in a frantic search for the last of her cash, which had turned up nothing but a roll of fifties, a couple of forks, and a remote control in her underwear drawer. "Here's your burglar," Seth had told Lydia, holding up said remote. "That old bat hid the stuff and forgot where she put it." Though Lydia wondered about the missing copy of *Great Expectations*, she kept it to herself. Seth never changed his mind.

"But we have the policy right here. It names us specifically." Though Lydia couldn't see him, she heard Seth hammering the paper with his index finger. "Seth and Lydia McKay. That's us."

She could barely sit still with Seth's sounds filling the

silence. She could read his footsteps like the weather. As brisk and uneven as a spitting rainstorm.

"Isn't there anything you can do to help us? Like give us some kind of advance on the money? We're in a tight spot here."

Like the rumble of thunder, his footfalls grew louder, more insistent, until she sensed the storm moving in. A ninety-nine percent chance of explosion.

"I understand. And you have yourself a nice *fucking* after- noon too." Seth loomed in the doorway, holding a bag of frozen veggies against the bump on his forehead. He glared at his cell- phone as he reared back and readied his lightning bolt, but Lydia stopped him.

"Don't. We can't afford to buy another one." Lydia held her breath, only releasing it when Seth's hand lowered to his side. "So, what did they say?"

"Tina *Bitchface* Moore of Pacific *Scam* Mutual said, and I quote, 'A claim is paid to the beneficiaries on the death of the policyholder. You can petition the court to declare Mrs. Duncan deceased. Otherwise, the presumption of death will only be made after a period of seven years has lapsed without word from her.' Seven goddamned years."

"Seven years?" Lydia acted surprised. Best not to tell Seth she'd already scanned the fine print of the policy.

"And she was a real cow about it too, treating us like crimi- nals trying to con the system. Like we're not entitled to that money. Hell, we worked hard for it. You know as well as I do, Iris could be a real slave driver."

Lydia winced, but she didn't dare correct him. Not when he'd finally released the death grip on his cell, setting it on the coffee table. Explosion averted for now.

"I wish we could sell this thing," he said, gesturing to the picture above the fireplace. "What kind of moron scratches off the artist's signature?"

She'd wondered that herself, but only shrugged. "You were being careful. You did what you thought you had to do."

"*See*, that's what I mean." He flashed her a grin. "Us McKays stick together. No matter what. I want to know you've got my back, Liddy."

"What if we get a loan from one of those cash advance places? Remember the one with the catchy jingle. *When you need cash, and you need it fast...*"

Seth took her cue, spinning as he sang, "*Call your friends at Fast Cash.*"

Though Lydia laughed, she felt dead inside, sitting here in Iris's house with that painting of the Golden Gate looming above them. A constant reminder of the past.

"Bad idea. Dad hated those places. He said they were nothing more than a racket."

Lydia anticipated a punchline—surely, Seth was joking—until she realized her brother wouldn't recognize irony if it smacked him in the face.

"We need free money," he said. "No strings attached. If I could just get my hands on ten grand, I know I could double it. Easy. Then, we could hire us a hotshot attorney to put these cops in their place."

"What if you took a little break from the racetrack? We've got the three hundred from the drawer. Plus, we can live here rent-free. And the pantry is stocked. If we bide our time—"

"What did you say?" And just like that, Seth thrust his gritted teeth in her face. His eyes burned through her, hot and black as coals, forcing her to retreat into the corner of the sofa.

"I—I just thought—it was only a suggestion. I'm trying to help."

"Well, keep your suggestions to yourself. Next thing, you'll be telling me I've got a problem. That I need that Gamblers Anonymous shit. Ain't that right? I saw you looking at that book Iris had. The one with the roulette wheel on the cover."

Lydia couldn't deny it. Iris owned books on every topic under the sun. "We don't have money for gambling right now. If you don't realize that, then maybe..."

"Maybe what? Go on, finish your sentence."

"Then, maybe you do have a problem."

It had been fourteen months since Seth hit her. Either she'd forgotten what it felt like or he'd been saving up. Socked her right in the stomach with his fist like a bowling ball. Lungs squeezed shut, she doubled over. When he reared back again, she found a trace of breath. "The baby..."

"The baby? *What baby?*" Hands around her neck. Big bear paws like her father's. "Don't try to play the victim. You made the whole thing up."

Lydia tried to shake her head, but his thumbs dug deep into her windpipe. She swatted at him, her eyes tearing and popping with desperation.

Seth addressed her in their father's voice. A voice made of ice. "Just remember, I know what you did to Dad. I saw all of it. And I'll bet you his bones are still out there too. The cops will call in those divers, and they'll haul him right up."

Finally, Seth released her, leaving her to suck in a greedy gulp of air. He curled his lip at her, disgusted.

"Look what you made me do."

She didn't move, didn't whimper. She tried to be as still as the painting on the wall. But her bottom lip trembled; her teeth chattered. Try as she might, she couldn't do a damn thing about it.

When Seth slunk back downstairs an hour later, still favoring his left knee, Lydia sat in the same spot, staring ahead blankly. Her whole world had gone off-kilter again, and she didn't quite remember how to set it right. As he came closer, she flinched.

"Shit, Liddy. Don't make me feel worse than I already do."

"Am I bruised?" She touched her neck gingerly, feeling an ache in her throat. She'd already raised her shirt to find a splotchy red mark on her flank where the blood vessels had burst.

"Only a little. It'll be gone by morning. Not like this goose egg on my head. Or hey, borrow one of those hideous turtlenecks in Iris's closet." He sat down next to her, maneuvering his head until she had no choice but to look at him. "So, are you pregnant? And no bullshit this time."

"You never asked before. You just assumed."

"Well, yeah. Because the old bag was itching to be a godmother. I figured you were bluffing. And frankly, I thought it was a horrible idea for a con. I mean, can you imagine? A fake pregnancy? You would've been stuffing a pillow in your shirt eventually."

Lydia needed to get it out before the rage wave swelled again. She thought of his anger like the ebb and flow of the tides. "Remember how we needed money real bad? Right before I met Iris."

"Sure, sure."

"And remember what you—I mean, what *we* did?"

She watched the realization contort Seth's face. To shock and horror, then pure revulsion. "Are you kidding me?"

"It's true. I took a test. He's the only one it could be."

"TMI, sis. I don't need to hear all that." One lip curled, as if he'd tasted worm meat. "Especially not about him."

"I'm just saying, there's nobody else."

After a long while, Seth's distaste faded, replaced by something new. Something worse. "I've got an idea."

Lydia couldn't stop the dread from blanching her face. Telling him about the baby hadn't made it better like she thought, but worse.

"You got yourself in this predicament, Liddy, encouraging him like you did. Dad always warned you he was a perv." Seth shuddered. As if something slimy had crawled up his pants leg. "Now, it's up to you. You need to handle it. You need to do whatever it takes."

His words spoke to a dark place inside her. A dirty place where shame rooted itself like a thorny weed. The hardy kind that even the harshest winter couldn't kill.

"Whatever it takes," she heard herself say.

TWENTY-SIX

Maureen parked the Volvo along California Street and hoofed it up the busy sidewalk, craning her neck up at the skyscraper where Craig Chalmers and Marty Pierce had set up shop years ago. According to their sleek website, the attorneys had taken over the firm in the late nineties after the prior named partners retired. Scrawled across the home page, the tongue-in-cheek slogan that made Maureen chuckle. *If We Can't Help You, No One Can.* As she pressed the elevator button for the 32nd floor, she hoped that tagline would prove to be more truth than bluster.

The elevator doors parted to reveal an expansive, modern lobby that practically smelled of money. All windows and shiny white floors and glass dividers meant to give the illusion of freedom to clients looking to avoid a lengthy stint without it.

Maureen showed her badge at the front desk and loitered nearby, studying the large portrait of Craig Chalmers that hung in the lobby. At a glance, Maureen understood why he'd been successful defending the scum of the earth. He had the chubby-cheeked face of a choirboy framed with snowy white hair, the very color of innocence.

"Detective Shaw, Mr. Chalmers will see you now." *Detective*. Maureen's little white lie echoed too loudly in the sparse waiting room.

The receptionist led her into the interior of the building, her heels clicking authoritatively against the marble. She stopped in front of the door at the end of the long hallway. "He only has a few minutes before his next client, so..."

"I understand. I'll keep it brief."

Satisfied, the woman left her there to gather herself before she gave a knock.

Chalmers had aged since his portrait. Hair thinning, wrinkles deepening across his forehead. But, when he smiled and ushered her inside, she half believed he could convince her of anything.

Maureen took the seat across from him and prepared to embellish the truth again. To call herself a detective. Just a small fib, really, but a crucial distinction to someone who knew the system.

"I'm glad to see you, Detective. I was wondering when someone would come by. I telephoned the station on Monday evening, as soon as I heard the story on the news. It's a damn shame about Iris. A lovely woman. Pigheaded, but lovely nonetheless."

"Thank you for calling in, sir. As you can imagine, we've been busy following up on all the leads. I understand you represented Mrs. Duncan in her dispute with the Home Owners Association."

"I did. But..." He puzzled, examining her street clothing as if for the first time. It took everything in her not to squirm in her seat. "Didn't you get my message?"

Maureen nodded. "Of course. I wasn't sure where you wanted to start."

"Well, Iris worked for me as a legal assistant for the better part of twenty-five years. I thought that might be more important than the nonsense with the HOA. Tyrants, those people. Just looking for someone to bully."

Legal assistant? Twenty-five years? The revelations dropped into Maureen's lap with the subtlety of a grenade toss. She hoped her face didn't give her away. "From what we've gathered, Mrs. Duncan kept her employment a secret, possibly even from her husband. Were you aware of that?"

Chalmers chuckled, a big belly laugh that shook his ample midsection. "Ah, Dean. Now, there was a guy stuck in the past. To hear Iris tell it, he would've preferred her barefoot and pregnant. And when that didn't happen, he expected her to be, at the very least, less successful than him. He told her to volunteer at the library, since she liked to read so much. Having her own money and working in a place like this—surrounded by criminal defendants, even the innocent ones—Dean would've never approved."

"And she volunteered at the library for a year or so, correct?"

"That sounds about right. She didn't have much work experience, but I hired her on the spot. I was an up-and-comer back then. Not much room on the payroll for a tenured assistant. And Iris was as smart as a whip. Good instincts, too. In fact, a few years before she retired, she'd even started to help with some of our investigations."

"Really? In what way?"

"Establishing alibis. Developing alternate suspects. Interviewing witnesses." He shrugged, as if to admit how unusual it sounded. "People see a lawyer coming a mile away. Especially an old white guy like me. But they'd open up to Iris. I first noticed how some of the clients took to her in the waiting room. She'd bring a cup of coffee and before you know it, the guy with a rap sheet longer than my arm would be telling his life story. Everyone trusts an older lady. I think she reminded them of their grandmother. And the way she grew up—in that orphanage in Mendocino—she had a way of understanding people."

Another grenade launched and landed, but Maureen didn't shrink away. "Do you think her work here could've put her in danger? Any clients she had a problem with? Someone we should be looking into?"

"No one I can think of. Most of our clients were quite fond of her. Every Christmas, Iris's desk was covered with cards and gift baskets. But it's been at least five years since she retired."

"Then, why call us at all, if you don't mind my asking?"

Chalmers took his time to answer. The quintessential attorney, weighing every word. "As you probably know by now, Iris didn't need to work. She *wanted* to. I paid her under the table, so Dean wouldn't find out, and as far as I know, he never did. But in a murder case, all the secrets start rising to the top, so I thought I'd better get ahead of it. To let you know I've got nothing to hide."

Maureen nodded, listening for what went unspoken. Like rests in a piece of music, the unsaid could be critical. Right now, she could only hear the rumbling of her mostly empty stomach and the static in her tired brain. "Well, I appreciate you calling. It certainly helps to know more about Mrs. Duncan."

"The couple who lived with her—have they been arrested yet?"

It pained Maureen to shake her head no.

"It sounds like you folks have your work cut out for you, Detective. It's not easy building a murder case without a body. *No body, no crime,* as we defense attorneys like to say."

Maureen hated that adage. No truth in it anyway. Adam Waddell had left a slew of bodies behind him and still gotten off with a slap on the wrist. Sentenced to a state mental facility, where he'd walk around like a free man. "You're right. This case is a challenge. And we need all the help we can get."

She paused for a moment, wondering how far to push.

"You've been on the other side of this. You've seen the worst humanity has to offer. You've shaken hands with it, looked it in the eye. Even defended it. So, what do you think happened to Iris?"

If Chalmers took offense, he didn't show it. He leaned back in his leather swivel chair and rested his hands on his stomach.

"In my forty-year career, I've learned one thing about murder. It's almost always the devil you know."

When Maureen closed Chalmers' door behind her, the fatigue of the last few days set in. Finally, she'd hit the wall. Like a zombie, she traipsed back toward the entrance but found herself turned around in the maze of empty corridors, where every door looked like the one before it. Except *that* one.

Maureen wandered into the open doorway of a large conference room. Past the head of the table, photographs covered one wall. At the center, Chalmers and Pierce posed arm in arm with matching grins. Maureen scanned the photos, searching for Iris's face.

There, at the company Christmas party, holding a glass of champagne.

There, looking up from her desk, with a slightly annoyed smirk.

She stopped in front of the last row of pictures, feeling a little seasick. Her boat, thoroughly rocked.

"Did you get lost?" The receptionist poked her head in, studying Maureen with suspicion.

"I think I went right when I should've gone left."

"It happens all the time."

Maureen glanced back at the photo, unable to walk away. "Do you happen to know this gentleman?"

The woman leaned in for a better look at the man standing outside the San Francisco Federal Building. The camera had captured his raw emotion, a fist pump in the air. Maureen located the same man in the background of the Christmas party photo. "Oh, of course. That's Antonio Matta, on the day Craig won his racketeering case."

Legs of jelly carried Maureen to the lobby and down the elevator. She barely took a breath until she stood on the sidewalk outside the building, trying to make sense of what she'd seen.

Just like the man Charlie Tallboy spotted in the park with Iris, Antonio Matta had only one ear.

Maureen waited until she arrived home to San Bruno. Until she had a hot shower and downed a Coke and a microwave pizza. Until she felt halfway human again. Then, she sat cross-legged on the bed with her laptop and typed *Antonio Matta* into the search bar.

As she scrolled down the results page, a 2008 headline from the *San Francisco Chronicle* caught her eye. CAR WASH FRANCHISE OWNER EXONERATED IN CASE WITH CARTEL CONNECTIONS. At the top of the article, the same fist-pumping image had been captured from another angle. Maureen scanned the page, looking for anything that might explain Matta's mysterious meeting in the park with Iris more than twelve years later.

> *Antonio Matta, owner of Matta's Shinetastic Car Wash, with multiple locations across the Bay Area, walked out of the San Francisco Federal Building a free man. Matta had been arrested on charges of racketeering after federal agents implicated him in a money laundering scam linked to Los Diabolitos, a local gang with reported ties to a Mexican drug cartel. Matta previously served time in state prison for forgery and narcotics trafficking, where he was the victim of a serious*

assault which left him disfigured. His attorney, Craig Chalmers, argued that federal agents used his client's past against him, charging him with a crime for which they had little evidence. In fact, Chalmers alleged that federal agents had manufactured evidence, paying a key witness for her false testimony. To reporters, Matta credited Chalmers for his freedom. "Mr. Chalmers saved my life. I owe him everything. He's like family to me."

Maureen closed her laptop. She set the alarm on her phone for 11 p.m.—which gave her a solid six hours—and laid back against the pillow, shutting her eyes with purpose. The faster she slept, the sooner she could hit the pavement again. The sooner she could find Iris. The sooner she could catch her killer.

TWENTY-SEVEN

BEFORE

Iris cursed at the mixing bowl on the counter as it wobbled toward the edge. Stirring took two hands, but she'd learned to manage with one. Iris considered her resourcefulness her best trait. If only she'd been part of a so-called normal family, with a mother and father who hadn't dumped her off like a stray puppy, she felt certain she would've made an outstanding Girl Scout. Still, capable as she was, she counted the days—only fourteen more—until she'd be free of this onerous fiberglass shell.

Through the kitchen window, she spotted Seth watering the planters, where the brightly colored fuchsia bloomed. The pink petals resembled a painting, too vibrant to be real. Even with Dean at the helm, the yard had never looked better. Finally, Daft Dorsey and his neighborhood cronies had taken their proverbial boots off her neck. But she'd asked Mr. Chalmers to craft a strong response anyway. Because no one likes a bully. Certainly not her. Though Dorsey had nothing on those rotten little creatures at Lost Pines.

Iris spooned the dough onto a cookie sheet in even dollops and donned the mitt to transfer the sheet into the warm oven.

"Lydia, dear?"

"Coming..." Lydia poked her head in from the hallway, where she'd been busy dusting the rare book collection. Dean never had understood that a dollar store paperback had just as much value to Iris as a first edition.

"Will you help me remember the cookies? They'll be done in about ten minutes. And you know how I am." Iris thunked her finger against her head, frowning. "Sounds empty up there, doesn't it? I'll bet that's what that neurologist will say. As empty as the Scarecrow. *If I only had a brain.*"

Lydia half laughed, but Iris knew she didn't like that kind of talk. "You're not so bad off. You still make the best chocolate chip cookies I've ever tasted."

"Flattery will get you..." Iris paused, winked. "Everywhere."

Just then, Seth opened the front door, poking his head. "Hey, Iris. I'm gonna pop over to the—*damn*, something smells good in here."

"I made another batch of those cookies you like."

"That's what I'm talking about. How 'bout you start paying me in cookies?" He chuckled at his own joke. "But, seriously, I'm heading to the hardware store again. We need a couple bags of fertilizer. Can I get some spending money?"

Iris nodded, casting a weary look up the steep staircase. Sometimes, she wished she'd let Dean build that elevator. "Lydia, would you run upstairs for me? Get five hundred from the hat box."

"Five hundred? That seems like a lot for fertilizer. I mean, it's just high-grade poop."

Seth blinked a few times, those blue eyes like still water. "Actually, five hundred should just cover it. Besides, what do you know about it, Liddy? I'm the one working my ass off out there. When was the last time you bought fertilizer?"

"Uh, never. But I can do basic math."

Playing peacemaker, Iris stepped in between them. Seth

seemed more on edge than ever. And Iris worried they might leave her. "It's not worth arguing about, you two. If there's any money left over, buy some fresh flowers for the kitchen. Maybe that will cheer us all up."

Lydia stomped up the stairs, leaving her alone with Seth. "Is everything okay?"

"She thinks she's smarter than me. She always has."

"I'm sure that's not true. But you could stand to be a little nicer to her, young man. After all, she's carrying your baby. Right?"

Seth groaned.

"How long will you be gone?" Lydia asked, shuffling down the stairs with a wad of money in her hand.

"A few hours, at least. Maybe longer."

"Of course." Lydia's voice dripped with sarcasm.

"What's that supposed to mean?"

Iris had had about enough. Throwing up her hands, she retreated to the kitchen, squeezing tears from her eyes.

"Now you've done it," Lydia said. "You've upset Iris."

Seth answered with the slam of the door behind him, so hard it rattled the windows.

Iris scooped two dollops of vanilla ice cream into matching bowls and joined Lydia at the counter. Since Seth had stormed out hours ago, the house felt strangely unsettled. Like the uncertain calm after a storm.

"Have a cookie sundae, dear. In my experience, chocolate makes everything better. And you can never have too much ice cream."

"Or too many Cheetos." Lydia barely managed a half-hearted smile, before she nibbled at the crispy edge of the cookie on her plate. "It's delicious. But..."

"But what?"

Heaving a sigh, Lydia turned to face her. "It's Seth. He's just so... infuriating."

"And you love him anyway. In spite of it all." Iris understood that kind of devotion. "Am I right?"

"I suppose. It's just that sometimes I wish I could have a do-over. A chance to see what my life would've been like without him in it."

"You feel trapped." That, too, Iris understood.

"I shouldn't be telling you this. Seth always says to keep our problems between us. My dad was like that too. *If you don't talk about it, it didn't happen.* He actually said that to me once."

"Well, that's hogwash. What is a friend for, if not to tell your problems? That's what I say."

Lydia took another bite, washed it down with a swig of milk, and rested her head on Iris's shoulder. "Is it weird to say you would have made a good mom?"

"And so will you." Iris smacked the counter and hopped off her stool, grabbing Lydia by the hand. "Come with me, dear. I have something I must show you. And we don't have much time."

Iris hurried out the back door and through the neatly trimmed grass, with Lydia trailing behind her. The sun had begun its steady descent, coloring the sky a dusky rose and leaving the yard in near darkness. Shadows gathered around the toolshed in the corner, and Iris felt a familiar nip of excitement at the back of her neck. It reminded her of her days at Chalmers and Pierce, where she'd rubbed elbows with criminals on the regular. Even murderers. It had been too long since she took a risk. Too long since her blood had whooshed through her veins.

"Do you have the key to the shed?" Iris whispered. As if Seth might be one step behind them.

"I think so." Fumbling in her pocket, Lydia produced the metal ring Iris had given her when they moved in. "But he'll be mad if we—"

Iris snatched it from her hand. "Nonsense. This is *my* property. And I do what I want. I'm a seventy-year-old woman, for God's sake."

Lydia giggled. So did Iris. Like two schoolgirls swapping secrets in the library. But, when Iris fitted the key and unlocked the door, the mood turned serious again.

She ushered Lydia inside the dark space and pulled the door shut behind her, with only the remaining daylight from the small window to illuminate their faces.

"I know you've been hiding something from me."

Lydia shuffled backward in a panic. "What—uh—I—"

"The baby doesn't belong to Seth, does it?"

"How did you know?" The words spilled out in a gust of relief, leaving Lydia slumped against the wheelbarrow as she wiped a stray tear from her cheek.

"It's as plain as day that you're displeased with him. You're certainly not in love."

"Are you going to tell him?"

Iris threw back her head, appalled. "Of course not, dear. That's why I brought you here. Now, help me move this thing."

At Iris's direction, Lydia worked to move the wheelbarrow aside, struggling to muscle the front wheel along the dirt floor. Finally, she managed to park it next to the tool rack. With the wheelbarrow out of the way, Iris studied the item that rested against the work table. It had been a while since Seth had lugged it back here from the bed of his pick-up truck. A canvas tarp lay draped across it. But one corner had caught under the wheel and fallen down with Lydia's effort, exposing the colorful surface of a painting beneath.

Crouching down, Iris pointed to the dim corner of the shed, where a few errant sprigs of grass sprouted up from the soil. Persistence at its finest. "There's a big glass jar buried beneath those weeds."

"What's in it?" Lydia asked. She seemed distracted by the

painting, tugging the tarp back over it.

"My 'get out of Dodge' money."

"Your *what?*" Now, Iris had grabbed her attention. "But I thought you were happy with Dean."

"I met Dean at eighteen. Just a couple of months after I left Lost Pines. I got a job as a server at one of those fancy company parties. Turns out Dean's father ran the company. Dean probably wouldn't have noticed me at all if I hadn't spilled a drink on him and got myself fired. Forty-seven years together—well, it's a lifetime. People grow. They change. I certainly did. In the end, Dean and I made better friends than bedfellows."

Lydia looked stricken. "Were you planning to leave him?"

"I'm not sure I ever would have. Dean let me have my own life, so I let him have his. After I couldn't give him a child, I'm sure there were other women. Many others. Strange how you can know someone like the back of your hand and yet, not at all. And somehow, you still need each other. Like two trees fused at the roots."

"I know what you mean. Seth and I are like that."

"That's why I'm showing you this. Don't get me wrong, Seth is a good man, but if he's not the one for you, I want you to have options. There's enough cash there to set you and the baby up for a long time."

"The money, was it from your job at the library?"

Iris thought of the crisp white envelope Mr. Chalmers placed on her desk every other Friday. "Something like that."

Lydia moved toward the door, opening it partway, but Iris stopped her, seizing her by the wrist. "One more thing. If you decide to leave, do it quietly. Don't tell me. I couldn't bear to say goodbye."

"Oh, Iris. You're just so..." Lydia pulled her in for an embrace, wetting the shoulder of Iris's blouse with her tears. "You're the closest I have to a mother. I'd never leave you."

"And as long as I'm around, you don't need to worry," Iris

told her. "But if something happens to me…"

"Don't say that." Lydia clutched her tighter.

"There, there, dear. Don't cry." After a moment, Iris freed herself. "Shall we tidy up a bit? Seth might notice if anything is out of place."

As Lydia returned the wheelbarrow to its prior resting place, Iris stepped to the side, lifting the tarp to reveal a painting of the Golden Gate Bridge. It stole her breath. "This is a lovely work of art. Where did Seth get it?"

"Uh—I—I don't—" Stammering, Lydia turned away. Like a bird that flew in through an open window, she struggled to find the exit right in front of her. Finally, she flung open the door, gasping for air, and ran straight into the wall of Seth's chest.

Iris couldn't say how long he'd been there. But she quickly understood he'd overheard her last question.

Pointing at the abstract piece with pride, he said, "I painted it."

Iris watched as Seth secured the painting on the picture hook above the mantel. It gave her peace to see it there in a place of honor. A work like that shouldn't be collecting dust in a toolshed.

"A little to the left," Lydia said. "*No.* Too far. Just a smidge to the right."

"Jeez, Liddy. This ain't a museum." But he followed instructions until Lydia pronounced it acceptable.

"It looks perfect," Iris told him. "I never would've imagined you had a hidden talent."

Seth turned back to the painting, admiring his work. "I guess we all have our secrets."

Iris risked a flickering glance at Lydia, but the poor girl avoided her eyes.

"We certainly do, dear. We certainly do."

TWENTY-EIGHT

AFTER

Wednesday evening

Lydia hardly recognized herself in the rearview mirror of the taxicab. The trappings looked familiar—red lipstick, black mascara, heavy makeup to cover Seth's handiwork—but the eyes had a strange hardness. She'd run out of tears. The heart, too, felt alien. It beat evenly, like a metronome in her chest, as she held tight to the purse in her lap. It would all be over soon.

The taxi glided to a stop in front of the grungy dive bar, where the neon sign bathed the sidewalk in an eerie red glow. "Here we are, darlin'. The Broadway Saloon and Sports Bar."

Lydia forked over one of the hundred-dollar bills from Iris's underwear drawer to cover the ride to the Mission District. She pocketed the change before she replied.

"I'm not your darlin'." To psych herself up, she slammed the door behind her, relishing the cabbie's flinch.

A quick scan of the lot revealed Vinnie Frank's gold-trimmed Chrysler. Like most nights, its large frame took up two spots at the edge of the small lot.

Lydia removed the prepaid cell she'd picked up at the Speedy Stop on the way and texted Seth, exactly as he'd instructed.

He's here. We're a go.

She tugged at the hem of her red dress and toddled inside on a pair of designer heels she'd discovered in the back of Iris's closet. She had her own cheap stilettos, but it gave her solace to bring a piece of Iris with her. Even if the size-too-small shoes scrunched her toes mercilessly.

When Lydia located Vinnie, perched on a corner barstool like an elephant on a circus ball, she nearly balked. But he'd already spotted her, scowling while he held a fat cigar between his stubby fingers. As he brought it to his mouth, his lips pursed obscenely, and it reminded her of the first time she'd seen him, standing outside her father's room at the Blue Bird and puffing on a Montecristo. *Home alone?* he'd asked, looking her up and down. And for once, Lydia wished Seth had been there. But after their father died, Seth had assumed his place. Spending his schooldays at the track and leaving her there alone to wait for him and his mercurial temper.

"Well, well, well. If it ain't the asshole's little sister. Does big brother know you're here?"

"*Seth?* Of course not. He's an idiot. Albany PD booked him for evidence tampering. We didn't have the cash to post bail, so I've got the whole night to myself."

Get him drunk and get him talking. Seth's voice coached her through it, though Vinnie looked well on his way to intoxication station. Lydia soldiered ahead into the plume of cologne that clouded Vinnie's personal space. She took a seat on the barstool next to him, flaunting her bare legs as she crossed them. Best to get this show on the road.

"Do you now? That sounds lonely."

"It doesn't have to be." Lydia leaned in closer, feeling Vinnie's eyes dip from the baseball game on the television screen straight to her cleavage. So, Seth had been right about the dress. "Buy me a drink. You know what I like."

"Yes, ma'am. One Sex on the Beach coming right up." He signaled to the bartender and a fruity cocktail appeared in front of her.

Lydia left the drink untouched. Instead, she grazed her finger across the scab above Vinnie's ear. "I'm sorry about what happened at the Blue Bird the other day. Things got a little out of hand."

"I blame your brother for that. He's a hothead. I don't know why you put up with him." Vinnie took her hand and placed it on his meaty thigh. Ignoring a wave of nausea, she massaged his knee.

"He's all I have, Vin. Always has been. Someone once told me that we're like two trees fused at the roots."

"If it was me, I'd take a goddamned chainsaw to that shit."

Lydia faked a laugh.

"Is that why you're here, then? To work off his debt like last time? Because it's gonna take more than one night, honey. We sure did have a lot of fun though, didn't we?"

"We did." But when Lydia tried to recall that night, she found only a black hole. At the frayed edges of her memory, a desperate Seth dropping her off at Vinnie's house in the same red dress, pleading with her. *Do this for me one time, Liddy, and I'll owe you forever.* The rest of the evening had dissolved into a dark pool of acid.

"That asshole owes me... *big*. And now, it ain't even about the money." When Vinnie lowered his voice, his pungent breath tickled her cheek. "The cops find out where he got that gun, and your problems become my problems. And I don't like problems."

"I came here because I need to talk to you. In private. Maybe we could go back to your place." Her hand moved up Vinnie's leg, and he groaned. "Then, whatever happens, happens."

Vinnie tossed back the rest of his martini and popped the olive in his mouth. "You're in charge, doll."

But he didn't really mean that. Like all men, Vinnie took whatever he wanted. However he wanted it. He only let her think she had a say.

Lydia grabbed his hand and tugged him off the barstool. "Let's get outta here."

Vinnie wasted no time. Pedal to the metal, he ran every stoplight between the Broadway Saloon and his studio apartment on Lake Merritt. Before he fitted his key into the lock, he already had one hand on his belt buckle, clumsily undoing the clasp. Inside the dark room, Vinnie's fingers sought Lydia out, roaming her body like tentacles, until she found the light switch and doused the mood.

"Slow down, cowboy. We've got all night. Let's have a drink first."

"Suit yourself." Vinnie loosened his tie and busied himself at his massive stereo, while Lydia beelined for the liquor cabinet in the corner of the kitchen.

"What's your poison?" she asked, trying not to look at the bed with its familiar oil slick black comforter. Or at the wall behind it, where Vinnie had hung an oversized photograph of a pair of blood-red lips. Or at Vinnie himself, draped across the leather sofa and leering at her, with Marvin Gaye crooning in the background.

"I'll have whatever you're having."

Lydia poured a splash of whiskey into a glass, sucking it down in one swallow. Just enough to get through this.

"So, Seth really doesn't know you're here?"

"No, he has no clue." Lydia offered Vinnie his own drink, which he promptly knocked back, before beckoning her over. She averted her eyes from his exposed mid-section, visible now that he'd undone the buttons of his dress shirt.

"Should we get a little more comfortable?"

Lydia stayed put, certain that Vinnie didn't have *her* comfort in mind. Being here, alone with him, more memories had started to surface. Like slimy, dead things dredged up from the bottom. The first time, the last time. All the times in between. Vinnie stripping her down, crushing her beneath him, breathing heavy in her ear while she'd lain paralyzed beneath him, praying for the world to end. "Can we talk first?"

He rolled his eyes, nodded. "You're such a tease, making me wait."

"I have to tell you something." Lydia clutched her purse to her waist like a shield. "I took a test."

"A test? *Shit*. Like for STDs or something? I knew I should've used a—"

"I'm pregnant."

"You're *what*?"

"And you're the father."

"I'm... *what*?" Vinnie sat bolt upright, his mouth hanging open like an old dog. "Have you lost your goddamned mind?"

"I'm telling you the truth." Lydia covered her face, letting her shoulders shake. It wasn't a stretch to feign complete misery. "I need to know, Vin. Are you gonna step up for your kid or not? It takes money to have a baby."

Vinnie stared at her for a moment. "Seth cooked this story up, didn't he? We both know I ain't nobody's daddy. Hell, a girl like you, always asking for it, I'm sure there's any number of fellas that could've knocked you up. You gonna ask for a paternity test?"

"I don't know. I don't know what to do. I thought you'd want to help. You always said you cared. That Dad asked you to look after me, if anything happened to him." Lydia rubbed her eyes, smearing her mascara, and sniffled. "Remember that day you came to the Blue Bird? You told me I could trust you. You promised you wouldn't hurt me. I was only fifteen."

"Yeah. Fifteen going on thirty. Besides, I didn't hear you complaining about those new clothes I bought you and your brother. Hell, if it wasn't for me, you kids probably would've gotten scooped up by social services and put in a home somewhere."

A home. The thought of it—an actual home—made Lydia sob. "Can I get a tissue?"

"Jeez, enough with the waterworks. I gotta take a leak." Vinnie disappeared into the bathroom, leaving Lydia alone. She poured two fresh glasses of Jack and Coke. She had to be quick.

Through the door, she heard the toilet flush. "Look, I can probably help you out with some cash, doll, but you know my money ain't free. Are you thinking of getting rid of it?"

Then came the sound of running water. Lydia removed the plastic baggie from her purse and held it, poised above Vinnie's drink.

"If you ask me, you'd be doing the kid a favor. Saving that baby from a lifetime of suffering. So, are we gettin' busy, or what?"

Like soft snow, the powder fell silently into the glass. She left none behind. "Let's have a toast first," she said, plastering on a smile, when Vinnie emerged from the bathroom, wearing nothing but his briefs.

"Should you even be drinking that?" he asked.

"To chainsaws," she answered.

Vinnie looked at her funny, but he clinked his glass against hers anyway. And when she gulped it down, he followed suit, the liquid snaking down his gullet. He wiped his mouth and drew Lydia to him. "Now, where were we?"

Lydia poked Vinnie's abdomen with her finger. He didn't move, didn't grunt. He looked smaller somehow, sprawled on the bed, head lolling. And she couldn't help but remember her father. How death had turned him from a tyrant to a useless sack of skin and bones that took her and Seth thirty minutes to carry the fifty yards from the Bulb parking lot to the cliff above the water.

Lydia forced her mind to travel back there to the ocean's edge. To relive the moment they'd heaved him in—wrapped in a tarp weighted with stones—and watched him sink. To the heady mixture of sadness, fear, and relief that followed. The tears came freely now.

She fished her new cellphone from her pocket, swiped past a text from Seth—*What's taking so long? I'm waiting outside*—and dialed. A groggy voice answered.

"Detective Casey, Homicide." You could always count on cops and criminals to answer the phone after midnight.

"I'm sorry to call so late," she sobbed. Outside, she heard the throaty rumble of Dean's Indian motorcycle but she didn't dare peek out the blinds. "It's Lydia McKay. I'm in trouble, and I need your help."

TWENTY-NINE

After 2 a.m., Maureen eased the Volvo up Archer Avenue, past Iris's Victorian and toward the Presidio gate, where she parked along the curb. So far, she'd been lucky to avoid the neighborhood patrols. On her nights off, she had to keep a low profile, especially with Casey and Diedrich riding her ass. But at least she'd managed to get some sleep. She had to be sharp now. Sharper than she'd ever been.

Her duty belt secured around her waist, she locked the car and ventured into the forest, taking the same route she and Walt had travelled. She cast the beam of her flashlight into the trees, scanning for signs of life beyond the small animals darting through the underbrush.

"Charlie?" Her own voice scared her a little. "Are you out there?"

The only reply came from a coyote yipping in the distance. Maureen shivered, suddenly wishing she'd invited Walt to come with her. *Keep moving*, she told herself. That's the best way to deal with fear. Outrun it.

A few steps up the trail, she spotted one Pabst can, then

another. She followed the breadcrumbs to Charlie's tent, pitched beneath a redwood. Its front panel, zipped tight.

"Charlie?" she called again. "Hello?"

When she reached the tent, she rapped the back of her hand against the nylon fabric and called out once more before she carefully undid the zipper. Holding her breath, Maureen lowered her head to peer inside but found only a dirty blanket balled on the tent floor. No shopping cart. No Charlie.

As she tucked her business card inside the inner screen, loud voices from the street pierced the stillness and started her heart thumping. Maureen ran toward the sound, pulling up short at the gate, breathless.

A parade of red and blue lights lined Archer Avenue, leading to Iris's house.

Creeping up the sidewalk, Maureen positioned herself within hearing distance of the commotion. A group of officers stood on the porch, at the ready, their weapons drawn. Several others positioned themselves around the perimeter, as the lead man pounded on the front door, announcing himself.

"San Francisco Police! Open up!"

Its secrets boarded up tight, the house didn't answer, and the windows remained dark.

"Seth McKay, we know you're in there. You're either coming out or we're coming in."

Keeping herself out of sight, Maureen edged closer. She needed to see the expression on his smug face as they cuffed him. To witness the moment the sword of justice sliced him clean through.

But the door stayed shut, even as the officers kept pounding. Even as a small crowd of sleepy neighbors began to gather on the sidewalk, their slumber interrupted by the drone of the bullhorn.

"Last warning, McKay. Come out now with your hands up."

Finally, the lead officer loosened the duct tape and removed the cardboard covering the hole in the stained glass. He reached inside and undid the lock, gaining entry. Her brothers in blue streamed in through the open door like ants at a picnic.

Lingering at the periphery, Maureen spotted Officer Morales. She slunk toward him, hopeful the homicide detectives hadn't made the trip, deeming themselves too important to get their hands dirty. "What's this all about?" she asked.

"McKay's got a warrant for his arrest. Conspiracy to commit murder."

"Of Iris Duncan?" She couldn't wait for him to say it. To confirm what she'd known all along.

Morales shook his head, looking puzzled. "Some scumbag named Vinnie Frank."

Maureen stumbled back to her car in disbelief. *Vinnie.* The baton-wielding creep from the Albany Bulb.

She leaned against the trunk of the Volvo, watching the cavalry drive away without Seth. A search of the house had yielded nothing. As she stared at the last of the taillights disappearing down the hill, a wave of guilt bowled her over. If only she'd done her job and arrested Vinnie, he'd probably be in jail right now. Alive. Instead, she'd set him free like a lamb to the slaughter.

No. She wouldn't do it. She wouldn't blame herself. Whatever Seth had done to Vinnie, the blame rested squarely on his shoulders. And Iris still needed her. Iris deserved justice.

Shrugging off her foul mood, Maureen surveyed the house. Since the cops left, there'd been no movement inside or outside as far as she could tell. No signs of Lydia either. Maureen headed back down the sidewalk, knowing she might never get another chance like this one.

As she approached the front door, Maureen ducked beneath the DO NOT ENTER tape strung across the steps. She donned a pair of latex gloves from her duty belt. With the precision of a surgeon, she turned the knob, taking a last look over her shoulder at the quiet street before she entered.

The door made no sound when she pushed it open. The house held its breath, waiting for her to break the silence.

"Hello? Lydia?"

No answer.

Maureen made her way up the dark staircase to the third floor, with only her flashlight to guide her. Iris's bedroom door stood ajar, beckoning to her like a crooked finger, but Maureen ignored her impulse, turning to the McKays' room instead. She had no idea what she might find. No idea what to look for, truthfully. But she'd know it when she saw it.

The bedside lamp bathed the room in soft yellow light. The rumpled blanket and flattened pillow proof that Seth had laid his head here.

Maureen ducked to avoid being seen from the window. Scanning the cluttered floor, her eyes settled on a red Ferragamo shoebox resting near the dresser. She felt certain it hadn't been there when she'd discovered the gun days ago.

She knelt down and lifted the lid, discarding it on the floor. Then, she removed the stack of papers and sat back against the bed to sort through them.

Stuffed carelessly inside a torn envelope was Iris's two-million-dollar life insurance policy. Reading the named beneficiaries, Maureen swallowed a hot ball of anger and disgust—there would be time for that later—and snapped photos of the pages with her cell.

At the bottom of the pile, she found Iris's birth certificate, the paper yellowed with age and creased at the edges. A baby girl, christened Iris Juniper Hill, born March 21, 1951 at Ukiah

General Hospital to Mary and Cyril Hill of Mendocino. Maureen ran a delicate finger across the top of the page, where two tiny feet had been inked.

Preparing to return the documents and continue her search, she spotted something shoved into the corner. The square of paper had been folded and refolded so many times Maureen worried it would rip clean down the middle. After she worked it open, she read.

> *On February 5th, 1959, minor child, Iris Hill, was surrendered by her widowed mother, Mary Hill, to the care and custody of Lost Pines Girls' Home due to financial hardship. Ms. Hill agreed to furnish proper and suitable clothing for said child upon her admission and to inform the Trustees of any changes in her address. She further agreed to allow said child to be subjected to any disciplinary measures deemed necessary and to remove said child at the Trustees request. Ms. Hill authorized the Trustees to place said child in another charitable facility or with a suitable family if one becomes available.*

Maureen wiped at her eyes, annoyed with herself. She needed to stay focused. But that shabby piece of paper with its cold language broke her heart. No wonder Iris had kept a part of herself hidden from the world. Her very own mother couldn't be trusted, would just as soon sign her away like a calf at the market. What else could a little girl learn from that?

From downstairs, Maureen heard a soft creak. Cursing herself for letting her guard down, she dropped the papers back into the box and pulled her gun. As she exited the bedroom door, she found herself hoping to confront a criminal. A burglar. A rapist. A crazy-eyed killer. Anyone but the uniformed officers of SFPD. She couldn't afford to be caught taking another risk like this one.

Maureen crept down the staircase, gun raised. When she rounded the final corner, in full view of the entry, a shrill scream staked her heart.

"Don't shoot! Don't shoot!" Bill Dorsey dropped to his knees, hands skyward. In his robe and fuzzy house slippers, he hardly looked like a criminal.

"Mr. Dorsey?" Maureen holstered her weapon. "What are you doing in here?"

He glanced her up and down, taking in her street clothes. Her latex gloves. "I could ask you the same question."

"You first." Maureen noticed the way Bill's robe sagged to one side as he stood. As if he carried something heavy in his pocket.

"After the police left, I thought I saw someone in the window. I figured it might be a prowler. An opportunist. Even a reporter. Naturally, as a member of the HOA, I felt it was my duty to investigate."

"And the item in your pocket?"

"But you haven't told me—"

Maureen withdrew her badge. "What's in your pocket, Mr. Dorsey?"

"It's only an old book." Which instantly convinced Maureen of its importance. "*See.*"

Bill placed the leather-bound copy of *The Tale of Peter Rabbit* on the hall table, tapping his foot nervously, while Maureen flicked on a light. Her eyes searched the nearby bookshelf, where she found a rectangular-shaped hole.

"Is this a first edition?"

He gave a small, pitiful shrug. "It's not what it looks like."

"It looks like you snuck in here and pilfered one of Mrs. Duncan's books."

"Okay, then I suppose it *is* what it looks like. But I can explain. Jacqueline, my wife, spent years scouring the Internet for a copy of *Peter Rabbit*. It was a childhood favorite of hers. When I spotted it on Iris's shelf last year, I offered to pay double. She refused, of course. She could see how much it meant to me."

Maureen gritted her teeth, barely containing her outrage.

"It's in excellent condition, and I thought it should go to a good home. To someone that cherished it as much as Iris."

"How much is it worth?" Maureen asked.

"The 1902 version, bound in the original publisher's brown boards like this could fetch up to twenty thousand dollars at auction." Bill gestured to the shelf beside him. "She had quite a collection. The bottom two rows are all rare first editions. But I'd say this one is the rarest."

The McKays had inherited a literary goldmine. "So, grand larceny, then? You should be ashamed of yourself. And something tells me this isn't the first time."

Bill's cheeks flamed, confirming the villainous "Ride of the Valkyries" as his theme music. Maureen's ear never steered her wrong.

"You're right, Officer Shaw. I only wanted to please Jacqueline. She can be quite demanding. But, if she knew about this... if the HOA knew. My employer. Oh God."

Maureen put him out of his misery before he started to beg. She knew the type. "And she will, *everyone will*, if I catch you here again. Understood?"

After Bill fled the premises, tail between his legs, Maureen retrieved the book from the table, intending to return it to the shelf. But curiosity got the better of her.

"Twenty thousand dollars?" she whispered to the empty house. "Let's see what the fuss is all about."

She ran a finger across the colorful illustration—Peter in his little blue jacket—and flipped open the cover. Taking in a sharp breath, the familiar drumbeat pounded in her head, pounded in her chest. It grew so loud, she couldn't deny it. *Find Iris!*

Maureen reached for the folded square of paper secreted inside. As she scanned the handwritten letter, she felt certain she'd been guided to this very spot. Not by Iris. But by the woman who'd painted hope for her when she'd all but lost it: Dolores Peck.

THIRTY

The desolation of the police interview room no longer unnerved Lydia. She felt grateful for the quiet. With the worst part over, she could only wait for Detective Casey's return. Her mind, a welcome blank. As the door opened, she thought only of the future. It looked like a stretch of lonely highway, so long she couldn't see to the end.

"We went to the house to arrest your brother." Detective Casey offered her a blanket and a hot cup of coffee. "We didn't find him or the motorcycle."

Lydia nodded and drew the blanket around herself, eager to hide the skimpy red dress that clung to her like the scent of Vinnie's cologne. Try as she might, she couldn't escape the cloying smell.

"We'll get him, I promise you that. But I want to hear your story for myself. To be sure the responding officers got it right." Sipping from his own steaming cup, Detective Casey lowered himself into the chair nearest her and withdrew a yellow notepad.

Lydia knew a test when she saw one. She'd always been an excellent student. "Seth told me we had to get rid of Vinnie."

"And why was that again?"

"Because he sold us the gun. A ghost gun, Vinnie called it. With no serial number to track. Since Seth couldn't come up with the money he owed, he got paranoid, thinking Vinnie might go to the police. And then, to make matters worse, Vinnie showed up at the Albany Bulb yesterday and beat Seth up. He took his money too."

"So, Seth was angry with Vinnie?"

"That's putting it mildly. 'I'm going to kill that asshole.' That's exactly what he said." Lydia lowered her eyes, gathering herself. "He was really worked up after we got home. It's been a few days since he had cash to gamble with, and he's hard up. He tore the place apart. When I told him I thought he had a problem... well, I should've known better."

"What happened? Did he hurt you?"

"It's not the first time." Lydia tilted her head back, certain the faint red marks would tell the story. "I have a bruise too. On my side."

She pressed a hand to her flank, where the mark had begun to purple.

"So, what was the plan tonight?"

"To dump the whole baggie in Vinnie's drink. All of it. Then, steal whatever I could find and meet Seth outside on the motorcycle. But after Vinnie collapsed, I couldn't go through with it. Like I told the officer, I tried to give him CPR. He was already gone."

"And then you called me?"

Lydia nodded, pulling the blanket tighter. "I didn't know what else to do. I couldn't go back to Seth empty-handed. He made that clear."

"He threatened you?"

"'Whatever it takes,' he said. I do it or else."

Detective Casey scribbled her quote onto the pad, underlining it twice. At least he appeared to believe her. "Where did Seth get the Baclofen?"

"It belonged to Iris's husband, Dean. Seth found it in the medicine cabinet in her bathroom and crushed it into a powder. He threw the pill grinder at the trash can, but it rolled under the dresser. It's probably still there." Lydia felt proud of herself for remembering the details. Details lent credibility. "I gave the used baggie to the officer at the scene."

"Had Seth ever done anything like that before?"

"Not exactly. But I had my suspicions. He had access to Iris's meds." Now that they were getting down to the nitty-gritty, Lydia needed to be sure. "Does your offer still stand? If I tell you everything I know, you'll help me? You'll help me get away from him?"

Detective Casey lowered his pen and met her eyes. She felt her bottom lip tremble. "I'll do what I can, Lydia. But it's complicated. You killed a man tonight. I can't just wave a wand and make that go away."

"I was in fear for my life. Seth told me that he would end me. What choice did I have?"

"Under California law, duress isn't an acceptable defense. Not for murder."

After Lydia hid her face in her hands, he added, "But I'll put in a good word for you, if you cooperate. The DA won't pursue any charges unless I give him the green light."

"You'd do that? For me?"

The detective measured his words carefully now, making it clear he wouldn't be swayed by her emotion. Not entirely. "On one condition. You need to tell me the truth. The whole truth. That's the first step. Without that, you're on your own."

"What will happen to Seth?" she asked.

"A lot of that depends on you."

A comet's tail of memories flashed before her, so flashbulb-bright it could've all happened yesterday. At eight years old,

Seth had distracted the cashiers with his smile, while she stuffed her bookbag with the loot their father would sell at the flea market. And later, with Dad gone, he'd done the same on the BART train. Flirting, while she'd slipped her slim hands into purses, pockets. Seth needed her. Without her, he'd crumble to dust.

"What do you want to know?"

Detective Casey wasted no time thinking. As if he'd already figured on her cooperation. Probably he'd seen a lot of girls like her. "Are you pregnant?"

"Yep. Two pink lines."

"And the father is..."

"*Was*. Vinnie Frank." Lydia hoped she would never have to say it out loud again. "I have Seth to thank for that too. He wanted me to work off his debt. It wasn't the first time Vinnie touched me. He's been hanging around since I was fifteen years old."

Thankfully, the detective said nothing. But a small frown conveyed his dismay.

"All I want is a fresh start for me and the baby. I want to break the cycle. I want to be better." Lydia cradled her stomach, her eyes welling. She reached for the detective's arm on the table, imploring. "You'll help us, won't you?"

"That depends on you, Lydia. Did your brother kill Iris Duncan?"

Lydia watched him retrieve the pen from the table. He held it poised above the page like a sword ready to strike.

THIRTY-ONE
BEFORE

Iris slid the photograph into the frame and positioned it on her nightstand, sitting back to admire her work. Lydia would be so pleased. She'd been pestering Iris to frame the shot since they'd taken it a week ago, posing on the front steps in front of Dean's camera to honor Iris's newfound freedom. Finally, she'd laid the fiberglass beast to rest.

Iris wiggled her fingers, waved her hand. Good as new, with a little physical therapy. Better, really. Since anything that broke healed stronger at the broken places. Hemingway had been right about that. Iris imagined the cracks in her heart soldered with steel.

"Iris said *no*, Seth." Lydia's voice travelled up the stairs, bringing Iris to her feet.

She called down to them from the landing. "Said 'no' about what?"

"This thing." Lydia held up one of those newfangled security cameras. "I told him you don't want it."

"She's right, dear." Iris put her hands on her hips, treating Seth to a disapproving headshake. "You'll have to return it."

Seth groaned. "But it makes no sense. If you think someone

is trying to creep around the house, a camera is the best way to catch him in the act."

"I don't *think*. I *know*," Iris told him, her voice raised above its usual pitch. "Yesterday, my reading glasses went missing. And he'll just figure out a way to block the camera. He's not a fool."

Lydia cut a razor-sharp glance at Seth, before she returned the apparatus to the box at her feet. "I told you so."

"You two are bonkers." Seth wound his index finger by his ear. "Totally bonkers."

Iris stomped down the last few stairs, her frown deepening to a scowl. "Are you saying I'm crazy? You think I'm making it all up, don't you? That I'm to blame."

"No one is saying that, Iris." Lydia tried to comfort her, but Iris pushed her aside with more force than she'd thought herself capable.

"Well..." Seth began.

Iris pointed at the door. "If you don't believe me, you may as well get out of my life. Both of you."

"I'm sure that's not what Seth meant. Is it, Seth?"

Grumbling, Seth collected the camera and headed for the door.

"*Is it*, Seth?"

"Of course not," he said, though his smile seemed forced. "I'm sure the burglar stole your glasses. And the silverware. And the remote control. It makes total sense. Now, can I get some gas money to take this back to Pro Tech?"

"I don't appreciate your smart mouth, young man." Iris spun around, giving him her back. "Pay for the trip yourself."

Iris spent the afternoon tooling around in her precious garden, waving Lydia off at any sign of a tentative approach. She didn't want to be bothered. Not after that display. Instead, she found refuge in her memories, which could grow as unwieldy as weeds when she let them. She travelled back to her last day at Lost Pines, the day after she turned eighteen. To the small suitcase she'd filled with her few possessions. To the beady eyes of the other girls, watching enviously from the windows. For ten years, she had dreamed of leaving that place, and yet, she clung to her friend like one of Harlow's wire monkeys. Sometimes, she could still hear her voice. *I'll always have your back, Iris. And you'll always have mine.*

After it grew dark enough for the automatic porch light, Iris shed her gloves and dragged herself up the steps and back inside, dog-tired. She found Lydia standing at the front door, peering out the window with palpable anxiety.

Iris gently cleared her throat. She didn't want to startle the girl. "I'm feeling tired, dear. I think I'll go to bed early tonight."

Lydia looked pained. "Seth's not back yet."

"Not back? It's been..."

"Six hours," Lydia finished her sentence. "He's never been gone this long."

"My goodness." Iris hung her head. "I can't help but feel I'm to blame for this. Me and that silly security camera. I suppose it wouldn't have done any harm to keep it."

Lydia retreated to the sofa, checking her cell. "I've tried calling, but his phone is turned off."

"Let's go up to the attic," Iris suggested. "Surely, we'll spot him coming from there. And in the meantime, we can spy on the neighbors. You haven't lived until you've seen Bill Dorsey get a good talking-to from his wife."

When she got like this, it was no small feat to make Lydia laugh, so Iris felt pleased with herself. Lydia followed her up the stairs and sat beside her on the banquette.

"Now, let's have a look-see." Iris raised the binoculars, scanning the street below. "Oh, goodie. Bill and his wife are in the living room. God bless that picture window. Here, have a gander."

Lydia accepted the binoculars but left them on her lap. Her breathing sounded shallow. "Seth has a gambling problem. I mean, he *had* a problem."

As soon as Lydia uttered the words, she covered her face with her hands. "I should've told you a long time ago. But I didn't want to worry you."

"And you suspect that's where he's gone?"

Lydia shrugged, wiping her eyes on her shirtsleeve. "You must think I'm a mess."

"Let me tell you a secret, dear. Everybody is. Take me, for instance. Dead husband. No friends. *Well, one.*" Iris patted Lydia's hand. "A brain like a sieve. And a body in desperate need of a tune-up. You know, there are a couple of books about gambling in the hall closet. If you're interested."

"There." Lydia straightened up, pointing out the window. "It's him. He's walking."

After Iris retrieved the binoculars, she spotted him straight-away, passing beneath a street light, red-faced. A sweat stain marked his gray T-shirt, and his hair stuck out in all directions. "He certainly looks the worse for wear. A bit like the mice Ginger used to leave on the stoop. *Little presents*, Dean called them."

Lydia sighed, her tears welling. "Jeez. *What now?*"

"It's okay. He's home. And he's safe. That's what's most important." Iris gave Lydia an earnest look. "Besides, Seth is no different than Ginger. Or those mice. He can only be what he is, dear."

By the time they reached the front door, Seth had already breached the threshold. He leaned over the sink, splashing his face. "Damn car broke down near Balboa Park," he said, wiping his face on a *Life's Too Short, Lick the Bowl* dish towel. "I had to walk back."

"Balboa Park?" Iris and Lydia exchanged a flummoxed look. "That's over eight miles from here. Why didn't you call?"

"I didn't think you'd answer. Didn't think you cared. Lydia either. I apologize for being a jackass." Seth gulped a handful of water straight from the tap, before Lydia handed him a glass.

"No need, dear. You were only trying to be helpful. And I went and bit your head off. I don't know what's gotten into me lately. I was just telling Lydia how off-kilter I've felt. You haven't been fiddling with my meds, have you?"

A sudden, hacking cough gripped Seth.

"Only kidding. It's just this old brain of mine. It doesn't run like it used to. Speaking of which, it's time to send that rust bucket to the graveyard."

"We can't afford a new car right now. Especially with a baby on the way. I'll get the car towed here tomorrow. I'm sure I can fix it."

"Never fear. Dean played golf with Freddie Mackey. He's the owner of Mackey's Motors over in Oakland. On Monday, I'll hire a taxi to take you and Lydia over there. Pick yourself out something sensible, reliable. Something safe. Something good for a family."

"Iris, we couldn't," Lydia said.

"You could, and you will. I insist." Iris wrapped an arm around Lydia, giving her a squeeze. "I won't have you and the baby stranded on the side of the road."

"You're too good to be true, you know that?" Lydia squeezed her back. "Like one of those fairy godmothers."

Chuckling, Iris pretended to wave a magic wand. "Now, if only I could make dinner appear."

"While Seth gets himself cleaned up, I'll heat some leftovers," Lydia offered. Already, she peered into the refrigerator, sorting through a stack of Tupperware. "It's the least I can do."

With a nod, Iris trailed Seth up the stairs to the third-floor landing. Before he disappeared into the bedroom, she tapped on his shoulder and beckoned him to follow. Even with the door to her room closed behind them, she spoke in a hushed tone. One couldn't be too careful.

"There's something else I want you to know. I haven't spoken about it with anyone. Not my attorney. Not my doctor. Not even Lydia. I don't want to trouble her with it. She can get a little anxious sometimes."

"A little anxious? Liddy's a complete nervous wreck. Always has been. So, what's on your mind?"

"Well, I'm sure you can tell I haven't been myself lately. And I'm certain that neurologist is going to tell me that it's only a matter of time before I'm completely off my rocker."

Seth didn't argue.

"I decided it would be prudent to make some changes to my will, while I'm still of sound mind. Like I told you, I want to be sure you and Lydia are provided for in the event of my untimely demise. So, I've named you and Lydia as my beneficiaries."

"What do you mean exactly?"

Iris laid it out as clearly as she could. She wanted no misunderstanding. "If I kick the bucket, you get it all."

Her belly full with yesterday's chicken casserole, Iris lay in bed, rereading Agatha Christie's *And Then There Were None*, when Lydia popped her head in. "Got a sec?"

Iris removed her spare set of reading glasses and rested the book on her stomach. "For you, of course."

"I just wanted to say... well, what I told you about Seth earlier, up in the attic. Maybe don't mention it to him. He'd be furious if he knew I told you. And we've already got enough problems between us."

"Whatever do you mean?" Iris sat up, frowning in confusion. "Attic? Are you sure? I don't recall being up there today."

Lydia thought for a moment, then waved her off. "Never

mind. You're right. I don't know what I'm saying. Ignore me, please."

"If you say so, dear." Unbothered, Iris returned to her book. She'd only just gotten to the fatal overdose of Mrs. Ethel Rogers. *And then there were eight.* "Good night, Lydia."

THIRTY-TWO

AFTER

Thursday, early morning

Under the dome light of the Volvo, Maureen inspected the letter again to reassure herself. That she hadn't lost her mind. That she hadn't dreamed the whole episode. But no, the long cursive strokes of the signature couldn't be denied.

My dearest Iris,

It was such a joy to celebrate your birthday last week. Moon Pies forever! My memory is not what it once was, but I do vividly recall the first one we shared by the lake. So sweet and gooey and perfect. As miserable as we were, no other Moon Pie has ever come close. I suppose that's the tragedy of youth. Nothing can eclipse its magic, though we do spend our lives trying. Don't we?

Listen to me, waxing philosophical again. I know how you hate that. But I must tell you that seeing you lifted my mood tremendously. You inspire me, friend. You make all my burdens lighter. Since seeing you last, I've started painting again. And what do you know, these arthritic hands still have some life left in them. It's not my best work, but it feels good to create again. I'm calling it "Iris's Bridge" because I've used all your favorite colors. We will have to plan another meet-up soon so you can see it for yourself.

And as I mentioned, please don't feel badly about the care-takers. You couldn't have known. I'm just grateful you set me straight before I gave it all away. I've gone soft in my old age. Lost Pines Dolores would've never allowed herself to get into such a predicament. Anyhoo, the young man promised to pay me back in full. He's coming over Saturday to discuss terms. I do believe I'll charge that rascal interest in the form of Moon Pies.

Love,

Your dearest Dolores

Maureen could hardly take it all in before a flash of move-ment drew her attention to the sidewalk. Neither Charlie "Tall-boy" nor his shopping cart could hold a straight line. As he swigged from a can of Pabst, he ambled past the Dorseys' mansion, swerving dangerously close to the flowerbeds. One wheel veered into the mulch before he managed to right his course. Dorsey's zinnias remained intact, much to Maureen's disappointment.

Through her open window, she hissed, "Charlie."

Tallboy rolled to a stop and cocked his head skyward. As if her voice had come from the heavens. "Charlie Cochise, reporting for duty. Beam me up, Scotty."

Maureen groaned audibly, then opened her door and

hurried over to him. "It's me. Officer Shaw. I need to show you something."

"Hey, I remember you. I got myself a steak and egg breakfast on your dime. And dessert." He raised his beer can to toast her. "Been waitin' for you to come back around. I'm glad you didn't bring that old curmudgeon with you."

"He's off duty tonight. We both are."

"Off duty, huh?" Charlie wiggled his eyebrows and flashed her a jack-o'-lantern grin. "Wanna split a cold one with me?"

"Sorry, Charlie. I can't. Not tonight." Maureen opened the 2008 article she'd saved to her phone and held the screen out to him. He leaned in close, steeping her in sour beer breath. "I want you to take a look at this photo for me. See if it's someone you recognize."

"Well, I'll be a monkey's uncle. That fella's only got one ear." Charlie took another swig, his eyes widening as he swallowed. He hammered the screen with a grubby finger. "Wait a minute. That's the guy. The one I saw in the park talking to that old lady."

"Are you sure?"

"As sure as I am that the Giants are due to win another pennant."

Maureen nodded solemnly. San Franciscans took their baseball seriously. "My dad went to every home game."

"Well, then you know how sure I am." Charlie pointed to the orange and black banner tied to the front of his shopping cart. "So, was the guy a PI like I thought?"

"Not exactly. But the information you gave us proved to be very helpful."

Charlie puffed up like a blowfish. "If you think that's good, wait till I show you what else I got. Always thought I coulda had myself a career in law enforcement. If it wasn't for..." His thoughts trailed off, and he set his beer can in the seat to rifle through the stash in his cart.

"The drinking?" Maureen suggested.

"Nah." With a straight face, Charlie offered her a dilapidated shoebox. Filled to the brim with junk, the bottom sagged, one trinket away from sheer collapse. "It's the uniform. After 'Nam, I can't bring myself to put one on. That's what got me."

"The uniform. Of course." Reluctantly, Maureen took the box in one hand. She held it a safe distance away from her, in case a critter had made its home among Charlie's wares. "What is all this?"

"This here is a box of evidence. I assembled it myself from my collection. It's all the things I gathered in Presidio Park around the time that lady got shot. I figured you might find something in here worth your while."

Maureen shook the box, watching the refuse shift and settle. Rising to the surface in turn, she spotted a red scarf, a cassette tape, a cigarette lighter, a comb, and a gold hoop earring. A smattering of bottlecaps glinted beneath like shale, catching the glow from the street light.

"Thank you. I'll take a look."

Teetering on the edge of the curb, Charlie saluted her before he resumed his drunken stroll up the sidewalk. Maureen carted the shoebox across the street, contemplating tossing it in the trash can at the curb. But then, Charlie stopped at the park's gate and called out to her. His words slurred but unmistakable.

"You're a righter of wrongs, Officer Shaw. Don't forget that."

Maureen opened the trunk of the Volvo and dropped the box next to her gym bag. Like the bags of her parents' clothes she kept in the garage, she knew she would toss it out one day. *Someday*, but not today.

Maureen watched the dash clock change from 4:00 to 5:00 a.m. The houses on Archer Avenue remained dark. The whole world slept but her. Every minute that passed, she asked herself the same questions. Questions for which she had no answers.

Did Dolores gift Iris the painting above the mantel? And why would she remove the calling card of her dear friend?

What was Iris doing in the park with a creep like Antonio Matta?

Who would bring Seth McKay to justice?

And the most insistent of them all: *Where was Iris?*

THIRTY-THREE

Detective Casey tapped his pen impatiently. His eyes homed in on Lydia's like a hawk hunting a rabbit. "I need an answer, Ms. McKay. Did your brother kill Iris?"

"I can't prove it," she said, finally. She wiped at her tear-stained cheeks with the edge of the blanket, leaving mascara streaks on the fabric.

"But you think he did?"

Unable to speak the word, Lydia only bobbed her head. *Yes.*

Satisfied, the detective leaned back, allowing her space to breathe. "Tell me everything you know."

"Well, for starters, I lied about Seth's alibi. He didn't sleep at the Blue Bird that night. We got into a fight about the way he'd treated Iris—calling her crazy—and he stormed out. Yesterday, when I asked him where he'd been, he gave me some cock and bull story about spending the night at the racetrack."

Lydia could still picture Seth, perched on Iris's bed, working the pill grinder. Of all they'd taken from Iris, somehow that worthless bottle of Baclofen hurt the most.

I got a tip on this horse, okay? White Lightning. He was supposed to be the fastest thoroughbred this side of the Rockies.

I had the stupid idea to sneak into the stables at the track to take a look at him myself. Like I already told you, I would've called but my cell died. Anyway, I got plastered and passed out. Woke up the next morning covered in hay and stinkin' to high heaven.

"And then, I found that bloody dish towel in the toolbox of his truck. He couldn't explain that either. Between our money problems and his temper, it's not such a stretch."

"Any chance Seth knew that Iris had changed her will?"

"Knowing Seth, he probably pressured her into it. He seemed surprised when I found the life insurance policy though. I assume you know about that too by now."

Detective Casey gave a solemn nod. "Pacific Mutual notified us yesterday afternoon. Apparently, Seth made a suspicious phone call, demanding an advance on the payout."

"I told him he was stupid to do that." Lydia sighed. "He never thinks anything through. He's always been that way. Live for today, you know. Probably, he got it from our dad. I mean, that deadbeat just ran off and left us to fend for ourselves."

The detective met her eyes, and for a moment, a cold flash of fear hit her skin. "Is there anything else you need to tell me, Ms. McKay? I mean *anything.*"

Lydia finally broke his gaze. She said nothing. The truth of her father's death stuck like a bone in her throat.

"There's something you should know," he told her, lowering his pen to the desk with the gravity of a mic drop. "We've charged Seth with murder."

"For Vinnie, you mean?"

The detective shook his head. "Not just Vinnie. We found rug fibers in Seth's truck bed consistent with the ones on the floor of Iris's bedroom."

"The missing blue rug. Iris loved that old thing."

"And a strand of gray hair coiled around a screw on the tailgate. We won't get the DNA results back for a while, but our expert says it's a presumptive match. Iris was in that truck bed, and I'm guessing she wasn't there voluntarily."

And just like that he'd knocked the wind from her once more. Cut her off at the knees with no warning. She started to cry again. Not for herself this time, but for Iris. Poor, sweet Iris. "If you catch him, he'll never confess."

"*When*. And we don't need a confession. We've got means, motive—and now, thanks to you—opportunity. All the evidence points to your brother like a big red arrow. But I'm not so sure he acted alone."

"What do you mean?" Lydia asked, sniffling.

"You know exactly what I mean. If you saw him pull the trigger, if you hid the gun, if you helped him move her body, I need to know. If you're not one hundred percent honest with me, our deal is off. Think carefully, Ms. McKay."

"The gun," Lydia offered. "I'm the one who hid it beneath the floorboard. That's why my fingerprints were on it. I should've told you from the very beginning. I put it there a couple days after Iris's birthday, because I was worried about her hurting someone or herself. But Seth knew where it was. He helped me find the spot. So, if he shot her, he must've worn his work gloves or something."

"I see." Detective Casey mulled it over. "And you think Seth would do that? Shoot an elderly woman?"

Lydia wrung her hands, though it was the easiest question he'd asked. "As much as it pains me to say it, he'd do anything for money. *Anything*. His whole life exists on that mile-long dirt racetrack."

"A desperate man, then. It's a good thing you came forward when you did. You might've been his next target. Are there any other victims we need to know about?"

In her mind's eye, Lydia watched Seth hurl the pill grinder toward the trash can, frustrated with her for bringing up the past.

How was I supposed to know what would happen? he'd yelled at her. *She was an old lady, Liddy. It was her time to go.*

And later, after she'd squeezed into the slinky red dress that barely fit her anymore, *You're in this with me, sis. All of it. From Dad to now. Don't think the cops are gonna let you walk just because you've got a nice ass.*

With Detective Casey watching her expectantly, Lydia knew what she needed to say. Seth had it right. The detective's sympathy would only extend so far. "No. No other victims."

THIRTY-FOUR

At exactly 9 a.m., Maureen dialed the number for the Shinetastic Car Wash location on the outskirts of San Francisco. Each ring of the telephone dispatched a zip of excitement up her spine. She felt on the verge of flight or fall. She couldn't tell which.

"Will Mr. Matta be in today?" she asked.

A disinterested voice informed her that Mr. Matta worked out of the Oakland office on Thursdays. No appointment necessary.

Maureen made quick work of the fourteen-mile drive, rolling down her windows as she sped across the Bay Bridge toward the port. She watched as the first employees arrived at the car wash and entered the white stucco office through a side door. Already, the early-bird customers had started to roll in. A sign informed her that a Prestige Wash and Wax was half off on Thursdays, which explained the line of vehicles forming at the entrance to the wash.

When a sleek black Mercedes pulled into the lot, skirting them all, Maureen felt certain those tinted windows hid Antonio Matta. A moment later, the door opened and a man stepped out, confirming her suspicions. He looked the part of a mid-level con man with the cowboy boots and the dark suit and the swagger in his walk.

As Matta waved to his crew, Maureen hurried after him. Better to confront him outside, catch him off guard, where she had the advantage. Seated in his own office, he'd be like a grizzly in the forest, comfortable in his domain and eager to take a swipe at her.

"Mr. Matta?" she called. "Could I have a word with you?"

He swiveled toward her, his eyes narrow slits. "You with the *Chronicle*? Over ten years later, and those vultures still won't leave me alone."

"No, no. Of course not. Officer Shaw." She flashed her badge, quick to add, "I'm off duty. I need to ask you a few questions about Iris Duncan."

With a nod, he beckoned her inside the store, where a massive window offered a view of the wash itself. A red Mini Cooper inched along the conveyor belt, soaked in brightly colored soap. Matta turned toward it, giving her a clear view of the shell of his ear. The rest of it, apparently lost at Crescent Bay State Prison, where he'd served his time.

"I'm not sure how I can help, Officer. But I'll do my best. Mrs. Duncan was like family to me. She never judged me. Treated me like a real person, not a common criminal."

Maureen took his cue and stared straight ahead while the soft cloths descended onto the car. "I appreciate your cooperation."

He laughed a little, all breath, but his gravelly voice came out as serious as a heart attack. "These days, I'm an honest businessman who fully cooperates with law enforcement. That's one thing my attorney, Mr. Chalmers, taught me. You never know when the Feds are watching. Walk a straight line. Mind your Ps and Qs. Don't give 'em a reason to haul your ass back to court."

She wanted to believe the guy. Even though the bulge in his back waistband hinted at a gun. And the CASH ONLY sign on the door reeked of tax evasion. "So, how did you know Iris?"

"She used to work for Chalmers. I saw the story on the news. A damn shame. What kind of asshole shoots an old lady? Especially a nice old lady like Mrs. Duncan."

"Good question."

"Streak-free shine every time. Ain't it something?" Matta pointed ahead, grinning like a proud father as water cascaded from above, rinsing the suds from the Mini Cooper. Finally, he turned to look at her. "He'd have to be heartless, that's for sure. Kids, old folks, and animals are off limits. Everybody knows that."

Maureen declared her empathic agreement. As if she'd written the criminal's handbook herself. "So, when was the last time you saw Mrs. Duncan?"

"A couple of weeks ago, actually. She called the office and asked me to meet her at Lafayette Park in the city. She said she needed my help."

"With what?"

"A burglar, supposedly. She seemed convinced that somebody was breaking in to the house and taking her stuff, just to mess with her. She wanted me to send a couple of guys over to watch the house over the weekend. To see if they spotted anyone. She insisted on paying me a couple hundred dollars for the job."

"And what happened?"

"I surveilled the place myself for a few days. Didn't see anything suspicious. To tell the truth..."

He hesitated, winced. Apparently, the truth hurt.

"She reminded me of my Grandma Matta. A bit confused. Forgetful. At the park, she didn't even recognize me at first on account of the hat I was wearing. I thought she might be getting a little long in the tooth. That she could be senile or something.

I know she'd hired a young couple to help her out with the house. I told her to be careful."

"What were you worried about?"

"Oh, c'mon, Officer. You know as well as I do that a rich, lonely old lady is an easy mark. Mrs. Duncan had big money from her husband. And she was on and on about the caretakers. How great they were. How they were her friends. It seemed fishy to an ex-con like me. Hell, I don't even trust my own mother. Anyway, that's the last time I saw her."

The Mini Cooper eased toward the exit, where a young man in a Shinetastic uniform waited for its arrival. He hopped in the driver's seat and advanced it a few feet to the lot, where he started to wipe it dry.

"What do you think happened to Iris?" Maureen asked.

"Between you and me, I think she was too generous for her own good. When a taker meets a giver, it never ends well. I should know. I used to be one."

Maureen raised her brows.

"Drug dealer," Matta said, pointing a thumb at himself. "Sacrificed seven years and one good ear over it. Anyway, I'd say you folks are on the right track. And between you and me, I'd like to meet that Seth McKay fella myself. In a dark alley. With a baseball bat."

"What about your straight line?" Maureen asked, averting her eyes from his clenched fist. But she couldn't ignore the smack of it against his palm.

"Screw it. For Mrs. Duncan, I'd go crooked."

Maureen understood exactly what he meant. It resonated right down to her core, to the vacuous space inside her, the anechoic chamber where no sound existed. The best she could hope for was revenge. But that too had been lost to her the moment Adam Waddell hung himself with his state hospital-issued bedsheet.

"She must've been one heck of a legal secretary."

"Truth be told, she's the reason I'm here today. A free man. The Feds' star witness—one of my employees, no less—said she spotted me taking bags of money from Juan De Leon, the shot caller for Los Diabolitos. And Mrs. Duncan, she didn't believe it for one second. Thanks to her, we found out that Fernanda had a little thing with the lead agent on the case. Turns out, she had an appointment to get her nails done at the same time she supposedly saw me and Juan. Their whole case blown wide open by a little gray-haired lady."

Trying to disguise her surprise, Maureen chuckled. "Well, I can certainly see why you'd cross the line for Iris. Especially if you thought Seth had hurt her."

"Hell, I'm looking for that little bastard... off the record."

"*Off the record...*" She risked a glance at Matta, only to find him looking back at her with similar intensity. "I need your help."

"Yeah, you do. That Volvo of yours has seen better days. What'd ya got on that thing? A couple hundred thousand miles?"

Maureen shrugged. She couldn't bear to part with it.

"Well, a wash and polish are a good start. It'll take those swirl marks right out of the paint. Restore her to her original luster. And I'll even give you the first responder discount. Thirty percent off a full detail. We can talk in my office while you wait."

Maureen fished her car keys from her pocket and dropped them into Matta's outstretched hand.

THIRTY-FIVE

After leaving the Shinetastic Car Wash in her newly spotless Volvo, Maureen headed up the freeway to Golden Gate Fields, her head spinning. Antonio Matta had been nothing like she'd expected. More teddy bear than grizzly, she could understand why Iris had turned to him for help. Little did the woman know, the real danger slept across the hall from her.

Maureen took the exit for the racetrack and pulled into the lot. She sat there, scanning the sparse rows for any sign of him. If Seth had a dollar to his name, he'd turn up here. She had no doubt about that.

When her phone alerted her from the seat, her stomach dropped into a freefall. On his days off, Walter Greer didn't lift a finger. Which meant his number on her screen spelled trouble. Big trouble.

"Hey, Walt. What's up?" She cursed herself for trying too hard to sound casual. An old-timer like Walt couldn't be fooled.

"'What's up?' I should be asking you that question. You're in hot water, Shaw. And as your partner and training officer, I thought I should let you know."

"Okay." But it definitely wasn't. Maureen readied herself for the worst.

"Iris Duncan's neighbor, Bill Dorsey, filed a citizen's complaint against you this morning. He said you unlawfully entered the Duncan house and threatened him when he confronted you outside."

"What a load of crap! I caught the guy trying to steal one of her rare books."

"So, you *were* inside?"

"That's not the point. I had a good reason to be there. Remember that painting on the wall? Iris knew the artist. She and Dolores were friends. And..." Maureen stopped herself. It seemed too much to explain, especially to Walt. Even his breathing sounded judgmental. He would never believe her. "Seth McKay did it. I know he did."

"You're grasping at straws here. They already issued a warrant for his arrest."

Maureen sighed. "Yeah. For the murder of Vinnie Frank. He killed *Iris*, Walt. And he's going to get away with it."

"Slow down. Don't you listen to the news? Apparently, the sister gave him up, and they cut her loose. As of this morning, they issued an APB for McKay and an Indian motorcycle. He's got two warrants. Conspiracy on the Frank case. And the first-degree murder of Iris Duncan. They've got divers out at the Albany Bulb right now looking for her body."

Drawing in a breath, Maureen rolled down her window and peered out beyond the high fence to the bay. The wind off the ocean whispered to her, compelled her. *Find Iris!*

"Now, this is serious, Shaw. If you want to keep your job, you need to—"

The call silenced, Maureen mouthed an apology to the screen and tucked her phone into her pocket. She flung open the door and took off in the direction of the Bulb, unable to stop herself from running.

When she spotted the cop cars at the Bulb's entrance, she pulled up short. A police boat idled in the water. Just beyond the rocky shoreline, two dark heads bobbed like seals in the choppy waves.

She observed from a distance while they went under. Gloved hands groping through the murk and sand and cast-off debris, searching for the corpse Seth had discarded as carelessly as a bag of trash.

Maureen felt a surge of anger that warmed her against the whipping gusts off the water. Iris deserved better than this. The divers resurfaced again and again, empty-handed. And Maureen kept watch as the minutes ticked by, uncertain whether to feel disappointment or relief. At least there'd been no sign of Casey or Diedrich, and she'd found a spot behind a live oak that kept her hidden from the wind.

When the divers finally hauled their slick bodies from the sea to the deck and the boat rounded the corner out of sight, Maureen's heart ached. She gazed out at the water, wondering what dark secrets still churned beneath it. Whether tiny fish hid in the safety of Iris's silver hair, hermit crabs picking the flesh from her bones. She could hardly bear the injustice of it.

As Maureen picked herself up and began the lonely walk back to the parking lot, her phone buzzed again.

What now? She'd already ignored three calls from Walt and another from the lieutenant.

A text had arrived from an unknown number. Matta had come through on his promise to keep her in the loop.

Target spotted in the Tenderloin, looking to trade a rare book for fake docs and a piece.

A sense of urgency bit at her heels, and Maureen's legs took off at a full sprint.

. . .

Maureen rolled down Ellis Street, scanning the sidewalks of the unsavory Tenderloin neighborhood for any sign of Seth McKay. She'd been at it for over an hour now, with nothing to show for her effort. It didn't help that everywhere she looked down here she saw signs of despair.

A figure huddled in the doorway of an abandoned storefront searched for a vein to stick a needle. Bearded and barefoot, a man berated his imaginary companion. A young girl in hot-pink heels sidled up to a slow-moving pick-up, ready to make a deal. Sirens, screams, tires screeching. She heard it all, and it sounded like the end of the world. Without her uniform, she felt like a soldier without armor, exposed and ill-equipped to handle the onslaught to her senses.

Maureen pulled off the street and flipped through her phone, quickly finding the news story Walt had mentioned.

WARRANT ISSUED IN MURDER OF PACIFIC HEIGHTS WOMAN, SUSPECT ALSO WANTED IN SEPARATE HOMICIDE

She closed her eyes and listened for Seth's music: "Flight of the Bumblebee," a disorganized melody of chaos and confusion. As she played a frantic air piano on her thigh, she pictured him in all his disguises. From his suited elegance, blending in with the Friends of the Symphony, to his primitive rage, screaming Iris's name as he obliterated the Kia's side mirror. His soul fed on anger and greed, and there was only one place he could satisfy both appetites.

Maureen jerked the Volvo into drive. Destination, Pacific Heights. She only hoped she'd get there in time.

THIRTY-SIX

BEFORE

A soft knock drew Iris's attention. It had been only ten minutes since she'd retreated to her room in a huff, slamming the door behind her.

"Come in," she called, straightening herself on the bed. A balled tissue rested in her lap.

Lydia stood there, shoulders drooping. She held a folder in her hand. "I'm sorry I yelled. It's not like me."

"It's no trouble, dear. I know you meant well." Iris kept her eyes on the floor, working the tissue in her hand like a stubborn knot. "You were right to be upset. I did it again. I wandered off and got lost. In my own neighborhood, for Christ's sake. What is wrong with me?"

"I'm just glad that you had money for cab fare."

"And that I remembered how to hail one." Iris managed a small snuffle.

"Still, I shouldn't have raised my voice. I sounded like..."

"Like *who*, dear?"

"You know who. Seth has the temper. I'm usually the calm one."

Iris patted the spot beside her, inviting Lydia beneath her

arm. "Sometimes, it's good to get angry. Don't ever let a man walk all over you. You're far too precious for that. Me being gone so long today, it triggered you. It reminded you of him, the ways he's hurt you. How unreliable he's been. You deserved to have a good yell about it."

"Where have you been all my life?"

"I'm right here, dear. Right here." As Iris pulled the young woman closer to her, she asked, "What's this you've got? Paperwork?"

"It's an intake packet. It came in the mail today from Golden Gate Neurology." Lydia spread the pages out on the bed in front of them and handed Iris an ink pen. "Consent forms, medical history. Those sorts of things. Since Seth left for God-knows-where again, I thought we could fill it out together. At least it will distract me."

"I hope the new truck didn't make things worse for you. I thought he'd get something a little more sensible like a minivan. But trust me, he'll learn to settle down eventually. One way or the other."

Lydia cocked her head. "Seth being sensible? Settling down? That'll be the day."

"Well, let's not waste too much time on this balderdash." Iris gave the folder an exaggerated frown. "I want to look through those paint samples Seth brought for the porch railing. Who would've thought there were so many shades of black and brown?"

Lydia read off the items one by one, ticking off Iris's answers. "Do you ever have trouble remembering events that took place in the past week?"

"Well, that's a yes."

"Inability to find important items?"

"Yep."

"Repeating questions more than once?"

"I'll let you answer that one." Iris made a sad smile.

"Obsession about the past? Emotional outbursts?"

"Sometimes." That one came with a twist in Iris's gut. The past felt too alive most days. Like a bloodthirsty parasite that had latched onto her as its host. "Goodness, this questionnaire is depressing enough to trigger one. Are we almost done?"

Lydia nodded her encouragement. "Last question. Difficulty remembering directions? Problems getting lost?"

They both paused for a beat before bursting into shared laughter. It had been too long, and Iris felt the thrum of it deep in her chest.

"Just one more signature at the bottom," Lydia told her, still chuckling, as she held the last of the pages out to her.

After Iris mindlessly scrawled her signature, she relinquished it all, leaning back with a sigh. "If I'm being honest, I'm scared about what comes next."

"*You?* Scared? You're the bravest person I know. Besides, it's just a doctor's appointment. Dr. DeBorg won't bite."

"I haven't always been brave, dear. But the times I've been the bravest, I've had a friend by my side. And without her, well, it's been mighty hard to be brave."

"You've got me now." Lydia gathered the papers, shoved them back into the folder, and laid it on the nightstand. She turned to Iris in earnest. "We're friends. And we always will be."

"Even if DeBorg says I'm a nutcase?"

"Are you kidding? *Especially* if DeBorg says you're a nutcase. I've been one of those as long as I can remember."

THIRTY-SEVEN
AFTER

Thursday, early evening

"Are you sure you want to stay here?" Detective Casey turned to her with newfound sympathy, while he piloted his unmarked sedan up the hill toward the old Victorian on Archer Avenue. Now that Lydia had earned the spot of star witness, he'd suddenly become a lot friendlier, even letting her nap for hours in the station breakroom and buying her an early dinner. "With Seth on the run, it's not safe. The department can put you up in a motel, if you like."

Lydia nibbled at the chicken sandwich from the fast-food place near the station. It smelled good, but it did her somersaulting stomach no favors. She dropped it back into the bag, uneaten. "No, I want to stay here. I'm tired of letting Seth win. Besides, he isn't coming back. When he saw the cops pull up to Vinnie's last night, he tore out of there like a wild banshee. He's probably halfway to Mexico by now."

No matter what she told the detective, Lydia didn't really

believe it. Seth had been tethered here, like a dog on a chain, just as long as she had. She couldn't imagine him picking up and starting over. People like them stayed put.

"It'll be dark soon, so keep the doors locked. Stay inside. And if you see or hear anything suspicious, call me immediately. I'll have a patrol car make the rounds every hour or so, just in case."

Lydia nodded, ready to be free of the detective's watchful gaze. But also, not. She recognized the uncertain confusion. Like a wild animal released from captivity. The last time she'd felt it—the day her father sank to the bottom of an ocean graveyard.

"What do you think will happen? With Iris's will, I mean?"

"Well, given what you've told me, I'd say it's likely to be thrown out. Unless there's something I don't know, you'll probably have to find yourself another place to stay soon."

When her eyes welled, he looked genuinely sorry for her.

"But don't go running off on me. We need your help to put Seth behind bars where he belongs. You may not realize how dangerous he is. Especially now that he's boxed into a corner."

"I know. I'll be careful."

Detective Casey stopped the car in front of the house, idling there. She followed his eyes to the bright yellow DO NOT ENTER tape strung across the door frame.

"Maybe go in through the back," he suggested, giving her knee a reassuring squeeze. His touch startled her. It had been a long time since a man offered her comfort. She decided that she liked it and squeezed his hand right back. "You'll need to get that door fixed ASAP."

Lydia retrieved her sandwich bag and purse from the floorboard. She made it halfway up the walk before she turned, forced a smile, and waved to the detective. He waited for a moment, then zipped away, leaving her alone.

. . .

Inside the house, it felt different. But she found everything in its place. Only *she* had changed.

Lydia shed Iris's heels and the clingy red dress, giving it an unceremonious burial in the garbage can, and dressed quickly in the dim light. She tossed a few things in her duffel, just enough to get her by, and hurried out of the bedroom, eager to leave it behind.

Outside Iris's room, Lydia paused. She nudged the door open and stood at the threshold, finally letting herself imagine what might have happened there. An angry Seth breaking in the front door and brandishing the ghost gun, demanding Iris's stash of hat box money. He didn't like to be told *no*, especially when he'd been drinking. Maybe they'd struggled. Maybe not. Either way, it wouldn't be the first time Seth had wrapped up a dead body. She pictured him pushing the heavy bundle down the stairs and into the garage. Loading it into his truck bed. Cleaning up what blood he could with a dish towel. She didn't need a badge to know where he'd dumped the body. Poor Iris, dead and cold, lay with the remains of Gene McKay. The salt water cleaning their bones.

Lydia shivered and shut the door. The sound echoed in the empty house. Down the steps she went, straight to the foyer, where she deposited her duffel for a speedy exit. She wanted nothing to slow her down. Then, to the kitchen, where she selected the sharpest knife from the hardwood block.

The clock on the mantel read 6 p.m. Soon, it would be dark out, allowing her the freedom to move unseen. Lydia waited on the sofa, holding the knife and staring blankly at the painting Seth had stolen from a dead woman.

THIRTY-EIGHT

From her perch on the sofa, Lydia witnessed the steady descent of nightfall, the languid crawl of the shadows across the sitting room floor. In time, they covered the coffee table and stretched toward the mantel, darkening the vibrancy of the painting to a muted hue.

How could Iris have ever trusted Seth's claim? *Him*, an artist? Laughable. He'd never created anything of beauty. Only destroyed. Only taken. But like their smooth-talking father, he had a knack for telling stories. *I'll take care of you, Liddy. Just one more bet, Liddy. You and me against the world, Liddy.* And she had a knack for believing them. Seth had once said it himself. *If you fall for a con, it's because you agreed to get conned. It takes two, Liddy. It takes two.*

As the last vestiges of light disappeared, Lydia's palms began to sweat. With the knife resting on her lap, she gnawed at her thumbnail until the patrol car Detective Casey had promised eased past the house. It would be an hour before it made another round. She couldn't delay any further.

Lydia retrieved a flashlight and slipped out the back door into the yard, where the night provided her cover. She zipped her sweatshirt against the crisp air and tugged the hood over her head, making her way toward the toolshed. The knife rested heavy in her kangaroo pocket.

Though only a few days had passed since Iris's death, it seemed a lifetime since Lydia had walked through the garden. The lawn, freshly mowed and raked; the bushes, trimmed. As pristine as Seth had left it, the place felt lonely and forgotten. And beyond it, the inky forest loomed like a cloaked figure.

Lydia plucked the key from her pocket and fumbled with the lock. While she worked it free, her imagination ran wild, raising the hair on her neck. With the door finally open, she spun around quickly, expecting Seth to be there, his eyes black with rage. But there was no one and nothing. Just the breeze swaying the branches above her. Even the night birds had stopped singing.

Lydia pushed her way inside, where she found the shed ten degrees cooler and much, much darker. Shutting the door behind her, she turned on the flashlight and set it on the ground, illuminating the weedy corner beneath the work table.

A full watering can and trowel in hand, she dropped to her knees and crawled to the spot. Already, the shed felt airless, but Lydia didn't have time to panic. She kept her focus on a single dandelion sprouting near the baseboard. It struck her as a hopeful sign.

The water softened the earth and muddied her hands. Eager now, she plunged the blade of the trowel into the ground as far as it would go, scooping out a fistful of dirt. She worked quickly, efficiently, building a small mound beside her. With each thrust, she anticipated the precious *clink* of metal on glass. The sound of her future.

Still, her heart nearly vaulted into her throat when she heard the sound, when she felt the hard edge beneath the blade. She'd found it. She'd *really* found it.

She used her hands now, clawing in the muck, until she

unearthed the large glass jar. Holding it to the light, it looked exactly as she'd pictured it in her daydreams. Except—

"What the hell are you doing?" Seth growled at her from the doorway. The light cast strange shadows on his face, hollowing his eyes. Perspiration beaded at his temples, and he mopped it with the corner of his sweat-stained shirt.

"Well?" he demanded.

"I—I don't know." Lydia cowered beneath the table. Her heartbeat pounded in her ears. Her mind went blank. "It's empty. Empty."

The word broke her heart in two. "I thought..."

"You thought *what*?" He stepped into the shed, eclipsing the doorway. For the first time, she saw the gun gripped tight in his hand. And then, she couldn't look away from it. Her skin buzzed with fear. "Where is it? Where's the money?"

Seth pushed aside the wheelbarrow with one sweep of his hand. Tossed a bucket at the wall behind her. It sounded like a gunshot.

"I know that old bag left you something. That's why you sold me out." He dropped down to his knees, baring his teeth at her. "Your own goddamned brother. Your flesh and blood."

The jar huddled against her, Lydia pushed back into the corner, like a broken-winged bird. Seth, a cat ready to pounce.

"You better start talking, sis."

"There's nothing here, Seth. I promise you. She lied to me." But already, Lydia wondered, doubted. Because Seth had burst in on them that day. Probably, he'd overheard the conversation, dug up the jar for himself weeks ago, and blown the money at the track like always. "You took it, didn't you?"

"That's rich. Blaming me, when you intended to leave me behind to fend for myself."

"You need to hit rock bottom, Seth. Or you'll never stop. I can't do it anymore. I can't keep paying for your mistakes."

"Give it to me. *Now*." He waved the gun at her, pointing to the jar until she surrendered it. In one violent motion, he ripped it from her clutches, raised it above his head, and hurled it against the dirt, the glass exploding at his feet.

"Get up."

Lydia knew better than to argue. Crawling from beneath the table, she struggled to stand. Her bones felt like rubber. But the weight of the knife made her brave. "The police are coming back, you know. They're patrolling the neighborhood. They're looking for you and the motorcycle."

"You think I don't know that? You think I'm a fucking idiot?" He grabbed her by the arm, dragging her forward, then peered into the empty hole she'd dug. "You do, don't you? You always have. Sneaking around behind my back with the goddamned cops. Thinking I wouldn't notice."

"I didn't do anything wrong."

He answered with a kick of his heel against the shed door. It flew open, barely clinging to its hinges. "The hell you didn't. How am I the one with two warrants on my ass? And here you are, prancing around free as a bird and digging for buried trea-sure. I warned you not to give Vinnie too much. I told you that stuff could kill an elephant."

"I did exactly what you said. Just a pinch. I don't know what happened. Maybe his heart gave out." Lydia decided she lied better when her life depended on it.

Seth shoved her out the door, and she stumbled, landing on her knees on the lawn. The grass crunched beneath his boots as he approached from behind her. She had to move fast.

"Hell, you probably killed Iris too," he said. "And you're letting me take the fall. Just like you made me clean up your mess with Dad. I should've turned you over to the cops right then and there. Would've saved me a helluva lot of trouble."

When Lydia sensed the heat of him at her back, she whipped her hand from her front pocket and slashed at him with the knife. The blade sliced through the skin on his arm, and he cried out like a wounded animal.

Lydia hauled herself up and ran for the house with Seth staggering behind her. If she could only reach the steps, she could open the door. She could lock herself inside. She could call for help.

Nearly there, she lunged forward, but her head jerked back. A sharp pain seared her scalp as Seth held tight to her ponytail.

"Drop the knife," he ordered, pushing the barrel of the gun into her back.

Lydia watched it fall from her hand into the grass, Seth's blood still staining the steel.

"I *will* kill you." The calmness of his voice scared her more than his yelling ever had. "But first, you're going to show me where she hid the rest of the money. I know it's here. And I know you know where."

Lydia thought of the empty glass jar. Of her dreams for the future. Of the promise of freedom. All of it shattered at Seth's hand.

"You're just like Dad," she said. "A loser. A perpetual, pathetic loser."

He slammed her head against the ground, then pulled her up again by her hair. Stars swam in and out of her vision, her ears rang. But knowing she'd raised his hackles felt like a small victory.

Seth jabbed the gun into her side, forcing her up the stairs and into the house. "So, where to, sis?"

Lydia swallowed hard, tasting metal at the back of her throat. Her arm bore Seth's handprint in his own blood. It trickled down his hand and onto the hardwood. "The attic," she said.

. . .

Lydia dragged her feet up the stairs with Seth's steps heavy at her back.

"There better be something good up here."

She didn't answer, only pushed the door open and pointed to the banquette benches. That would keep him busy.

"Which one?"

"I told you, I don't know."

Holding the gun in one hand, he reared back and whacked her across her face with the other. "Don't lie to me. And don't play games."

"Let me look," she said, ignoring the fire that blazed across her cheek. "I just—I don't remember where. But I'll find it."

Lydia moved like a zombie, slow and steady toward the windows, hoping someone down below would be looking up.

THIRTY-NINE

BEFORE

On the morning of her death, Iris had never felt more alive. She woke before sunrise with a jolt of nervous energy. For so long, she'd been plotting and scheming, and now the time had arrived. By tomorrow, the bed where she lay would be soaked with her own blood. The two pints of blood she'd harvested herself months ago. And she'd be safe in Tony's basement until she hopped a plane for anywhere but here. Someplace quiet where she could smell the ocean from her window.

While the rest of the house slept, Iris popped her pills and dressed quickly. She found her precious butterfly atop the dresser and pinned it to her lapel.

"I've got your back, Dolores," she whispered. "Always." But it came with a pang of guilt. She'd been the one to encourage her friend to hire those bloodsuckers. Dolores had met Seth at the Friends of the Symphony, after he'd worked as a driver for an elderly couple. Later, he'd introduced her to his little sister. The way Dolores had described them—a sweet pair of siblings, orphaned and down on their luck—she should've known from the start. *A sweet pair, my patootie.*

Newly focused, Iris retrieved a set of tweezers from the

bathroom and crouched down next to her favorite blue rug. The one she and Dolores had picked out together at the Berkeley Flea Market on a perfect spring day. She plucked at least fifty small fibers, dropping them into a plastic bag that she tucked into her pocket. Then, she padded down the stairs, careful not to make a sound.

Retrieving Seth's truck keys from the kitchen drawer, Iris snuck out the front door and crept toward it, parked at the curb in front of the house.

"Morning, neighbor."

Like a skipping stone, her heart missed a beat. Bill Dorsey waved to her from his porch, his Sunday newspaper in hand. Iris grumbled at him, pretending to be confused. Leave it to Daft Dorsey to throw a wrench in her plan.

"Who are *you?*" she asked. "I thought I saw someone sneaking around out here."

"It's me. Bill. I live here." He pointed to the disgustingly extravagant mansion behind him, and Iris fought the urge to roll her eyes. "I help you sometimes. You like me. I'm a member of the HOA."

Iris wondered how long it would take him to bring *that* up. She nodded warily, giving him a tentative wave, and waited for him to go away. Finally, he took the hint, disappearing inside his castle. But not before he asked, "Are you sure you're okay?"

After you reach a certain age, everyone assumes you're as helpless as a hog on ice, especially when you pretend to forget a few things, let your house go to pot. Invent a burglar who never existed. Though she still hadn't found that damn copy of *Great Expectations*.

Iris scurried around to the bed of the truck, thankful she'd thought to tell Seth to leave the paint cans till the morning. If Daft Dorsey planned to spy on her through the window, he'd see nothing more than a sad old woman trying to prove her independence. Everyone underestimated Iris. Her plan depended on it.

Iris lowered the tailgate and sat atop it, scooting inside the truck bed and hoisting herself upright. At her age, the task took effort, and by the time she'd climbed to her feet, her lungs burned.

With her back to Dorsey's house, she carefully spread the tiny rug fibers. So insignificant, no one would spot them until it mattered. Not unlike herself, she thought. Blending into the world when she should have been standing out. But no matter, her time would come. Even if it was a little late.

Then, she pulled a couple of strands of silver hair from her head and wound them tightly around the base of the nearest screw. Last, she approached the toolbox and opened it with the smaller of the two keys, stuffing the bag as far down as she could. Inside it, the dish towel Seth had brought to mop up her blood after her so-called accident with the hoe. Hacking her foot like a weed certainly hadn't been pleasant, but *no pain, no gain,* as the youngsters say. Satisfied with her work, she started to heave the first can of paint from the bed.

"Iris! What are you doing?" Seth frowned at her from the doorway, rubbing his sleepy eyes.

"What does it look like?" she huffed. "I'm getting the paint."

"By yourself?"

Iris shrugged, awkwardly working her way down from the truck bed. She carried the can toward the steps. "Now that I've seen the colors up close, I reckon I prefer the black. What do you think?"

"Whatever you like. Your house, your decision. But don't strain yourself." As if the bastard cared about her at all beyond her pocketbook. Yesterday had been proof of that. Seth had gobbled up the money—twenty thousand bucks!—she offered him for the "baby" with no shame. As if the world owed him. "I'll get the other one."

Iris looked on with slight trepidation, while he ambled bare-foot to the truck bed and retrieved the second can. When he returned up the sidewalk, she realized she had no reason to worry. The man had the brain of an ostrich. "Well, aren't you helpful this morning?"

"Careful, he only helps when he wants something." Lydia caught Iris by surprise, winking at her when their eyes met. That one she had to watch out for. Claiming to be pregnant with her brother's child, now that took guts. Iris only wished she could be there if and when Lydia decided to cut her losses. To dig up the jar Iris had emptied months ago. She could admit she envied that girl one thing: Lydia had choices. Unlike Iris—and women of her generation—whose life resembled a train on a track with its predictable stops, its predetermined destination.

"You two are up early this morning." Iris tried not to sound annoyed. After all she'd sacrificed—she'd stuck a needle in her vein, for Christ's sake—she couldn't get sloppy. Not today.

"Couldn't sleep," Lydia admitted. "Not with Seth out here making a ruckus."

"Oh, go easy on him. He was only looking out for me." Iris studied the paint cans on the porch. "I've decided on the black," she told Lydia.

"Black it is. The color of sophistication, elegance, power."

"And mourning," Iris added, with a childish giggle. She couldn't help herself. She'd been sad for too long.

Lydia made a face. "Jeez, someone's in a weird mood today. You didn't take too many pills again, did you?"

Iris froze on the stoop, arranging her face the way she wanted it—bewildered. She felt a bit like her tabby, Ginger, batting around an unsuspecting mouse. She'd been playing this game since the day she walked into the Sunrise Café decked out in her best jewelry, since the phone call to Burt that afternoon that got Lydia fired. "*Pills?* Uh-oh. We better check to make sure I took them at all, dear."

.   .   .

The hours crawled. Iris tried to savor her last moments in the only real home she'd ever known, but she found herself checking the clock and willing its hands to move faster. To be honest, the house didn't feel like hers anymore. It belonged to another Iris. The *before* Iris, who had one true friend. The *after* had no one but herself.

While Seth prepped and stained the railing, Lydia coached Iris through her PT exercises—the wrist extensions, the forearm rotations, the single-finger bends. Then, they holed up in the kitchen, where they baked two dozen of her chocolate chip cookies. Baking always quieted her mind. But today, it felt like a chore. Just one more thing to get through. Her mind wandered to all the usual, awful places.

Call me if you need me, she'd told Dolores that fateful Saturday morning. *And be careful. People behave badly when they feel trapped in a corner.* No call ever came. And the neighbor found Dolores's body a week later after her mail started to pile up in the box. *Suicide,* they said. *Overdose.* But Iris knew better. Because Dolores would never leave her. Because Dolores had started painting again. Because she and Dolores had made a sacred pact years ago at Lost Pines, when Iris felt herself sinking into the murk of it all, barely able to keep her head above water, not even wanting to. *Never one without the other. We go together or not at all.*

When Seth finally called Iris out to the porch to survey his work—"One side done!"—Iris sighed with relief. Memory lane, permanently closed to visitors. All aboard at retribution station.

"Well, let's go check out the new railing, shall we?"

"I'm right behind you," Lydia said, transferring the last of the cookies into the metal tin and depositing it in the pantry.

Iris stood at the front door, her hand on the knob. As she opened it, she glanced over her shoulder into the foyer at

Dolores's painting. The one called "Iris's Bridge." Too big to carry, she would have to leave it behind. With them. The thought of it, nearly unbearable, gave her the fuel to stoke the fire.

"You stained it black." Iris glared at the painted half of the railing as if it had insulted her personally.

"*Riiight*. Black. Just like you asked."

"No, I wanted brown. I said brown." Iris drew from the well of rage inside her. The deep, dark hole where she kept them all. Her good-for-nothing mother. Wicked Sister Frances and the horrid wenches at Lost Pines. Bill Dorsey and his crew of white-collar bullies. Even Dean, who hadn't viewed her as an equal but a good little wife who should stay in her place. If she hadn't been so hell-bent on proving herself—that unlike her mother, she would honor her commitments, no matter the cost—Iris would've been gone years ago. Her job at Chalmers and Pierce had been her way of telling Dean to go squat in a cactus patch.

"Brown! The railing should be brown!"

Lydia reached out a hand to calm her. "It's okay. He's only done one side anyway. It's an easy fix. You probably just forgot."

She slapped it away. "Don't placate me. I didn't forget anything. I hate black. It's the color of death."

Seth puffed his cheeks and blew out a frustrated breath. Just then, Daft Dorsey poked his head out his front door, no doubt concerned about the volume of her yelling. Surely, it violated the neighborhood noise ordinance.

"Everything good out here?" Dorsey asked.

"It's fine, Bill," Iris spat back. "Stop spying on me."

Seth dared to step in front of her. "You're acting crazy, Iris. You told me to paint it black, so I painted it black. You forget things. That's what you do. That's why you have to see that head doctor in a few days. *Remember?*"

"I am not crazy, young man. And if that's what you think of me, then get out. Get the hell off my property."

"Huh?" That threw him for a loop.

"You heard me. *Out*. And I want your key back."

"Fine." Seth tossed the key ring at Iris's feet and tugged at Lydia's arm. "Let's go, Liddy. Pack a bag. We don't have to deal with this nut job."

Lydia looked stunned. Seth, irate. And Bill Dorsey had witnessed the entire show. Iris had to admit it couldn't have gone any better.

"Are you okay?" Dorsey asked her, after the McKays sped away in the truck she'd bought them. "I can help you bring the paint inside."

Iris shook her head stubbornly. "It's Seth's responsibility. He has to face the music. He'll do it in the morning."

Her neighbor watched her with concern until his wife called him inside like a schoolboy.

"Take care, Iris. Get some sleep."

When the door had shut at his back, Iris spoke her last words to him. "Kiss off, Bill."

With the McKays banished, Iris went to work, approaching the task the way she had for decades at Chalmers and Pierce. Diligent and meticulous, she dotted every *i*, crossed every *t*.

First, she dealt with the pillbox, adding three Valium in each remaining slot. After her not-so-accidental overdose on blood pressure pills, with Seth and Lydia managing her meds at their request, the cops would surely suspect she'd been drugged to make her more compliant. And in downtown San Francisco, benzos were easy to come by for the right price. No prescription needed. And whatever pills she didn't use, she flushed right down the toilet.

Then, she opened the hat box, stuffing most of the money she'd gradually withdrawn over the past year into her go-bag. The rest, she spread in the bedroom and down the steps, leaving a trail for the cops to follow. Of course, she'd wisely left enough in her bank account not to arouse suspicion.

Iris retrieved a pair of heavy-duty scissors from the kitchen and sliced her beloved rug into manageable strips that she deposited in a trash bag. A necessary sacrifice that would explain how the McKays had transported her body.

Finally, for the pièce de résistance, Iris padded to the fridge, where she loosened the seal of the door and carefully removed it. Though she knew it would still be there, she felt relieved to see it all. Two pints of refrigerated blood. *Hers*. Two spent shell casings she'd collected from her clandestine target practice with Seth. And her brand-new passport, courtesy of Tony Matta. She retreated to her bedroom with the goods to await her own demise.

At 2:40 a.m., Iris slipped on a pair of winter gloves and trashed her bedroom. It didn't trouble her as much as she expected. In fact, she rather enjoyed rumpling the bedcovers, flinging open the doors, tossing her clothing like a child in the middle of a tantrum. She took particular pleasure in smashing the photograph of the three of them, relishing the deep crack down the center of the frame. If only the McKays could see her now. Their sweet moneybags gone wild.

By 2:47, she had placed the shell casings on the floor and opened the window.

Moving quickly now, Iris retrieved the blood bags. She didn't have time for disgust, though the smell of the blood quickly overwhelmed her. Workmanlike, she soaked one side of the bedding, hoping it would be enough to convince the authorities of her passing. Then, she deposited the used bags in her suitcase for disposal.

Iris headed downstairs one last time for the riskiest part of the whole operation. Thankfully, she had experience with faking forced entry. The burglary in March had been an inside job, intended to give her a legitimate reason to invite Seth and Lydia to move in across the hall. She knew what to do and how to do it.

Iris wrapped her gloved hand in a dish towel—she couldn't afford to nick her skin on the glass—and let herself onto the porch. Peering across and down the street, only the blank faces of dark houses bore witness. She counted in her head. *One... two...* On three, she jabbed the butt end of the pair of scissors through the stained glass, the broken fragments scattering on the hardwood of the foyer. Iris carefully stepped over the threshold and left the door partway open behind her.

As Iris summited the steps again, still gripping the scissors, her heart beat heavy in her ears. She felt like a little girl, holding her breath under the icy water of the lake, her foot brushing against something slimy. Now that she'd come so close, a strange sense of panic overtook her.

Only amateurs panic, Iris reminded herself. That's what Tony had told her. He'd warned her this would happen. *You're no amateur, Mrs. Duncan.* Easy for him to say. Working for a criminal defense attorney didn't mean she knew how to commit a crime, much less how to get away with one. But she'd already lined up the dominoes. She only needed to push the first and let momentum take care of the rest.

While Iris stood there, paralyzed, a blackbird fluttered in through the window. It hopped on the windowsill, pecking at the wood, and cocked its head at her. Iris had never been superstitious, but the sudden appearance of that little bird spoke to her. It made her feel less alone.

Nodding at the bird as if she understood its message, Iris placed the tape recorder on the nightstand beside the old rotary phone. With one hand, she clutched the receiver to her ear. The other hand waited, index finger poised above the button marked *play*. As soon as she'd done it, she would stretch the phone's cord to the side of the bed and sever it with the scissors.

Three numbers. That's all it took. Her fingers trembled as she dialed. Her breath quickened with each shrill ring.

"Nine-one-one. What is your emergency?"

Iris clung to her bags, moving so fast her bones creaked. She rushed through the yard and out the back gate, scurrying like a squirrel toward Presidio Park. She dropped the trash bag into a neighbor's garbage can for Monday morning pick-up and pressed on. She didn't need to hurry, but her fear propelled her. Her fear of being caught. Of her whole plan blown to bits. Of the McKays walking away unscathed, while her precious Dolores turned to worm food in Piedmont Cemetery.

The redwoods wrapped their arms around her like a blanket, hiding her from the world. The farther she travelled from the glow of the street, the darker it became. Until only the moon lit the way. Iris looked up ahead, trying to find the path that would lead her to Crissy Field and Tony Matta. As she squinted into the murk, a coyote let out a mournful howl. Her eyes darted to the shadows flitting between the trees, and she picked up her pace, her bag jostling on her shoulder. She should've known better than to hurry. *Haste makes waste*, a Sister Frances favorite, usually punctuated with a smack of the ruler.

Suddenly, Iris's foot caught the edge of a downed limb. She stumbled forward and landed on her knees. The impact sent her bag flying. Shockwaves of pain juddered her body, but she sealed her mouth shut. She wouldn't let herself cry.

Iris struggled to her feet, her legs like jelly beneath her. She stared in horror at her go-bag. One side had busted open, and its smarmy contents spilled around her. Blood bags and benzos. It sounded like the title of a bad Lifetime movie. The sort of movie she and Dolores should've watched together, snuggled side by side on Iris's bed. But that would've required Iris to tell her friend the truth. That she'd wasted years waiting for the courage. That she'd lived most of her life in secret. That she'd loved her—*really loved her*—since they'd shared that first Moon Pie on her eighth birthday. Since they'd twirled together years later, two girls on a makeshift dance floor. *What a wonderful world.*

Cursing herself for all of it, Iris stooped to gather the evidence. At least she'd avoided another broken appendage. She stuffed what she could into the bag and kept looking. The tape recorder, the last item in, had travelled the farthest. It lay on its side in a pile of leaves with the deck sprung open. The tape, nowhere in sight.

Iris heard the sirens. So close, they seemed to come from someplace inside her. If she didn't go now, she risked losing everything.

Holding the bag like a baby to her chest, Iris kept moving. She didn't stop until she saw the Mercedes parked off the road with its headlights darkened. It felt fitting that he'd driven the black one.

Her hearse awaited.

Iris didn't bother looking back.

FORTY

AFTER

Thursday evening

Maureen drove past Iris's house and parked in her usual spot near the Presidio, overlooking the street. She rolled down her window, her ears pricked like a watchdog. Though the neighborhood appeared serene, the air pulsed with electricity, charged with the energy that pulsed through Maureen's veins.

Lights glowed from the lower floor of the Dorsey mansion, and Maureen fought the urge to knock on the door and give him a piece of her mind. But she stayed put, eyes laser-focused on the Victorian.

A flash of movement drew her attention to the attic. The windows remained dark, but a shadow flitted inside. Lydia stood there for a moment, looking pale as a ghost, before she disappeared again.

Unease crept up Maureen's spine, raising the soft hairs on her neck. Armed with her Glock, she cracked the door and slunk toward the house. Maureen approached on high alert, skirting the front entrance and heading toward the backyard instead. As she reached over the fence to unlatch the gate, a familiar voice stopped her.

"You have some nerve coming back here, Officer Shaw. I've already reported you to your superiors."

Maureen spun around, holding a finger to her lips. But Bill Dorsey didn't take kindly to being told what to do.

"I will not *shush*. I happen to know that you are violating police procedure. The lead detective told me to contact him immediately if I ever see you here again. And I am—"

Gun aimed at Dorsey's kneecap, she waved him off again. This time, he complied, scampering back across the street. Maureen recognized the fear in him, and she knew she'd crossed another line. But it didn't stop her, didn't even slow her down.

She entered through the gate and padded across the lawn toward the back door. Her stomach flip-flopped when she spotted the blood dotting the stoop. Nearby, a knife lay discarded in the grass. Its blade, slick.

Maureen crouched near the steps, quickly dialing Walt's number. The old grump answered on the first ring, warming Maureen's heart.

"Shaw, what in God's name are you—"

"Call Casey. I need backup at the Duncan house."

"Jeez Louise. You are in such big—"

"Just do it, Walt." She silenced her phone and turned the knob, letting herself inside.

The blood trail led the way. Through the kitchen, into the foyer, and up the stairs, Maureen followed. Inside the belly of the house, Maureen heard nothing. Not a footstep or a whisper or the creaking bones of the foundations. Only her own breath, which she tried to quiet.

By the time she reached the third floor, she had to search for the blood drops in the dim light of the evening. She continued up toward the attic, finding a red smear on the knob of the closed door.

Maureen positioned herself to the side and gingerly worked the door open. Seth stood at the center of the circular room, clutching Lydia against him. His own gun, boldly pointed at the side of her head. Maureen's eyes darted from Seth's bloody arm to the strewn-about banquette cushions. To the terror that blanched Lydia's face.

"Don't come any closer or I'll blow her brains out."

"Understood." Maureen sounded steadier than she felt. She only had to buy time. "I know you don't want to hurt your sister."

"That's where you're wrong. This little bitch thinks she's better than me." Lydia trembled beneath his tight grasp. Though she stayed stock-still, the vein on his forearm bulged with the effort of holding her. "Just because she went to community college. Community college, for God's sake. They don't even have a football team. And she didn't even graduate. But she walks around with her nose up in the air like she earned a doctorate degree from Harvard."

"She's your flesh and blood, though. There's no getting around that. Trust me, you don't realize what a gunshot to the head looks like. It sticks with you forever. It doesn't let you go." Maureen still couldn't unsee it. It stained every memory of her parents, leaving its black rot just beneath the surface.

"Fine. I'll shoot her in the chest then." He relocated the gun, aimed it near her heart. "That works too."

"Do you really think shooting her will solve your problems?" Maureen risked a small shake of her head. "It will only make things worse. The best you can do is to let me help you. Put down the gun and talk to me. Tell me what Lydia's done to you. How she's treated you unfairly. I'll hear you out, I promise."

Seth's grip relaxed a bit, allowing his sister to suck in a

breath. "She told the cops I killed Iris. But I didn't. *I didn't!* Sure, I took the old broad for whatever I could, but the whole scam was her idea. Admit it, Liddy. It was your idea."

Lydia stared ahead blankly, tears streaming down her cheeks. Maureen willed her to agree with him.

"It was my idea," Lydia repeated. Like the words were foreign to her.

"See, your sister cares about you, Seth. She won't let you take the fall for something you didn't do. So, just let her go, and—"

From down below, Dorsey shouted at the house. "I called the cops on you! Do you hear me, you lunatic? You can't just go pointing your gun at civilians."

Maureen met Seth's panicked gaze. He flung Lydia forward, straight at Maureen's chest, and the two women stumbled to the ground, sending Maureen's Glock sliding across the hardwood. Seizing his chance, Seth fled the attic before Maureen could scramble to her feet and retrieve her weapon.

Down the stairs they ran, Seth one flight ahead of her. Each time Maureen tried to aim her gun, he skirted out of sight. Her chest heaving with the effort, she chased him out the front door and down the sidewalk. The commotion had drawn out the neighbors, who gawked at the scene, following the action with their cellphone camera lenses.

"Stop, or I'll shoot," Maureen yelled.

Seth didn't listen. He sprinted across the street and flicked a stunned Bill Dorsey to the ground as he ran. Dorsey cried out in pain, holding his limp wrist against him.

Still in pursuit, Maureen surveyed the path ahead of them. Her heart dropped to her knees when she spotted Charlie "Tall-boy" and his shopping cart weaving a zigzagging line up the sidewalk, heading for the Presidio.

She stopped and raised her gun. But Seth had gone too far

for a clear shot. It felt familiar, this helplessness. She swallowed hard. As he barreled straight for Tallboy, she could only watch.

At the last second, Tallboy casually extended his sneaker, and Seth took flight, landing with a thwack on the sidewalk. He didn't move.

"I got him! I got him!" Tallboy grinned at her, raising his fists above his head in victory, as the onlookers cheered. Unmanned, his shopping cart rolled off the sidewalk and spilled onto the street. But he didn't seem to care. "I got him, Officer Shaw!"

Maureen couldn't speak. Her mouth gaped open, while Seth raised up and aimed his gun at Tallboy's back. No time to think, only time to act, she pointed her Glock and pulled the trigger.

Maureen sat on the curb and looked on while the ambulance sped down Archer Street en route to San Francisco General, sirens blaring. Minutes after she fired her gun, her hands still shook in her lap. She couldn't decide what that said about her. Did it mean she wasn't cut out to be a cop? Or that she was?

After Detectives Casey and Diedrich motioned her over, Maureen forced herself to stand. Each step in their direction felt like walking the plank.

"Congratulations, Shaw." She flinched when Detective Casey patted her shoulder. "Impressive police work."

"Really?" She searched his face for signs, but he remained stoic. Diedrich, on the other hand, couldn't contain his shit-eating grin. A cloud of dread passed over her.

"Absolutely. Following your intuition. Nabbing our suspect. I couldn't be happier. You even left him alive. I gotta say that must have been some shot."

"Lucky shot," she said, still in disbelief. "The responding

officer said it looked like a ricochet off the sidewalk. And Lydia? Is she okay?"

Maureen looked to the attic, lit up now, where several officers and paramedics moved about inside.

Diedrich regarded her like a fly he couldn't swat. "It's not your problem anymore, Shaw. We got it covered." Sensing her confusion, he turned to his partner. "Are you gonna tell her? Or should I? Time to rip off the Band-Aid."

With a sigh, Casey delivered the news. "You're suspended pending termination, Maureen. You'll need to turn over your badge and service weapon."

Practically gleeful, Diedrich held out his hands.

"Now? Can't I bring them to the station?"

"Given your track record of insubordination, I'm afraid not," Diedrich answered. "I warned you this would happen. But you can speak with the lieutenant if you need clarification."

Maureen unholstered her weapon. She knew it would hit her in the morning. Right now, she just felt numb. As she surrendered her badge to Diedrich's outstretched palm, Tallboy wandered over, reeking of booze and good fortune.

"That's what you call a travesty right there." Tallboy pointed at the badge that didn't belong to her anymore. "Officer Shaw is a damn good cop. Hell, she saved my life. She's a righter of wrongs, an avenger of justice, a patron saint of hopeless cases like me."

"You're welcome to lodge a formal protest of her suspension." Diedrich wrinkled his nose in disgust. Before he left them there, he added, "But I wouldn't waste my time."

Detective Casey offered Maureen a sad smile that stabbed her in the heart. It felt as final as goodbye. Then, he turned to Tallboy and shook his hand. "For the record, sir, I don't disagree."

PART II

FORTY-ONE

Six Months Later

As soon as the Crescent Bay State Prison correctional officers completed their morning count, Seth retrieved the letter from beneath his mattress. He sat back on his bunk and unfolded the paper, trying to ignore the throbbing in his left shoulder. Sure, the doc had stitched him up, but the damn thing still ached when it got cold. And in prison, it was always colder than a polar bear's toenail. Unless it was sweltering hot. *Fucking cop.*

At least Seth had managed to negotiate the top bunk, trading the pain meds he cheeked for the privilege of sleeping above a three-hundred-pound bank robber who called himself Slim. They had a mutual understanding, the two cellmates. Seth shared the proceeds of his dice throwing in exchange for Slim's much-needed protection. Old-lady killers don't do so well in the joint. But nobody could shank him up here, not without going through Slim's Mack truck of a body first. It turned out gamblers like Seth could make fast friends, as long as he kept throwing sevens.

"Hey, Flea." Slim pounded against the bottom of the bed, creating a small earthquake. "You got my money?"

"I'll have it, man. I'm good for it. Plus interest." Seth knew why his bunkmate called him Flea, and he didn't like it. But he'd let it slide, because even he'd admit he could be annoying sometimes. And Slim could punch a hole through his chest without breaking a sweat. *So, Flea it is.*

"That's what you said yesterday. And the day before that."

"Well, I've had a few bad breaks. But I'm due, Slim. I'm due."

Seth ignored his cellmate's cynical grunt and turned his attention back to the letter. While he read it for the umpteenth time since its arrival last month, he could barely contain his glee. He ran his finger over the Innocence Project logo in the corner. The return address, a PO box in New York. Finally, *finally*, he had a winning ticket. And today was the day he would cash it in.

Dear Mr. McKay,

I hope this letter finds you well. I first became aware of your case in August, when I read a San Francisco Chronicle *article about your conviction for the first-degree murder of Iris Duncan, which appears to have been largely based on circumstantial evidence, as the alleged victim's body was never found. I also understand that charges against you in another homicide were dismissed, given the lack of available evidence. My examination of the facts in the Duncan case strongly suggests the possibility of other suspects, including your sister. I read your statement to the judge following your conviction, and I was stunned by your emphatic assertions of innocence. Assuming you are not still represented by your public defender, I would*

> like to assist you, pro bono, on behalf of the Innocence Project,
> in appealing your case. At your request, I will arrange to visit
> you as soon as possible. Please reply to the address below.
>
> Regards,
>
> Ms. E. Danvers, Attorney at Law

Seth could hear his father now. *All you need is one sucker.* But, this time, he didn't need to lie. All the things he'd done wrong, all the crimes he'd gotten away with, and he wound up doing time for the one he hadn't. *Life ain't fair, son. If it was, I'd be sittin' at the banquet table instead of fightin' for the scraps.* Touché, Dad. Touché.

"Attorney visit, McKay." The officer waited for him outside the cell, flashing him the usual look of disgust. Like he'd just found a wad of gum stuck to the bottom of his shoe. "Hurry up."

After slipping the letter into his pocket, Seth climbed down from the bunk and straightened his prison blues. He wouldn't let on how excited he felt. How today's visit was his first. Ever. Even his lousy public defender had abandoned him after the verdict.

"See ya, Slim. Enjoy those foxes."

Slim grinned at him over the cover of *Fish and Game* magazine—the cover story, *A New Generation of Fox Hunters*—behind which Seth had hidden the pages of a *Playboy* spread. "Will do, man. And don't forget..."

Seth nodded and followed the officer down the hallway toward the confidential attorney visiting booths at the entrance. Until he could walk out of here a free man, he hoped this Danvers chick would get him a single cell in a cushy prison down south like Valley View. He'd pretend to be a nutjob if it came down to that. *Yes, Doctor, I do hear voices.* Hell, he'd even cluck like a chicken.

"In here, McKay. She's waiting for you."

With a quick breath, Seth sauntered into the room. The woman had taken the seat nearest to the door—*smart lady*—so he dropped into the plastic chair. He hadn't expected an old broad like this one. Though she'd dyed her long hair a black-cherry red, her heavy makeup couldn't disguise the worry lines on her forehead. The crow's feet visible behind her horn-rimmed glasses.

"Not what you expected, dear?" she asked, giving a smile that unnerved him.

"Are you Ms. Danvers? With the Innocence Project?" Seth dropped his gaze to his hands. Something about her face bothered him. He didn't want to look at it.

"Indeed. Ms. E. Danvers, at your service. The E stands for Edith, in case you wondered." She laughed a little under her breath. Like she'd cracked a funny joke. "So, you're innocent, then?"

"Well, yeah. I thought you already knew that. Isn't that why you're here?"

"Tell me, in your own words, why you're innocent."

"Sheesh, Ms. Danvers." Seth swallowed a curse word. He hadn't planned on writing a goddamned essay. "I guess you would want to hear it from the horse's mouth. To put it plainly, I did not murder Iris Duncan. But to be fair, my sister and I did take advantage of her financially. That was wrong of us. I hope you know I've learned my lesson. I've even started going to the Gamblers Anonymous meetings in the day room. Anyway, they never found Iris's body. The only evidence they had against me... well, I think someone planted it."

"Really? A set-up? Do tell."

"You know how crooked the cops are these days. I wouldn't put it past that detective. Mark Casey. I'm pretty sure he had a thing for my sister. I saw the way he looked at her. If she had anything to do with it, he would've buried that evidence six feet deep."

"So, you've never killed anyone?"

That threw Seth for a loop. She couldn't know. Not that. No way. Only Lydia knew about Dolores, and only what he'd told her. Certainly not that he'd mixed a shit ton of Valium in her tea. That he'd never intended to pay her back. That he'd only planned to give her a smidgen, like usual, and slip a couple hundred from her pocketbook. But then, she got ornery and threatened to go to the police.

"Of course not," Seth said. "I'm a lot of things, Ms. Danvers. A gambler. A con man. But I am *not* a killer."

"I see." With a nod, Ms. Danvers reached down into her leather briefcase. Finally, they could get down to business, plan his appeal. She placed a folder on the table and slid it over to him. "Go on, dear. Open it."

Seth couldn't say why he felt afraid. Only that this old lady and her terms of endearment got under his skin like a ringworm, itching his insides something awful. Suddenly, that folder loomed larger than anything in the room. But it seemed stupid not to look. How bad could it be?

His mouth went dry at the sight of the photo. His eyes pinballed between Dolores Peck and another woman he recognized all too well. They had their arms slung around each other, laughing like the best of friends.

"Are you sure you're not a killer, Seth?"

"How did you—" His gaze landed on Ms. Danvers' lapel. "Shit."

"Excuse me?"

"That brooch. Where'd you get it?"

Ms. Danvers laid a hand on the butterfly pin—its body white diamonds, its wings mother-of-pearl. Her lips curled into a smile sweeter than her chocolate chip cookies. A shiver zipped up Seth's spine.

"This old thing?" she asked.

An hour later, Seth sat in the infirmary, waiting for the shrink to finish his evaluation. But he could barely focus on the doctor's questions. He kept replaying the visit, the trial. Everything that came before it. His whole sorry goddamned life. He never got a fair shake.

"Mr. McKay, I realize that being incarcerated can be overwhelming for the psyche. Are you thinking of hurting yourself?"

"No! For the last time. I am not suicidal. But I know what I saw."

"A dead woman?" The doctor gave him a patronizing little smirk. And Seth thought about ripping that awful tie from his neck and choking him out with it.

"I'm telling you, Doc. It was her. It was fucking Iris Duncan."

"Watch your language, please. Or I'll have no choice but to write you up for disrespecting staff."

Seth heaved an exasperated breath. "Watch my language? I'm in here for killing someone who IS NOT DEAD! That bitch set me up. And you're worried about an f-bomb."

The doctor scribbled a few more lines on his notepad. Each stroke of the pen rubbed Seth the wrong way. What bothered him most was his own failure to act. He'd just sat there like a schmuck, stunned speechless, while the old crone gloated. *You must be mistaken. I don't know any* Iris. Finally, after he'd lunged at her, she'd called for the officer, giving him a dainty wave as she watched the COs cuff him up and cart him away.

"What are you writing?" Seth stood up from the chair and tried to see for himself. "What does that say? *Paranoid? Delusional?*"

"Mr. McKay, I'm going to have to ask you to sit down.

Unless you prefer to spend the afternoon in four-point restraints. Now, what did you say her name was?"

Seth dropped back into the chair, defeated. "*Iris Duncan.* For the fiftieth time." Now that he thought about it, she'd probably been the one to get Lydia fired from the Sunrise Café. Taking money from the till wasn't his sister's style. Iris must have been running her con from jump street.

"No, no. The woman who came to see you."

"Edith Danvers. Or that's what she said it was, anyway." Seth pulled out the letter from his pocket and slapped it on the table. "From the Innocence Project. But let me tell you, she was no lawyer."

"Mrs. Danvers," the doctor repeated. "Like the character in the gothic novel, *Rebecca*?"

"Gothic *who*? Do I fu—freakin' look like I've read *Rebecca*? I don't know what you're talking about." Seth's anger boiled to the surface. He couldn't stop his hands from shaking. He needed to hit something. Someone. Bad. "Get me out of this place! I don't belong here."

The doctor called out to the nurse in the next room. "Get me the Haldol."

Seth got in one good shot to the doctor's jaw before two burly nursing assistants pinned him to the examining table. He felt the needle prick his skin. Then, a warm sensation spread through his body, and his legs grew so heavy he couldn't move them even if he tried.

"I'm innocent," he heard himself say. But now, even to him, it sounded like a lie.

FORTY-TWO

"To your retirement." Maureen winked at Walt as she clinked her glass of iced tea against his lager.

Since her dismissal, she'd been meeting the old codger for lunch at Betty's Diner most Thursdays. She suspected Walt considered himself her unofficial therapist, even though she'd found an official one of those too. Last week, she'd even started job-hunting again, which Dr. Marsha called real progress.

"It's been a good run. Thirty-five years' worth of memories." Half laughing, Walt swallowed a gulp of beer. "May I never have to transport another puking drunk."

"May you never have to direct traffic in the rain," Maureen countered.

"May I never have to pull a twelve-hour shift on Christmas."

Maureen lowered her eyes, speaking to the table. "May you never get stuck with such an impetuous partner."

"Oh, c'mon. You weren't so bad. At least you didn't shoot yourself in the leg."

"True. But it's my fault you got stuck with that guy. Your

last six months on duty with a boot named Preston Hamilton, the Third. It's a travesty."

"That it is." Walt took another swig and leaned back in his chair. "You know, I've been meaning to ask you. Did you hear about Tallboy?"

Maureen's stomach clenched. "Nothing bad, I hope."

"On the contrary." Walt fished his cellphone from his pocket and tapped at the screen, holding it out to her. "I meant to send it to you last night. It's hot off the presses. Came out in yesterday's paper."

HOMELESS MAN UNMASKS PRESIDIO RAPIST

Sixty-two-year-old Charles "Tallboy" Cochise is being hailed a hero by San Francisco police after evidence he collected from the Presidio Park led to the unmasking of serial rape suspect, James Davis. In the early-morning hours of October 6th, Cochise located a distinctive ski mask in the vicinity of his encampment. "Everything I stumble across out here, I always think it might be important. It might mean somethin' to somebody. Turns out that somebody was the cops." After Cochise spotted a Crime Stoppers bulletin that described the rapist's black and neon-green mask, he contacted police. One month later, DNA from the mask led police to their suspect. "Just happy to help," Cochise said. Earlier this year, Cochise put on another display of heroics when he tripped since-convicted murderer, Seth McKay, leading to McKay's arrest and the hashtag goldenfoot trending on social media. Through it all, Cochise, a Vietnam War veteran, remained humble. "Right place, right time, right person."

"And look, he's all cleaned up." Walt pointed to the photo of Tallboy, freshly shaven in his ill-fitting suit and sandwiched between the Mayor and the Chief of Police. In front of him, he displayed his Citizen Hero plaque.

Maureen's eyes welled, which Walt graciously ignored. "I wonder if that's why I got a call from SFPD on Monday. Maybe they thought I'd come to the ceremony."

Walt raised his eyebrows. "Did they leave a message?"

"Between you and me, I couldn't bear to listen to it. It still stings, Walt. I thought being a cop and catching a killer would fix all this." She wound a hand across her heart. "But it turns out I'm still as broken as ever."

"Aren't we all?" Walt patted her hand that rested on the table, reminding her that her parents were right there with her. They always had been. "Now, let's listen to that message. Together."

Maureen rolled her eyes, but Walt insisted. "It could be important."

"Alright, alright." She placed her cell between them, engaged the speakerphone, and hit play. Detective Casey's gruff baritone filled the booth. But it didn't make her as sad as she'd expected. Not with Walt making faces at the phone.

'Hello, Ms. Shaw. It's Mark Casey, Homicide. I don't want to bother you, but I thought you might've seen the story about your friend, Charlie. He told us he gave you a box of evidence related to the Duncan case. No rush, but I'm gonna need you to turn it in. We'll sort through it and file it away. It's probably all junk anyway. Like I said, there's no hurry. McKay's not going anywhere for the next fifteen to life.'

Maureen tried not to look disappointed. A part of her wished he'd said something else, something more personal. More substantial. She *had* brought down their perp, after all. With the assistance of #goldenfoot.

"Hey, Maureen. I've been thinking." Walt downed the last dregs of his beer. "We're both wannabe detectives, right?"

She couldn't believe he'd admitted it, and she didn't dare agree.

"I'm not so sure I'm ready to give this all up. But I have to confess, I'm not as spry as I used to be. I need somebody *impetuous* to keep me on my toes."

"What are you saying, Walt?"

"I'm saying, how would you feel about Greer and Shaw Private Investigators?"

An hour later, Maureen parked in the garage and headed straight for the shelves behind the piano, searching for the shabby shoebox Tallboy had given her. The entire drive home she couldn't get it out of her mind. And seeing it again, she felt anxious. It represented the old Maureen. Desperate Maureen. Wounded Maureen. Still, she had to look at it. She couldn't *not*.

Maureen emptied the contents of the box onto the cement floor and sifted through the refuse like an archaeologist hunting for a rare fossil.

"Junk," she said out loud, sorting through Tallboy's collection. Besides, Seth had already been convicted. Maureen hadn't attended the trial, but she'd followed the media coverage. The jury brought back a guilty verdict in less than two hours.

As she returned the items to the box one by one, the unmarked cassette—wound a quarter of the way—caught her eye. Curious, Maureen carried it back to the car. The 2006 relic Volvo that had belonged to her parents still had a tape deck. It was one of the many things Dr. Marsha hoped she would part with eventually.

After starting up the engine, she slid the tape into the deck and hit rewind, praying to God the thing still worked. Right now, listening to the soft whirring of the reel, Maureen could almost picture her mother beside her in the passenger seat, beaming with pride as they listened to the tape of her first solo performance. And she felt grateful that she'd held on a little longer.

Maureen pressed play and cranked the volume.

At first, she heard only the crackling of white noise. Then, a voice.

'Alright, Mrs. Duncan. You ready? Two shots, with a break in between. It's gonna be loud, so cover your ears.'

'I'm ready, dear.'

The first gunshot shook Maureen to the core. Like a whip, it cracked the silence, and she stiffened in the seat, her hands gripping the wheel.

After a long pause came the second. Then, moments later, *'It's perfect, Tony. You're a lifesaver. Dolores would've loved you.'*

'Aw, anything for you, Mrs—'

Hard and sudden as the break of a bone, the tape ended with a click.

Maureen couldn't say how long she sat there, rewinding and replaying. Long enough to memorize their words. She catalogued the facts, one by one, leapfrogging toward a conclusion that left her reeling. As shocking as a gut punch, it sucked the wind from her.

Dolores, Iris's best friend, dead by an apparent Valium overdose. Seth McKay, the thieving rascal in her letter.

Iris's body, never found.

All the evidence—the bloody rag, the hair, the rug fibers, even the shell casings—inferential. Easily planted.

The gunshots on the 911 call, staged by Iris and Tony Matta. No wonder Matta had been so keen to help Maureen find Seth, the perfect fall guy.

The truth unfolded itself to her like a blossoming flower, and it made so much sense that she wondered why she hadn't considered it before. Self-contained and secretive, Iris had planned her own murder to avenge the death of her dearest childhood friend.

Maureen packed up the rest of Tallboy's box and dropped it in the trunk. She would bring it by the station tomorrow. But the tape, she held back. She studied it and felt the great weight of her decision.

When she dropped it on the concrete and smashed its shell beneath her heel, she thought of her parents, of Adam Waddell. Of Dolores and Tallboy. Mostly, she thought of Iris. How the universe would only bend toward justice with a hand willing to bend it.

Her shoulders unburdened, Maureen dialed Walt's number. The moment he answered, she said two little words.

"I'm in."

Then, she blew the dust off the fallboard of the Steinway and opened it. Taking a deep, cleansing breath, she listened for the music. She set her fingers on the keys and began to play.

FORTY-THREE

Lydia cooed at the baby in the stroller. "Aren't you a cutie," she said, rubbing his chubby cheek with her finger. He giggled as a Barbie doll went flying past them, landing unceremoniously beneath a nearby table. Lydia retrieved the doll, combing its blonde hair with her fingers.

"And you." Returning the Barbie, she grinned at the little girl. "That's quite an arm you've got."

The kids' harried mother shook her head. In one hand, she held a menu. In the other, a pacifier. "Cute little tyrants, that's what I say. They could get away with murder."

"Well, lucky for them, they are adorable." Lydia pulled the pad and pen from her waitress apron.

"Do you have kids?"

And just like that, her head started spinning. Even an innocent question could set her off.

"*Kids?*" the woman asked again, unaware she'd just thrown another pebble into Lydia's festering pit of guilt. She wondered if God would punish her for lying about the pregnancy, first to Iris, then to Seth. For telling Detective Casey—Mark, as she called him now—that she'd "lost" the baby. But she'd only done what she had to do. Surely, he would understand that. He liked her fighting spirit. Her survival instincts. That's what he'd told her the first night she'd spent in his bed.

"Someday. I hope."

"Well, we'll take one large pepperoni and one small cheese. My husband should be here any minute."

Lydia stared ahead, blank-faced. For a moment, she'd gotten lost in the quagmire of the past.

"*Our order*," the woman said, her friendliness already wearing off. Lydia found herself smack dab in the here and now. Halfway through her eight-hour shift in a pizza dive in the middle of downtown Oakland.

"Oh, right. Of course. I'm sorry. Coming right up."

Lydia slunk into the kitchen, embarrassed. After putting in the order, she watched the family through the pass with envy. When the husband arrived, he leaned down to kiss his wife's cheek. He tickled the baby, ruffled his daughter's hair. And as the Barbie dipped her toes in Dad's soda, they all laughed together.

A *real* family. Lydia had never had anything like it. Sometimes, she pretended Iris was still alive. She talked to her at night. She made her the God-awful low-fat lemon ricotta pancakes. Iris had wanted the very best for her. Iris had believed in her. Iris would've never wanted her to settle for a mundane existence like this one.

"Hey, you sleepin' on the job again? Pizza's up. I'm not paying you to stand around."

Lydia gritted her teeth. She'd planned on waiting until the end of her shift. But her boss's tone reminded her of Seth. Of Vinnie. Of her father. And suddenly, one more hour of servitude seemed like one too many. She'd put them all exactly where they belonged.

"I quit."

"Excuse me?"

But Lydia had already untied her apron and tossed it in a heap on the counter. She gave no answer as she flung open the door and stepped into the new life that awaited her.

Mark carried Lydia's duffel bag up the porch stairs, depositing it on the stoop. He waited while she slipped the key from her pocket. The key she'd picked up that morning from the probate attorney after all the assets had been transferred to her name. Hers and hers alone.

"Are you gonna stand out here all day?" Mark asked. "Let's see your place. Your fresh start."

"It's weird," she confessed. "It feels like a dream. All of it. *You*, too."

When he pulled her against the solid wall of him and kissed her forehead, Lydia melted. She didn't care about the age difference—twenty-one years. Or his bald head. Or his bitter ex. Not even his coffee-stained teeth. He felt safe. And that, she would kill for. Besides, it couldn't hurt to have an officer of the law in her corner just in case she messed up again. He'd already followed through on his promise to keep her out of jail.

Lydia inserted the key into the lock and pushed the door open, marveling at how familiar it felt. How familiar and how new. Not a *house sitter*, Seth. *A home owner*. One little signature from a clueless Iris at the bottom of a blank page hidden in a stack of neurology intake forms was all it took. After Iris had been adjudicated deceased at Lydia's request, Lydia had presented her newly inked will—the one she'd told Mark she found hidden in the attic—and claimed her rightful place on Archer Avenue. With no one to contest the document and Mark's lawyer buddy on her side, it had been deemed valid by the court. The whole thing couldn't have gone better if she'd planned it herself. And she'd had no need to wait around for the old lady to kick the bucket. *Thanks, Seth.* Finally, her big brother had done her a solid.

Her bag in tow, Mark crossed the threshold. Lydia paused, looking over her shoulder and across the street. She waved at her neighbor. "Hey, Mr. Dorsey. It's nice to see you again."

When he shook his head and turned his back with no reply, she gave him her middle finger. Then, she followed Mark inside.

"Home, sweet home." She spun around the sitting room, then collapsed onto the sofa, giddy. But her spirits dampened when her eyes met the Dolores painting above the fireplace. It marked the wall, like a spot of blood she couldn't rub out. "Now, I think it's time for some remodeling."

A LETTER FROM ELLERY

Want to keep up to date with my latest releases? Sign up here! We promise never to share your email with anyone else, we'll only contact you when there's a new book available, and you can unsubscribe at any time.

www.bookouture.com/ellery-kane

Thank you for reading *The House Sitter*! With so many amazing books out there, I am honored you chose to add mine to your library.

One of my favorite parts about being an author is connecting with readers like you. You can get in touch with me through any of the social media outlets below, including my website and Goodreads page. Also, if you wouldn't mind leaving a review or recommending *The House Sitter* to your favorite readers, I would really appreciate it! Reviews and word-of-mouth recommendations are essential, because they help readers like you discover my books.

Thank you again for selecting *The House Sitter*! I look forward to bringing you many more thrills, chills, and sleepless nights.

www.ellerykane.com

facebook.com/TheLegacyBooks
twitter.com/ellerykane

ACKNOWLEDGMENTS

Like many of my novels, *The House Sitter* was born, in part, of my own experiences. Several years ago, like hundreds of thousands of other elderly individuals, a close family member fell victim to financial exploitation by a young couple who preyed on his kind heart and declining cognitive abilities. I always knew I would write the story of that young couple. Because writing is often therapeutic. And sometimes, writing is revenge. So, I must first acknowledge them—the real-life "Seth" and "Lydia." May you only get what you deserve.

Of course, I owe a tremendous debt of gratitude to you, my avid readers, for joining me on my writing adventure. Hearing that my words have impacted you is a little bit of magic, and knowing that my stories have a special place in your heart makes it all worthwhile.

I am fortunate to have a fabulous team of family, friends, and work colleagues who have always been there to support and encourage me on this journey. Though my mom is no longer with me, she gifted me her love for writing, and I know she's cheering me on even though I can't see her. Thanks, too, to my dad, who's never been a reader but thinks I'm brilliant anyway.

To Gar, my special someone and partner in crime, thank you for patching all my plot holes without complaint; for being my navigator to the Beseeching Woman and beyond; for cheering me on when I need it most; and for championing my dreams as much (and sometimes more) than I do. I know you don't believe me, but I couldn't do any of this without you.

I have been unbelievably fortunate to be matched with an amazing editor, Helen Jenner, and a fantastic publisher, Bookouture, who truly value their authors and work tirelessly for our success. It's been a pleasure to team up with Helen and the entire Bookouture family, including Kim, Noelle, Jess, and Sarah, who have worked so hard to spread the word about my books.

Lastly, I have always drawn inspiration for my writing from my day job as a forensic psychologist. We all have a space inside us that we keep hidden from the world, a space we protect at all costs. So many people have allowed me a glimpse inside theirs—dark deeds, memories best unrecalled, pain that cracks from the inside out—without expectation of anything in return. I couldn't have written a single word without them.